Marion Zimmer Bradley
The Heirs of Hammerfell

THE FOUNDING:

A "lost ship" of Terran origin, in the pre-empire colonizing days, lands on a planet with a dim red star, later to be called Darkover.
DARKOVER LANDFALL

THE AGES OF CHAOS:

1,000 years after the original landfall settlement, society has returned to the feudal level. The Darkovans, their Terran technology renounced or forgotten, have turned instead to free-wheeling, out-of-control matrix technology, psi powers and terrible psi weapons. The populace lives under the domination of the Towers and a tyrannical breeding program to staff the Towers with unnaturally powerful, inbred gifts of *laran*.
STORMQUEEN!
HAWKMISTRESS!

THE HUNDRED KINGDOMS:

An age of war and strife retaining many of the decimating and disastrous effects of the Ages of Chaos. The lands which are later to become the Seven Domains are divided by continuous border conflicts into a multitude of small, belligerent kingdoms, named for convenience "The Hundred Kingdoms." The close of this era is heralded by the adoption of the Compact, instituted by Varzil the Good. A landmark and turning point in the history of Darkover, the Compact bans all distance weapons, making it a matter of honor that one who seeks to kill must himself face equal risk of death.
TWO TO CONQUER
THE HEIRS OF HAMMERFELL

THE RENUNCIATES:

During the Ages of Chaos and the time of the Hundred Kingdoms, there were two orders of women who set themselves apart from the patriarchal nature of Darkovan feudal society: the priestesses of Avarra, and the warriors of the Sisterhood of the Sword. Eventually these two independent groups merged to form the powerful and legally chartered Order of Renunciates or Free Amazons, a guild of women bound only by oath as a sisterhood of mutual responsibility. Their primary allegiance is to each other rather than to family, clan, caste or any man save a temporary employer. Alone among Darkovan women, they are exempt from the usual legal restrictions and protections. Their reason for existence is to provide the women of Darkover an alternative to their socially restrictive lives.
THE SHATTERED CHAIN
THENDARA HOUSE
CITY OF SORCERY

AGAINST THE TERRANS
—THE FIRST AGE (Recontact):

After the Hastur Wars, the Hundred Kingdoms are consolidated into the Seven Domains, and ruled by a hereditary aristocracy of seven families, called the Comyn, allegedly descended from the legendary Hastur, Lord of Light. It is during this era that the Terran Empire, really a form of confederacy, rediscovers Darkover, which they know as the fourth planet of the Cottman star system. It is not apparent that Darkover is a lost colony of the Empire, until linguistic and sociological studies reveal that Darkovans are of Terran extraction—a concept not easily or readily acknowledged by Darkovans and their Comyn overlords.

> THE SPELL SWORD
> THE FORBIDDEN TOWER

AGAINST THE TERRANS
—THE SECOND AGE (After the Comyn):

With the initial shock of recontact beginning to wear off, and the Terran spaceport a permanent establishment on the outskirts of the city of Thendara, the younger and less traditional elements of Darkovan society begin the first real exchange of knowledge with the Terrans—learning Terran science and technology and teaching Darkovan matrix technology in turn. Eventually Regis Hastur, the young Comyn lord most active in these exchanges, becomes Regent in a provisional government allied to the Terrans. Darkover is once again reunited with its founding Empire.

> THE HERITAGE OF HASTUR
> SHARRA'S EXILE

THE DARKOVER ANTHOLOGIES:

These volumes of stories written by Marion Zimmer Bradley herself, and various members of the society called The Friends of Darkover, strive to "fill in the blanks" of Darkovan history, and elaborate on the eras, tales and characters which have captured their imagination.

> THE KEEPER'S PRICE
> SWORD OF CHAOS
> FREE AMAZONS OF DARKOVER
> THE OTHER SIDE OF THE MIRROR
> RED SUN OF DARKOVER
> FOUR MOONS OF DARKOVER

**Other DAW titles by
Marion Zimmer Bradley:**

Marion Zimmer Bradley
The Heirs of Hammerfell

DAW BOOKS, INC.
DONALD A. WOLLHEIM, PUBLISHER

NEW YORK
1989

For Betsy, a chip off the old block.

1

Storm raged over the Hellers; lightning split the sky asunder, followed by thunder rolling in long echoing crashes through the valleys. The driven clouds revealed ragged patches of lurid sky still lighted with the last rays of the swollen crimson sun, and, hanging near the tooth of the highest peak, the crescent rim of the pale turquoise moon. Near the zenith, a second moon hung violet and day-pale, hiding behind the racing clouds. Snow lingered on the peaks, and occasional patches of ice endangered the precarious footing of the small horned riding beast that fled along the narrow path. Neither of the other moons was visible at the moment, but the solitary rider who traveled by their light did not care.

On the chervine's back, the old man clung to his seat in the saddle, all but unaware of the blood that still flowed sluggishly, mixing with the rain to stain the front of his shirt and cloak. Moaning cries es-

9

caped his lips as he rode, but he was no longer aware of the lament that flowed as unheeded as the blood from the wound he had all but forgotten; and in any case there was none to hear.

So young; and the last, the last of my lord's sons, and dear as a son to me, too; and so young, so young . . . so young to die . . . not much farther now; if I can only make it back before those folk of Storn realize that I managed to get away. . . .

The chervine stumbled on a rock loosened by the up-thrusting ice and nearly went down. He recovered; but the old man was jarred from his seat; he fell hard and lay still, without strength to rise, still whispering the half-voiced lament.

So young, so young . . . and how shall I bring the news to his father? Oh, my lord, my young lord . . . my Alaric!

His eyes lifted painfully to the rough-hewn and battle scarred castle high on the crags above. It might as well have been on the green moon for all he could do to reach it now. His eyes closed reluctantly. The beast, aware of the loss of his burden but still held by the weight of the saddle binding him to his rider's will, nosed gently at the old man who lay on the icy, wet trail. When he scented the others of his kind moving down the steep pathway the old man had been climbing with such toil, he raised his head and whickered softly to attract the notice which he knew would mean food, rest, and freedom from the saddle's weight.

Rascard, Duke of Hammerfell, heard the sound and held up his hand, bringing the little procession following him to a halt.

"Hark, what's that?" he asked the paxman who

rode behind him. In the dim storm-light he could just see the riderless beast and the slumped form lying in the road.

"By the Dark Gods! It's Markos!" he cried out, flinging himself heedlessly from his saddle, and down the steep, slick path, falling to his knees beside the wounded man. "Regis! Lexxas! Bring wine, blankets!" he bellowed, bending toward the wounded man and gently drawing away the cloak. "He's still alive," he added more quietly, hardly able to believe it was true.

"Markos, old friend, speak to me! Ah, Gods, how did you come by such a wound? Those bastards of Storn?"

The man in the roadway opened dark eyes, blurred now more with confusion than pain, as a dark form bent over him with a flask and held it to his mouth. He swallowed, coughed painfully, and swallowed again; but the duke had seen the bloody foam at his lips.

"No, Markos, don't try to speak." He cradled the apparently dying man in his arms; but Markos heard, with the bond between them that had endured for forty years, the question the Duke of Hammerfell forbore to speak aloud.

What of my son? What of my Alaric? Ah, Gods, I trusted him to you as to my own self . . . never in a lifetime have you betrayed that trust. . . .

And the link bore to him the semiconscious man's thoughts;

Nor now. I do not think he is dead; but the men of Storn came upon us unseen . . . a single arrow for each . . . curse them all. . . .

Duke Rascard cried out in pain.

"Zandru's demons seize them all! Oh, my son, *my son!*" He held the fallen man in his arms, feeling the old man's grief as sharply as the arrow wound that burned as if it were in his own body.

No, my old friend, my more than brother, no reproach to you . . . well do I know you guarded him with your own life. . . .

The serving-men were crying out with dismay for their master's grief, but he silenced them with a stern command.

"Take him up—gently, now! His wound need not be mortal; you will answer for it if he dies! That blanket over him—yes, like that. And a little more *firi . . .* careful, don't choke him! Markos, where lies my son? I know you would not abandon him—"

"Lord Storn—that elder son of his, Fionn—carried him off—" The harsh rasping whisper failed again, but Duke Rascard heard the words he was too weak to speak aloud, *I thought it was indeed over my dead body . . . then I recovered consciousness and came to bear you word, even with my last breath. . . .*

"But you will *not* die, my friend," the duke said gently as with giant strength the horse-master Lexxas lifted the wounded man. "Set him on my own beast— gently, as you wish to go on breathing the air of this world. Back now to Hammerfell . . . as swiftly as we may, for the light is failing, and we should be within doors before nightfall."

The duke, supporting the fainting body of his oldest retainer in his arms as they slowly moved back up the pathway to the heights, saw in his mind the picture in Markos's as he lapsed into unconsciousness; his son Alaric, lying across Fionn's saddle, with a Storn arrow in his breast, latest victim of the blood feud which had raged between Storn and Hammerfell for five generations, a feud so ancient that no living man now remembered its original cause.

But Markos, though grievously wounded, still lived; was it not possible that Alaric, too, might survive, even be held for ransom?

If he dies, I swear I shall not leave a single stone of Storn Heights heaped upon another, or a living man of Storn blood anywhere in the Hundred Kingdoms, he vowed as they crossed the ancient drawbridge and reentered the gateway so recently closed behind them. He called aloud for serving men as they bore Markos into the Great Hall, and laid him down gently on a rough settee. Duke Rascard stared around wildly and commanded, "Send for *damisela* Erminie."

But the household *leronis*, crying out in dismay, had already hurried into the Hall and kneeling on the cold stone of the entryway, she bent over the wounded man. Duke Rascard swiftly explained what was needed, but the young sorceress, too, had dwelt lifelong with this blood feud; this slight girl was a cousin of the duke's long-dead wife, and had served him at Hammerfell since childhood.

She leaned over Markos, drawing out the blue starstone from the folds of her dress; focusing on the stone, she ran her hands down his body without touching him, holding them about an inch from the wound, her eyes remote and unfocused. Rascard watched in frozen silence.

At length she straightened, her eyes full of tears.

"The bleeding is stanched; he breathes still," she said. "I can do no more now."

"Will he live, Erminie?" asked the duke.

"I cannot tell; but against all probability, he has

lived this long. I can say only it is in the hands of the Gods; if they continue to be merciful he will survive."

"I pray so; we were children together, and I have lost so many . . ." said Rascard. Then he broke out in a great shriek of long-held-back fury, *"I swear before all the Gods! If he dies, such vengeance shall be taken . . ."*

"Hush!" said the girl sternly. "If you must bellow, Uncle, go and do it where you will not disturb this wounded man."

Duke Rascard flushed and subsided, walking toward the hearth and dropping into a deep chair, marveling at the composure and quiet competence of this chit of a girl.

Erminie was not more than seventeen, slim and delicate with the bright new-minted copper hair of a telepath, and deep-set gray eyes. Except for these she had not a single regular feature; with them, she was almost beautiful. She followed the duke toward the fire and looked levelly into his eyes.

"If he is to live, he must be kept quiet . . . and you, too, must leave him in quiet, sir."

"I know, my dear. You were right to scold me."

Duke Rascard, twenty-third Duke of Hammerfell, was past forty, in the fullest strength of middle age. His hair, once dark, was gray as iron, his eyes the blue of copper filings in the flame. He was strong and muscular, his weathered features and the twisted ropy muscles displaying the contours of the dwarfish forge-folk from whom he derived his heritage. He looked like a once active man who had softened a little with age and inactivity, and his stern face was softer than usual as he looked on the young girl; she was not unlike the wife he had lost five years ago, when Alaric, their only son, was barely into his teens.

14

The two had been brought up almost as brother and sister; and the duke almost broke down, thinking of the two red heads—cropped curls, long braids—bent together over a lesson-book.

"Have you heard, child?"

The young woman lowered her eyes. No one for a thousand leagues who possessed a single scrap of telepathic awareness, far less a *leronis*, intensively trained in the use of the psychic powers of her caste, could have been unaware of that agonized interchange in which the duke had learned the fate of son and old servant; but she did not say so.

"I think I would know if Alaric were truly dead," she said, and the duke's harsh face softened.

"I pray you are right, *chiya*. Will you come to me in the conservatory, when you can leave Markos?"

He added unnecessarily, "And bring your starstone."

"I will come," she said, understanding what he wanted, and returned to bend over the injured man once more, without looking again at Duke Rascard as he left the Hall.

The conservatory, a standard feature of a mountain household, was high up in the castle, with double-thick windows, heated with several fireplaces, and even during this inhospitable season thronged with green leaves and flowers.

Duke Rascard had seated himself in a very old and battered armchair where he could look out over the entire valley below him. He stared at the road winding up to the castle, remembering more than one pitched battle which he had fought there in his father's lifetime. So intent was he on memory that he did not hear the soft step behind him until Erminie came around the chair and sat on the little hassock at his feet.

"Markos?" he asked.

"I will not deceive you, Uncle; his wound is very serious. The arrow pierced his lung, and it was hurt worse when he pulled the arrow forth. But he still breathes, and the bleeding has not begun again. He is sleeping; with rest and good fortune, he will live. I left Amalie with him. She will call me if he wakes; for now, I am at your service, sir." Her voice was soft and husky, but quite steady. Living with hardship had matured her beyond her years. "Tell me, Uncle, why was Markos on the road and why did Alaric go forth with him?"

"You might not have known; but the men of Storn came last moon and burned a dozen ricks in the village; there will be hunger before seeding-time, so our men chose to go forth and raid Storn itself for food and seed for the burned-out houses. Alaric need not have gone with them; it was Markos's place to lead the men; but one of the burned houses belonged to Alaric's foster-mother and so he insisted that none but he himself should lead the raid. I could not refuse him this; he said it was a matter of honor." Rascard paused for an unsteady breath. "Alaric was not a child; I could not deny him what he felt he must do. I asked him to take one or more of the *laranzu'in* with him, but he would not; he said he could deal with Storn with armed men alone. When they had not returned at twilight, I grew anxious—and found Markos alone escaped to bring word; they were ambushed."

Erminie covered her face with her hands.

The old duke said, "You know what it is that I

16

need from you. How is it with your cousin, my girl? Can you see him?"

She said softly, "I will try," and brought out the pale blue stone from its hiding place at her throat. The duke caught a brief glimpse of the twisting lights in the stone and turned his eyes away; although he was an adequate telepath for one of his caste, he had never been trained to use a starstone for the higher levels of power, and like all half-trained telepaths, the shifting lights within the starstones made him feel vaguely ill.

He looked at the soft parting of Erminie's hair as she bent her head over the stone, her eyes serious and remote. Her features were so fresh, so young, untouched by any deep and lasting grief. Duke Rascard felt old and wearied and worn with the weight of the many years of feud, and the very thought of the clan of Storn who had taken from him grandfather and father, two elder brothers, and now his only surviving son.

But, please the Gods, Alaric is not dead and not lost to me forever. Not yet, and not ever. . . . He said hoarsely, "I pray you look and give me word, child . . ." and his voice trembled.

After an unusually long time Erminie said, in a soft, wandering, unfocused voice, "Alaric . . . cousin . . ." and almost at once, Duke Rascard, dropping into rapport, saw what she saw, the face of his son; a younger version of his own, save that his son's hair was brilliant copper and curled all over his head. The boyish features were drawn with pain, and the front of his shirt was covered with bright blood. Erminie's face, too, was pale.

"He lives. But his wound is more serious than

17

Markos's," she said. "Markos will live if he is kept quiet; but Alaric . . . the bleeding still goes on within the lung. His breathing is very faint . . . he has not yet recovered consciousness."

"Can you reach him? Is it possible to heal his wound at such a distance?" the duke demanded, recalling what she had done for Markos, but she sighed, tears flooding her eyes.

"Alas, no, Uncle; I would willingly try, but not even the Keeper of Tramontana could heal at such a distance."

"Then can you reach him and tell him that we know where he is, that we will come to rescue him or die in the attempt?"

"I am afraid to disturb him, Uncle. If he wakes and should move unwisely, he could tear his lung past healing."

"Yet if he wakes alone and knows himself in the hands of our enemies, could not that also prompt him to despair and death?"

"You are right. I will try to reach his mind without disturbing him," Erminie said, while the duke dropped his face in his hands, trying to see through the young girl's mind what she saw; the face of his son, pale and worn with pain. Although untrained in the healing arts, it seemed to him that he could see the mark of mortality on the young features. At the edge of his perceptions he could sense Erminie's face, tense and searching, and heard, not with his ears, the message she was trying to insinuate into a deep level of Alaric's mind.

Have no fear; we are with you. Rest and heal yourself . . . again and again the soothing touch of warmth, trying to carry reassurance and love.

The intimate feel of Erminie's mind touched Rascard. *I did not know how much she loved him; I thought they were simply as brother and sister, children together; now I know it is more than that.*

He became slowly aware of the young girl's blushes; he knew that she had overheard his thoughts.

I loved him even when we were children together, Uncle. I do not know if I am more to him than a kind foster-sister; but I love him much more than that. It does not . . . it does not make you angry?

If he had learned this any other way, Duke Rascard might indeed have been angered; for many years he had given much thought to a great marriage, perhaps even to some lowland princess from the Hastur lands to the South; but now fear for his son was all he knew.

"When once he is safe again with us, my child, then if that is what you both wish, it shall be done," said the stern-faced duke, so gently that Erminie hardly recognized the gruff voice she knew so well. For a moment they sat silent, and then, to his great joy, Rascard felt another touch within the rapport, a touch he recognized; weak and faltering, but unmistakable; the mental touch of his son Alaric.

Father . . . Erminie . . . can it be you? Where am I? What happened? What of poor Markos. . . ? Where am I?

As gently as she could, Erminie tried to inform him what had happened; that he was wounded, and within the keep of Storn Heights.

And Markos will not die; rest and heal yourself, my son, and we shall ransom or rescue you or die in the attempt. Do not be troubled. Be at peace . . . peace . . . peace. . . .

Abruptly into the soothing pattern of the rapport tore a great explosion of fury and the blue flare of a

19

starstone. It was like a blow struck into his heart, a physical pain.

You here, Rascard, you prying thief . . . what do you in my very stronghold? As if before his eyes, Rascard of Hammerfell could see the scarred face, the fierce eyes, of his ancient enemy; Ardrin of Storn, lean and panther-fierce, ablaze with rage.

Can you ask? Give me back my son, wretch! Name your own ransom, and it shall be paid to the last sekal, but harm one hair of his head and you will pay a hundredfold!

So you have threatened every moon for the past forty years, Rascard, but you now hold nothing I wish save for your wretched self; keep your wealth, and I will hang you beside your son from the highest tower of Storn Heights.

Rascard's first impulse was to strike full strength with *laran;* but Alaric was in his enemy's hands. He countered, trying to be calm, *Will you not allow me to ransom my son? Name your own price and I swear it shall be yours without haggling.*

He felt the glee of Ardrin of Storn; clearly his enemy had been waiting for just such a chance.

I will exchange him for you, was Ardrin's answer through the telepathic link. *Come here and surrender yourself into my hands before tomorrow at sunset and Alaric—if he still lives, or his body if he does not—shall be handed over to your people.*

Rascard knew he should have expected this. But Alaric was young; he himself had lived out a long life. Alaric could marry, rebuild the clan and kingdom. He answered after only a moment.

Agreed. But only if he lives; if he dies in your hands, I will burn Storn around your ears with clingfire.

Father, no! Not at that price! It was Alaric's voice crying out, *I cannot live so long—nor will I have you die for me.* Rascard felt the voice strike through his son's weak defenses, felt the bursting blood as if in his own veins, then Alaric was gone, dropped from the rapport—dead or unconscious—he could not tell.

There was no sound in the conservatory but Erminie's quiet sobbing, and another outburst of rage from the Lord of Storn.

Ah, you have cheated me of my revenge, Rascard, old enemy! It was not I who dealt him death. If you wish to change your life for his body, I shall honor the bargain—

Honor? How dare you speak that word, Storn?

Because I am not a Hammerfell! Now get out! Do not presume to come into Storn again—even in spirit! Ardrin flung at him. *Go! Get out!*

Erminie threw herself to the rug and wept like the child she was still. Rascard of Hammerfell bowed his head. He was numb, empty, shattered. Had the feud ended, then, at this price?

2

The forty days of mourning wound slowly to an end. On the forty-first day, a caravan of strangers wound its way slowly up the winding rocky track toward Hammerfell Castle and when welcomed proved to be a relative of the duke's late wife along with his retinue. Duke Rascard, more uncomfortable than he cared to admit in the presence of this sophisticated, finely dressed city-dweller, received him in his Great Hall, calling for wine and refreshments.

"My apologies for the insufficiency of this entertainment," he remarked, ushering him to a seat near the carved mantle which bore the crest of Hammerfell, "but until yesterday this was a house of mourning, and we have not returned to our normal state."

"I did not come for cakes and wine, kinsman," said Renato Leynier, a lowland cousin from the Hastur countries to the south. "Your mourning is all our family's mourning as well; Alaric was my kinsman,

22

too. But there is a purpose to our visit—I have come to reclaim my kinsman's daughter, the *leronis* Erminie."

Renato looked at the duke. If he had expected—as was the case—to see an old, broken man, ready to collapse at the death of his son and see Hammerfell fall into the hands of strangers, he was cheated. If anything, this man seemed to have grown stronger through his rage and pride; a vital man, still in command of those armies of Hammerfell through which he had marched for many days. Power spoke in the man's every small gesture and word; Rascard of Hammerfell was not young, but far from broken.

"But why do you seek to reclaim Erminie now?" Rascard asked, feeling the question like a stab of pain. "She is well in my household. This is her home. She is the last living link with my son. I would prefer to keep her as a daughter to my family."

"That is not possible," said Renato. "She is no longer a child, but a marriageable woman nearing twenty, and you are not so old as all that." (Until this very moment he had indeed thought of Rascard of Hammerfell as old enough to need no chaperone where a young woman was concerned.) "It is scandalous for you two to live alone together."

"Surely there is nothing so evil as the mind of a virtuous man, unless it is the mind of a virtuous woman," said Rascard indignantly, his face flushing with anger. In all truth this interpretation had never occurred to him. "Almost from infancy she was my son's playmate, and in all the years she has lived here, there has been no dearth of chaperones and duennas and companions and governesses. They will tell you that not twice in all these years have we been so much as alone in a room together, save when she brought me news of my son's tragic death; and then, believe me, we both had other things on our minds."

"I doubt it not," Renato said smoothly, "but even so, Erminie is of an age to be married, and while she dwells beneath your roof, however innocently, she cannot be properly married to any man of her station; or do you design to degrade her by marrying her to some lowborn paxman or servant?"

"No such thing," the old duke retorted, "I had designed to wed her to my own son, had he but lived long enough."

An awkward, and for Rascard, sad silence followed. But Renato would not back down.

"Would that it might have been so! But with due respect to your son, she cannot marry with the dead, more's the pity," Renato said, "and so she must return to her own kinfolk."

Rascard felt his eyes flooding with the tears he had been too proud to shed. He looked up at the dark coat of arms above the hearth and could no longer hide his bitter sorrow. "Now I am indeed alone, for I have no other kinsman; those folk of Storn have had their triumph, for there is no living man or woman of the blood of Hammerfell besides myself anywhere in the Hundred Kingdoms."

"You are not yet an old man," Renato said, responding to the terrible loneliness in Rascard's voice. "You could yet marry again and raise up a dozen heirs."

And Rascard knew that what Renato said was true; yet his heart sank; to take a stranger into his home, and wait, wait for the birth of children, wait for them to grow to manhood, just to risk seeing this blood feud wipe them out again . . . no, he might not be all that old, but he was definitely too old for *that*.

Yet what was the alternative? To let the Storns have their triumph, to know that when they followed the murder of his son with his own murder, there would be none to avenge him . . . to know that Hammerfell itself would be in Storn hands, and no trace of the Morays of Hammerfell would remain anywhere in the Hundred Kingdoms.

"I *will* marry, then," he said in a moment of bra-zen desperation. "What bride-price do you ask for Erminie?"

Renato was shocked to his core.

"I did not mean to suggest *that,* my lord. She is not of your station, she has been a common *leronis* in your household. It is not suitable."

"If I intended to marry her to my own son, how could I possibly claim she was not suitable for me? If I scorned her, I would never have thought of such a marriage," Rascard insisted.

"My lord—"

"She is of an age to bear children, and I have no reason to believe her other than virtuous. Once I married hoping for the great alliances a noble bride would bring; where are they, now that my son lies dead? At this point I wish only for a healthy young woman, and I am accustomed to her as my son's playmate. She will do well, better than most; and I will not need to accommodate myself to the ways of a stranger. Name her bride-price: I will give her par-ents whatever is customary and reasonable."

Lord Renato looked at him in dismay. He knew that he could not summarily refuse this marriage without making a formidable enemy. Hammerfell

25

was a small realm, but Renato was realizing how powerful it was; the Dukes of Hammerfell had reigned long in this part of the world.

He could only temporize and hope that the old duke would think better of this latest whim while the purely practical difficulties and delays were being dealt with.

"Well," he said slowly, at last, "if that is your wish, my lord, I will send a message to her guardians asking their permission for their ward to marry you. There may be difficulties; she may have been hand-fasted elsewhere as a child, or something of that sort."

"Her guardians? Why not her parents?"

"She has none, sir, that is why, when your late wife, my cousin Ellendara, wished for a companion of her own blood for Alaric when he was but a child, Erminie was sent here since she was in need of a home. As you surely remember, my lord, Ellendara was a trained *leronis* from Arilinn, and she wished, since she had no daughter, to train Erminie in those skills."

"I do not see the difficulty, then, since no loving parents await her," the duke remarked. "Is there a mystery or scandal about her parentage?"

"None whatever; my own sister Lorna was her mother, and her father was my paxman and a Hastur guardman, Darran Tyall. The girl was born outside the *catenas*, it is true; they had been handfasted when they were but twelve years old, and when Darran was killed on the border, my sister was wild with grief. All too soon we knew she was carrying Tyall's child. Erminie was born in my own wife's arms, and

26

we loved her well; that is why Ellendara so gladly welcomed her to this household."

"So she is your niece," said Rascard. "Is her mother living?"

"No, Lorna outlived her promised husband by less than a year."

"Then it seems you are her closest kinsman and her guardian too, and this talk of permission from 'others' is nothing but a device to delay my suit," Rascard said, angrily rising from his chair. "What objection have you to my marrying Erminie, when I was good enough for your cousin, my wife?"

"I will tell you truthfully," Renato said somewhat abashed. "This feud with Storn has grown from a smoke signal to a forest fire; it displeased me then, but it displeases me far more now. I would no longer willingly marry any kinswoman of mine into a clan so riddled with blood feud." He saw Rascard's jaw clamp down sternly and said, "I know your ways in the mountains; it saddened me that Ellendara came to be part of such a feud, I would not wish to entangle any more of my family in it. While Erminie was no more than a guest in your household, I told myself it was none of my concern; but marriage is another thing. And more than this; the girl is too young for you. I would not care to see any girl so young married to a man of an age to be her father, or more. . . . But let the girl herself decide, if she has no objection, I'll make none. Though I'd still rather see her married into a house less encumbered with blood feud."

"Send for her, then, and ask her," said Duke Rascard.

"But not in your presence," Renato insisted. "She

might hesitate to say before her friend and benefactor that she wishes to leave him."

"As you will," said the duke, and summoned a servant.

"Kindly request the *damisela* to attend her kinsman Renato in the conservatory." His eyes were icy, and Renato, as he walked down the dark hall behind the servant, found it difficult to imagine that any young woman could wish to marry this elderly and irascible man. He felt secure in the belief that his young kinswoman would welcome the news that he had come to take her away.

Rascard watched as Erminie went down the corridor toward the conservatory to confront her kinsman. He looked at her with considerable tenderness and for the first time he could see her as a desirable woman instead of the child who had been his son's companion and playmate. He had been thinking of marriage as a desperate necessity; now for the first time he realized it might have some compensations.

After a time they reentered the Great Hall. Renato was scowling angrily, while by Erminie's blush and the faint smile she gave Rascard behind her kinsman's back, the duke realized with a warmth in his heart that she must have looked kindly on his proposal.

He asked with great tenderness, "Are you willing, then, to be my wife, Erminie?"

"The girl's a fool," Renato growled. "I told her I'd find her a husband who'd be better suited to her."

Erminie smiled and said, "Why do you think you could find anyone who would suit me better, kinsman?" She smiled sweetly at Rascard, and the duke, for the first time since he had seen his dead son's

28

face through the starstone, felt light break through the dark shroud of his frozen misery.

He took her hand and said softly, "If you will be my wife, *chiya,* I will try to make you happy."

"I know," said the young woman, gently returning the pressure of his fingers.

"Erminie," Renato said, struggling to recapture his calm, "you can do better than this. Do you truly want to marry this old man? He's older than your father ever lived to be; he's older than I am. Is this what you want? *Think,* girl!" he demanded. "You are being offered freedom as few young women are given choice! No one has demanded that you must marry into Hammerfell."

Erminie took the duke's hand. She said, "Uncle Renato, this is *my* family, too, and my home; I have been here since I was a little girl, and I have no wish to return and live off the charity of kinsmen who are now strangers to me."

"You are a fool, Erminie," said Renato. "Do you wish to see *your* children wiped out in this mad feud, too?"

At this she looked sober. "I confess I would rather live at peace, but which of us would not, if given the choice?" she said.

And the duke, seized by something for a moment stronger than pride, said, "If you ask it of me, Erminie, I will even sue for peace with Lord Storn."

She looked gravely at the backs of her upturned hands and said, "It is true I long for peace. But it was Lord Storn who refused even to return the body of your son; I would not see you humbled before him, my promised husband, nor you going to him humbly as a suppliant to sue for peace on his terms."

"A compromise, then," Rascard said. "I will send him an embassy politely asking him for the return of my son's body for a decent burial, and if he does so, we will have an honorable peace; if he refuses, it is war between us forever."

"Forever?" Erminie asked, sobered, and then sighed. "So be it; we will abide his answer."

Renato scowled. "I realize now you are *both* hopeless fools," he said. "If you truly wished for peace you would somehow overcome this pride which threatens to wipe out both Storn and Hammerfell, and make both your castles into deserted eyries where ravens cry and bandits lurk!"

Rascard shivered, for there was a tone of prophecy in Renato's words, and for a moment as he gazed up into the cavernous beamed ceiling of the Hall it seemed he could indeed see the crag and deserted ruin which once had been the proud keep of Hammerfell. But when Renato went on to ask, "Can't you conquer that damned pride of yours?" he bristled, and Erminie drew herself up with a touch of arrogance.

"Why must it be *my* husband who conquers pride?" asked Erminie with a flare of anger. "Why should it not be Storn, since he has had the triumph of all but wiping out my husband's clan? Is it not for the victor to be magnanimous?"

"You may be right," Renato said, "but it is not right that will end this feud. One of you must sacrifice your pride."

"Perhaps," Rascard said, "but why must it be I?"

Renato shrugged and walked to the window. He said with a resigned gesture, "Erminie, you have made your bed; for what it is worth, you have my permission to lie in it. Take her, kinsman; you deserve one another, and much good may it do you both."

Rascard said with a dry smile, "May I take that for a blessing?"

"Take it as a blessing, a curse, any damned thing you please," Renato said angrily, and gathering his belongings, unceremoniously exited the room.

Rascard put his arm around Erminie and laughed.

"He was so angry he forgot to ask a bride-price," he said. "I fear you have alienated your kinsfolk when you marry me, Erminie."

She smiled up at him and said, "Such kinsfolk as that are better alienated than friendly; at least we will be spared many unpleasant family visits on that account."

"So that he stays long enough to play a kinsman's part at our wedding, he may go where he chooses—to hell, if Zandru will take him in, and may the devil take more pleasure in his company than we do," Rascard agreed.

3

At Midsummer, the marriage of Duke Rascard and Erminie Leynier was held. The wedding was a small one for mountain nobility, for the bride's kinsfolk refused to come, except for less than a dozen of Lord Renato's paxmen, to signify that Erminie was being married into Hammerfell by consent of her kin. Anything less would have been scandalous, but it was obvious that Renato grudged this duty, and there were few bride-gifts from her kin for the newly-made Duchess of Hammerfell. As if to compensate for this miserly show, the elderly duke endowed his young wife with all of the fabled jewels of the duchy. The few distant allies of Hammerfell who attended the ceremony were grim and disgruntled, for they had hoped, in the absence of an heir or any close kin, that one of them might inherit the title and lands of the duke; this new marriage to a young woman who might reasonably be expected to bear children put a stop to all of their hopes.

"Cheer up," said one of the duke's compatriots to another. "It may not mean anything. Rascard is not young; this marriage may well be childless."

"No such luck," replied the other, cynically, "Rascard looks older than he is since the death of his son; but he is in the fullness of his strength, no more than five-and-forty; and even if it were not so, you mind the old saying: 'A husband of forty may not become a father; a husband of fifty years is sure to do so.' " He sniggered and said, "It's a pity for the girl, though; she's young and hearty and deserves a better husband. I'd be tempted to seek a post here, to comfort her in the long winter nights."

"I doubt you'd have much luck," said the first, "She seems a modest girl, and truly fond of the old fellow."

"As a father—I doubt it not," replied the second, "but as a husband?"

This was typical of the conversation; and Erminie, who was a strong telepath, and whose barriers were not accustomed to the company of so many people, had to hear all this without betraying that she heard. It was all she could do not to show her outrage— and on her wedding day! When the time came for the women to take her away to the bridal chamber— they were mostly her serving-women, for none of her aunts or cousins had bothered to make the long journey—she was all but in tears, and had no heart for the typical game of protesting and struggling as they led her out of the room, though she knew she could be accused of being less than a properly modest bride.

Though it was midsummer, the chamber felt chill and drafty as Erminie was stripped to the revealing bedgown traditional for a bedding-ceremony (by old custom, so that the bride might be seen to be healthy and free of hidden deformity or defect); she waited, shivering and trying to keep back her tears—she did not wish Rascard to think her unwilling. Stern as he seemed, she knew well that he had a gentler side; she felt that this was a good marriage for her, whatever her kinsfolk said; being Duchess of Hammerfell was nothing to be despised. She would have had to marry sooner or later, and better an elderly man she knew would at least be kind to her, than to be given over to some complete stranger, however young and handsome he might be. Many a bride had been left alone in the arms of a man she had never met—she was desperately glad this was not to be her fate.

The jewels of Hammerfell were cold and heavy about her neck; she wished she could take them off, but as her serving women stripped off her clothing they would not let her take off the heavy stones;

"The duke will think you disdain his gifts," they warned her. "You must wear them tonight, at least."

So she endured the weight and cold of the stones cutting into her, wondering how long it must go on. They gave her a goblet of wine, which she was glad to have. She was faint after standing through the ceremony and sick at heart from all she had overheard. She had not been able to eat much of the wedding supper. The wine warmed her quickly and she felt some color coming back into her cheeks; so when Duke Rascard was led into the chamber, robed in a fur-lined bedgown (Erminie wondered why custom did not require a bridegroom to exhibit himself free of physical defect or deformity, for the benefit of the bride's family), he saw her sitting up in the high, curtained bed, her cheeks flushed a lovely pink, the shapeliness of her young body revealed by the thin gown, her loosed copper hair flowing over her breasts. He had never seen her hair unbound before, only in the severe braids she wore for every day; it made her look so young and innocent that his heart ached in his chest.

As the serving-folk left them with many rude jests, the duke held one of them back with a gesture.

"Go into my dressing room, Ruyven, and bring me the basket there," he said, and when the man reappeared with a huge basket in his arms, he said, "set it there. Yes, at the foot of the bed. Now go."

"Good night, me lord an' lady, and I wish you both much happiness," the man said with a broad grin, quickly withdrawing. Erminie stared curiously at the big basket, covered by a piece of blanket.

"This is my true wedding gift to you, my lady," Rascard said softly. "I know jewels mean naught to you, so I found you a personal gift which I hope may please you a little more."

Erminie felt the blood flooding into her face again. "My lord, please do not think me ungrateful—it is only that I am not used to wearing jewels and they are so heavy—I would not ever wish to displease you—"

"Here, what's this? Displease me—?" he said, taking her gently by the shoulders. "Do you think I want to be loved for the jewels I give you, girl? I'm flattered that you treasure your husband more than your bride-gift. Let's have them off, then." Laughing, he unfastened the massive gold clasps of the emeralds and helped her to lay them aside, hearing her sigh of relief. When all the necklaces and heavy bracelets had been unfastened and laid in heaps on the night table, he quietly asked, "Now will you open my other gift to you?"

Erminie sat up in bed and eagerly drew the basket toward her. She pulled the blanket aside and with a single small cry of delight she reached into the basket and drew forth the large furry puppy.

"What a darling he is," she cried, hugging the puppy close in her arms. "Oh, thank you!"

"I'm glad you're pleased, my dear," said Rascard, smiling, and she flung her arms round him, kissing him impulsively.

"Has he a name, my lord Duke?"

"No; I thought you would like to name her yourself," said Rascard, "but *I* have a name, and you must call me by it, my dear."

"Then—Rascard—I do thank you," she said, shyly. "May I call him Jewel, because I love him better than any jewels you could give me?"

"*Her*," Rascard said, "I got you a female; they are gentler and more even-tempered house dogs. I thought you would like a dog who would stay home and keep you company, and a male would be out running about and exploring the countryside."

"She is a darling, and Jewel is a better name for a female than a male," said Erminie, eagerly hugging the sleepy puppy, whose shining coat was almost the same color as her own bright hair. "She is the choicest of my jewels, then, and shall be my baby till I have one of my own."

She rocked the puppy, crooning over it happily, while Rascard, watching her with great tenderness, thought, *Yes, she will be a good mother to my children; she is gentle and loving with little things.*

He tucked the puppy in beside them, and she came willingly into his arms.

Midsummer quickly faded, and snow once again lay in the passes of Hammerfell. Jewel grew from a lollopy puppy, all big feet and floppy ears, into a sleek and dignified bitch, the constant companion of the young duchess as she went daily about the castle. With growing confidence that she could fulfill the duties of her new position, and basking in the knowledge that her marriage was a happy one, Erminie seemed prettier; and if now and again she mourned for the young playmate who should have been her husband, she did so in secret and with the full knowledge that her husband mourned no less.

One morning, as she bid him sit for the breakfast they always took together in a high room overlooking the valley, Rascard looked down from the heights and said, "My dear, your eyes are better than mine; what is it I see below?"

She came and looked out over the frosty crags where a small party labored up the icy trail. "There are riders; seven or eight of them, and they bear a banner of black and white—but I cannot see the device." What she did not say was that she felt an undefined sense of impending trouble; and even as she spoke, her husband said with a note of trepidation, "We have heard too little of Storn since we were married, my love."

"Did you expect him to come and eat a piece of our wedding cake, or to send us send us wedding gifts?"

"No more than I expect him to send our son a silver porringer as a naming-gift," said Rascard, "but these days have been too peaceful; I wonder what he is planning?" As he looked at the loose gown she wore, his face darkened with worry, but at mention of her child, Erminie smiled in peaceful self-absorption.

"With the new moon our son may be with us," she said, looking at the orb of violet hanging in the day-sky, pale and shadowy and waning from full. "As for Storn, his capture of Alaric was the last move; perhaps he feels that the next move in the game should be yours. Or maybe he has grown tired of the feud."

"If he wished for peace, he need only have returned Alaric's body," said Rascard. "There is no glory in revenge against the dead, and Lord Storn knows it as well as I do. As for tiring of war, I expect that of him when berries grow on the ice of the Wall Around the World."

Although she shared his views, Erminie turned away from her husband; kind as he had always been to her, she still felt a touch of trepidation when he glowered like this.

"Is it yet time to summon the midwife to stay inside the castle?" he asked her.

She said, "You need not trouble yourself with that, my husband; I can manage with my own serving-women. Most of them have borne children and helped to bring others into the world."

"But it is your first, and I am worried for you, my dear one," said Rascard, who had known too much loss of loved ones. "I'll hear of no denial; Markos shall set forth before this moon wanes to the Lake of

Silence, where he can summon a priestess of Avarra to care for you."

"All right, Rascard, if it puts your mind at ease, but must Markos go? Can you not send a younger man?"

Rascard chuckled and teased, "Why, my dear, such tenderness for Markos? Have I been unfortunate enough to have a rival within my very household?"

Erminie knew he was joking, but she was serious. "Markos is too old to defend himself if he should be set on in the hills, by bandits or—" She stopped there, but Rascard heard what she did not say as well as the spoken words.

Or by our foes of Storn.

"Well, then, we cannot endanger your cavalier," said Rascard genially. "I shall send some of the young men to guard him against danger on the way." He looked again out of the window. "Can you see the device of the riders now, my dear?"

Erminie looked out, and her eyes were troubled, "I can see now that it is not black and white but blue and silver; the Hastur colors. What in the name of all the Gods could bring a Hastur-lord to guest at Hammerfell?"

"I do not know, my love; but we must welcome them suitably," said the duke.

"So it shall be," Erminie agreed and hurried off to her pantries, calling the serving-women to make ready for welcoming strange guests. She felt concerned, for in all the years she had lived in these hills she had never set eyes on any of the Hastur-lords.

She had heard that the Hastur-lords had attempted to join all of the Hundred Kingdoms under their protection in one giant kingdom, and had also heard so many tales of their descent from the Gods, that she was almost surprised when the Hastur-lord turned out to be no more than a tall, slim man, with flaming copper hair and eyes of almost metallic gray not unlike her own. His manner was mild and unassuming; Erminie felt that even Rascard looked more like an offspring of the Gods than he did.

"Rascard of Hammerfell is honored to welcome you to his keep," the duke stated formally once they were comfortably seated before a warm fire in the morning room. "This is my lady Erminie. May I know the name of the guest who honors me with his presence?"

"I am Valentine Hastur of Elhalyn," said the man. "My lady and sister—" he indicated the lady beside him who rode crimson-robed, her face concealed by a long veil, "is Merelda, Keeper of Arilinn."

Erminie's cheeks flushed and she said to the woman, "But I know you, surely."

"Yes," Merelda said, putting her veil aside to show a stern and dispassionate countenance. Her voice was pitched remarkably low and Erminie realized she was an *emmasca*. "I have seen you in my starstone. That is why we came here—to meet with you and perhaps to bring you to the Tower to be trained as a *leronis*."

"Oh, I should like that above all things," Erminie exclaimed, unthinking. "I had only such training as my foster-mother, she who was duchess here before me, could give—" Suddenly, her face fell. "As you can see, I cannot leave my husband and—my baby who will be born soon." But she looked truly disappointed and Lord Valentine smiled kindly at her.

"Of course your first duty is to your children," Merelda said, "Yet we have great need of trained *leroni* in the Tower, there are never enough *laran* workers for our needs. Perhaps after your children are born, you could come to us for a year or two. . . ."

The duke interrupted with anger, "My wife is no homeless orphan for you to offer her an apprenticeship! I can care for her appropriately without help from any of the Hasturs. She need serve no man other than myself."

"I am sure of that," said Valentine diplomatically, "We are not merely asking you to give of yourself without recompense; the training you would receive there would benefit your family and all of your clan."

Rascard saw that Erminie looked really disappointed. Could it be that she was willing to leave him for this "training," whatever it was? Feeling unnerved, he said brusquely, "My wife and the mother of my child shall not pass from under my roof; and there's an end to talking about it. Can I serve you in anything else, my lord and lady?"

Valentine and Merelda, who knew better than to provoke their host, let the matter rest.

"Perhaps you can indulge my curiosity," said Lord Valentine. "What of this blood feud with the people of Storn? I have heard that it was raging even in my great-grandsire's time—"

"And in mine," said Rascard.

"Yet never have I known whence it came, or what began it. As I rode through these hills I saw Storn's men on the march, out for raiding, I suppose. Can you inform me, my lord Duke?"

"I have heard several tales," Duke Rascard said, "but I can offer no guarantee that any one and no other is the true tale."

Valentine Hastur laughed. "Fair enough," he said. "Tell me what you believe."

"What I heard from my father was this," Rascard said, absentmindedly petting Jewel's head which was resting in his lap. "In his grandfather's time, when Regis the Fourth held the throne of the Hasturs at Hali, Conn, my great-grandsire, had contracted to marry a lady of the Alton kindred, and he had word that she had set forth from her home, with her baggage and horses, and three wagons containing her goods and her dowry. Weeks passed, yet no further word came, and the lady arrived not at Hammerfell. After forty days, the lady finally arrived, but with a message sent from Storn, that he had taken the bride and her dowry; but that the girl did not please him, so he was returning her to Hammerfell, and that my forebear had permission to marry her if he wished; but he would keep the dowry for his trouble in trying out the bride. And since the lady was pregnant with the son of Storn, he would thank them to send his son along sometime before his naming-feast, with an appropriate following."

"I am not surprised that this resulted in blood feud," Lord Valentine said, and Rascard nodded.

"It might even then have passed as the most unseemly of all jests," said Rascard, "but when the child was born—and they say he was the very image of Storn's elder son—my grandsire sent back the child and a bill for the wetnurse who carried him, and for the mule she rode. And that spring Storn sent armed men against Hammerfell, and war it has been ever since; when I was but a lad of fifteen, scarce proclaimed a man, Storn raiders killed my father, my two elder brothers, and my younger brother, a boy of nine years. The Storn kin have left me alone in the world, my lord, save for my dear wife and the child she bears. And I shall guard them with my life."

"No man living could fault you for that," said Lord Valentine Hastur somberly, "surely not I; yet I would wish to see this feud mended before I die."

"And I," said Rascard. "Despite all, I would have been willing to put aside my ill will to the Storns until they attacked my paxman and killed my son, I would have forgiven the deaths of my other kinsmen. But not now. I loved my son too dearly."

"Perhaps your children may end this feud," said the Hastur-lord.

"Perhaps it may be so. But it will not be soon; my son is yet unborn," said Duke Rascard.

"The children Erminie bears—"

Erminie interrupted. "Children?"

"Why, yes," said the *leronis*. "Surely you know you are bearing twins."

"N–no, I did not know," said Erminie, stammering. "How can you tell that?"

"Have you never monitored a pregnant woman before this?"

"No, never; I have not been taught—sometimes I thought my mind had touched the child, but I could not be certain—"

Rascard was frowning.

"Twins?" he said, troubled, "I hope, then, for all our sakes that one of them is a daughter."

Valentine asked with lifted brow, "Well, Merelda?"

She shook her head. "I am sorry," she replied, "You have two sons. I thought—I was sure that would please you; it is terribly sad when only the life of a single child stands between an ancient line and its extinction."

But Erminie's eyes were bright. "I am to give my lord not one son but two!" she exclaimed. "Did you hear, my lord?" Then she saw the scowl on his face. "Does it displease you, Rascard?"

Rascard forced himself to assume a more amiable smile. "I am pleased, of course, my dearest; but twins always create confusion as to which of them is eldest, or best fitted to rule; and it is all too likely that they might become enemies and bitter rivals. My sons must stand together as strong allies against the dangers from our foes of Storn."

Seeing her distress, he added, "Still, you must not let this spoil your happiness in our children. We shall contrive something, I am sure."

Lord Valentine said, "I wish you would let your lady come to us, for a time at least; at Arilinn there is a notable college of midwives, so that she could be delivered safely, and we could insure that the twins would receive every care and consideration."

"I am sorry; but I cannot even consider it," said Rascard. "My sons must be born under their own roof."

"Then there is no more to be said," replied Lord Valentine, and rose to take his leave. Duke Rascard objected that they should remain for entertainment and perhaps a banquet in their honor, but they refused politely and took their leave with many expressions of esteem on either side.

As they rode away from Hammerfell, Rascard noticed that Erminie looked sorrowful.

"Surely you did not want to leave me alone, my wife, nor have our sons born among strangers!"

"No, of course not," she said, "but—"

"Ah, I knew there must be a *but,*" said the duke. "What could win you away from me, dearest? Have you anything to complain of in my treatment?"

"No, nothing, you have been the kindest husband one could imagine," Erminie said. "Nevertheless it is tempting to me that I might have complete training as a *leronis.* I am all too conscious that there are possibilities in my *laran* which I do not even know how to imagine, far less do."

"You know far more of it than I, or than anyone within the boundaries of all Hammerfell," said Rascard. "Can that not content you?"

"I am not discontented," said Erminie, "but there is so much else to know—this much I have learned from the starstone itself—and I feel ignorant compared with what I might be. With the *leronis* Merelda, for instance, she is so learned and wise—"

"I have no need for a learned wife, and you suit me exactly as you are," Rascard told her, and embraced her tenderly, and she said no more. With her husband, and her coming children, she was content, for the moment at least.

4

The violet moon waned, then waxed again; and three days after the new moon Erminie of Hammerfell was brought to bed and, as the *leronis* had prophesied, gave birth to twin sons, identical as two peas in a pod. Small wiry babies, red and squalling, each little head covered with thick dark hair.

"Dark hair," Erminie frowned, "I had hoped that at least one of our sons, my lord, would bear the *laran* gift of our family."

"From what I have heard of the *laran*-gifted," Rascard said, "we—and they—are better without it, my dearest. *Laran* was not too much known in my line."

"One or both may still be red-haired, my lady," said the midwife, bending near. "When babes are born with such an abundance of dark hair, it is in no way uncommon for it all to fall out and come in again fair or red."

"Truly?" Erminie asked, then paused, absorbed in thought. "Yes, my mother's closest friend said that when I was born my hair was dark, but it fell out and grew in bright red."

"Well, so it may be," Rascard said, and bent to kiss his wife. "My thanks for this great gift, my dearest lady. What shall we name them?"

"That is for you to say, my husband," said Erminie. "Would you name one of them for your son who perished at Storn hands?"

"Alaric? No, I like not the omen of giving my son the name of the dead," said Rascard, "I will search in the archives of Hammerfell for names of those who were healthy and lived to a ripe old age."

Accordingly, he came to her room that evening, where she lay with the babies tucked in one to either side of her, with Jewel, now a very large dog indeed, across the foot of her bed.

"Why have you tied a red ribbon around one son's wrist and not about his brother's?" asked Duke Rascard.

"It was I who did that," said the midwife. "This little man was the elder of his brother by almost twenty minutes; he was born just as the clock was striking midday, while his lazy brother delayed a few more minutes."

"A good thought," said Rascard, "but a ribbon can fall off or be lost. Call Markos," he added, and when the old paxman entered the room, bowing to the duke and his lady, he said, "take my elder son there— the little duke, my heir—he with the ribbon about his arm—and see that he is marked so that he may never be mistaken for his brother."

Markos bent and lifted the baby. Erminie quavered fearfully, "What are you going to do with him?"

"I'll not hurt him, my lady; not for more than a moment. I'll but tattoo him with the mark of Hammerfell, and bring him back to your breast. It won't take but a minute or so," said the old man, lifting the well-wrapped baby, despite pleas from his mother, and left the room.

Soon he brought him back, and, unfolding the blanket, revealed a tattoo in red on the small shoulder, the hammer-mark of the Duchy of Hammerfell.

"He shall be called Alastair," said Rascard, "after my late father; and the other shall be Conn, after my great-grandsire, in whose time the feud with Storn was made, if you have no objection, my dear."

The baby slept fitfully, and woke wailing, his face flushed and angry.

"You have hurt him," Erminie accused.

Markos laughed. "Not much, nor for long; and even so it is a small price to pay for the heirship of Hammerfell."

"Hammerfell and heirship be damned," Erminie said wrathfully, hugging the shrieking Alastair to her breast. "There, there, my little love, Mother has you now, and no one shall touch you again."

At that moment, Conn, in the cradle across the room, woke and began squalling an angry echo to his brother's cries. Rascard went to pick up his younger son, who was thrashing fitfully in his blankets. Rascard observed with surprise that Conn was clawing frantically at his unmarked left shoulder; no sooner did Conn begin crying than Alastair dropped off to sleep in Erminie's arms.

Over the next days, Erminie noticed it more than

once; that when Alastair cried, Conn woke and whimpered; but even when Conn was sorely pricked with a pin in his breechclout, Alastair continued to sleep peacefully. She remembered what had been said in her family, that of twins in *laran*-gifted households, one always had a little bit more than his share of psychic power, and the other a bit less. Obviously, then, Conn was the more telepathic of the twins, and she spent more time holding him and soothing him. If he were sensitive to his own pain and also to his brother's, he must therefore need more love and tenderness. So for the first months of his life, Conn became his mother's favorite, while Alastair was the duke's favorite because he was his heir and because he fussed less and smiled more at his father.

Both twins were handsome and healthy children, and grew like puppies; and when they were only half a year old, were taking unsteady steps about the house and courtyard, sometimes clinging to the great dog Jewel who was their constant companion and guard. Alastair was a few days quicker to walk, but was still only crying and cooing when Conn first babbled a sound that could have been his mother's name. As their midwife had predicted, their downy toddler's hair was the color of living flame.

No one but their mother could ever tell them apart; even their father sometimes mistook Conn for Alastair, but their mother never made a mistake.

They had rounded a full year, and several moons beyond when, on a dark cloudy afternoon, toward evening, Duke Rascard burst into his wife's sitting room, where she sat with her ladies, the twins playing with wooden horses on the floor. She looked up at him in surprise.

"What's the matter?"

The duke said, "Try not to be too alarmed, my dear; but there are armed raiders approaching the castle. I have rung the bell for folk on the outlying farms to come inside the keep; I have ordered the drawbridge to be raised. We are secure here even if they try and hold us under siege for a whole season. But we must be prepared for anything."

"The men of Storn?" she asked, her face betraying no fear or dread; but Conn, evidently sensing something in her voice, dropped his wooden horse and began to wail.

"I fear so," Rascard said, and Erminie went pale.

"The children!"

"Yes," he said, and kissed her quickly. "Take them, and go as we planned. God keep you, my dear, until we are reunited."

She snatched up a twin under each arm and retreated into her own room, where she quickly packed a few necessities for each child; she sent one of her women to the kitchen for a basket of food, and went swiftly down to a back entrance; the plan had been made that if anyone actually broke into the fortress, she would leave at once with the babies, and try to make her way through the woods to the nearest village where they would be safe. Now it struck her that perhaps it would be the greatest folly to leave the shelter of the castle for the woods and wilds; whatever came, she should remain in safety here; even under siege she would at least be with her husband.

But she had promised Rascard to follow the plans they had made. If she did not, he might not be able to find her afterward and they might never be to-

gether again. Her heart seemed to stop inside her
breast; might that hasty kiss have been her last farewell to her children's father? Conn was wailing in-
consolably; she knew he must be picking up her
fears, so Erminie tried to summon up courage not
only for herself but for her frightened children. She
wrapped them in their warmest cloaks and set them
down beside her, the basket on her arm and a hand
to each.

"Now come quickly, little ones," she whispered
to them, and hurried down the long twisting stairs
toward the back gate of the castle, the twins stumbling on unsteady little feet.

She pushed open the long-disused entrance, which
nonetheless was kept oiled and in order for just such
an eventuality as this; she looked back toward the
main court and saw the sky darkened with flights of
arrows, and somewhere, flames rising. She wanted to
run back, screaming her husband's name, but she
had promised.

*By no means return, whatever happens, but await me in
the village till I come to you. If I do not meet you there at
sunrise, you will know I have perished; then you must leave
Hammerfell and take refuge in Thendara with your Hastur
cousins, and appeal to them for justice and revenge.* She
hurried along, but her pace was too much for the
children. First Alastair tripped and sprawled shrieking on the cobblestones, then Conn stumbled; she
picked them both up in her arms and hurried on.
Something big and soft bumped her in the darkness;
she put out a hand and almost burst into tears.

"Jewel! There, good dog, good dog," she whispered, through tears tearing her throat. "You came
with me, then, oh, good dog!"

She stumbled over something frighteningly soft, and almost fell; recovering her balance in the semi-dark of the courtyard, she felt a man's body under her feet. She had fallen to her knees and could not avoid seeing the man's face. To her shock and horror it was the groom who had led her children's ponies out that very afternoon. His throat had been cut, and Erminie cried out in dismay, then stopped as Conn began to sob in accord with her fear.

"Hush, hush, my little son; we must be brave now and not cry," she murmured, patting him to quiet him.

In the dark, a voice spoke her name, so softly it could hardly be heard over the child's sobbing.

"My lady—"

She barely withheld a scream; then, even as she recognized the voice, she made out the familiar face of old Markos in the deepening firelit darkness.

"No need to fear; it's only me."

At his familiar touch, Erminie let out her breath in relief.

"Oh, thank the Gods it is you! I was afraid—" Her voice was drowned out by a great crash somewhere as of falling masonry, or thunder. Markos came close to her in the darkness.

"Here, let me carry one of the babes," the old man said. "We can't go back; the upper courts are all afire."

"What of the duke?" Erminie asked, trembling.

"When I saw him last all was well; he was keeping the bridge with a dozen of his men. Those fiends set it afire with *clingfire* which burns the very stone!"

"Ah, the devils!" Erminie's voice was a wail.

"Devils indeed!" the man muttered with a grim

stare at the heights, then turned to the woman. "I should be at the fighting, but His Grace sent me down to guide you to the village, lady; so gi' me one of the babes and we'll go faster." She could hear the creaking of some huge siege engine over the roar of the flames, and looking back saw it outlined against the dark sky, huge like the skeleton of some monstrous unknown beast, with dark missiles bursting out of the giant's maw and exploding into flame in midair. The twins in her arms were struggling to get down, and Erminie handed over one of the twins to Markos. She was not sure in the dark which one she had given to him. It was growing cold, and the night was dark and rain was beginning to make the path slippery underfoot. Clutching the remaining twin, she hurried after the shadowy form of Markos down the hill. Once she stumbled over the dog and dropped her basket; she had to retrieve it, and almost lost sight of her protector. She wanted to cry out to him to wait, but she did not want to hold him back, so she tried to keep him in sight, stumbling along without really taking much heed of where she was going. Before long she was completely lost, hampered by the dog who kept blundering under her feet and the weight of the heavy child in her arms. At least there was only one to carry and the other was safe with the only man save her husband whom she absolutely trusted.

Slipping and sliding on stones and grass, she somehow reached the bottom of the hill, where she called softly, "Markos!"

But there was no answer.

Again she called, afraid to raise her voice too much, for fear of attracting the attention of the enemies she knew must be all around her in the woods. Above her, at the top of the hill, Hammerfell was burning; she could see the flames rising as if from a volcano. Nothing could live in that inferno; but where was the duke? Had he been trapped within the burning castle? Now she could see that it was Alastair clinging round her neck, whimpering. Where was Markos with Conn? She sought to try and find her bearings by the terrible light of her home burning above her. She called again, softly; but all round her in the woods she could hear strange steps and unknown voices, even laughter. She was not even sure whether she heard the voices with her ears or with her *laran*.

"Ha, ha! So ends Hammerfell!"

"That's the end of 'em all!"

She watched, paralyzed with dread, as the flames rose higher and higher and finally, with a great crash like the end of the world, the castle fell in and the flames began to subside. Shaking in terror, she fled through the woods till she could no longer see the sun rising over the ruin that had been the proud fortress of Hammerfell. By early morning she was all alone in a strange wood, with the dog huddled against her legs and the tired child clinging round her neck. Jewel whined in sympathy as if trying to comfort her, nudging so close that she almost pushed Erminie off her feet. Erminie sat down on a log, Jewel cuddling close to her for warmth, and tried to avert her eyes from the dying fire of what had been the only home she had ever known.

As the light of the new day strengthened, she drew herself wearily to her feet and, hoisting the heavy weight of the sleeping twin, she trudged into what was left of the village at the foot of the hill. Horrorstruck, she realized that Storn's men had been here first; house after house lay in smoldering ruins, and most of the people had fled—except for those who lay slaughtered. Weary and heartsick, she forced herself to search throughout the remains of the village, the few houses left standing; to ask anyone she recognized of Markos and Conn, who had been in his arms. But nowhere did she hear any news of the old man or her child. She carefully avoided being seen by any stranger—if any Storn follower recognized *her,* she knew she would be killed at once without mercy, and her child, too. Till near noon she waited, still hoping that the duke had escaped that last conflagration and would join her there, but everyone she asked in the wood now filled with homeless villagers regarded the sad-faced, bedraggled woman with her dog and her heavy child with pity and kindness as they denied any sight or word of an older man bearing a year-old child in his arms.

All day she persisted in her search, but by sunset, she knew that what she most feared had indeed come to pass. Markos was vanished, dead or slain, or else he had abandoned her for some reason, and since the duke had not come for her at sunrise, he must have perished in the fall of the burning castle.

And so, filled with despair and the dawning of terror as the last light died, Erminie forced herself to sit down, to straighten and braid her long, disheveled hair, to eat some food from her basket, then feed some bread to her dog and her hungry child. At least she was not completely alone, but left with her firstborn, now the Duke of Hammerfell—and where, *where* was his twin? Her only support and protection was a witless dog. She lay down and wrapped herself in her cloak, creeping close to Jewel for warmth, sheltering the sleeping Alastair in her arms. She fervently thanked the Gods the winter had passed. At first light, she knew that she must look about carefully and take her bearings, then set out on the long road that would bring her at last to the faraway city of Thendara, and to her kinsmen in the Tower there. Alastair was rocked in her embrace as her body was wracked with sobs.

5

Thendara lay nestled in a valley of the Venza Mountains, the great Tower rising over the heights of the city. Unlike other, more secluded Towers which housed all the telepaths working there—monitors, Keepers, technicians, and mechanics—the Tower in Thendara did not serve to isolate the inhabitants from the people of the city, but as in all the cities of the lowlands, tended to set the tone of social life in general.

The Tower workers mostly had residences in the city itself, sometimes very elegant and splendid ones. However, this was not the case with the widowed Duchess of Hammerfell. Erminie, who had shed that identity for the simple one (which carried even higher prestige in the society of Thendara) of Second Technician in Thendara Tower, lived modestly, in a small house off the Street of Swordsmiths, whose only luxury was a garden filled with scented herbs, flowers, and fruit trees.

Erminie was now thirty-seven years old, but she was still slender, swift-moving and bright-eyed, her splendid copper hair as new-polished as ever. She had lived alone with her only son all these years; no breath of scandal had ever touched her name or reputation. She was seldom seen in any company save that of her son, her lady housekeeper, or the great old rust-colored mountain dog who accompanied her everywhere.

This was not because she was shunned by society; rather, it was she who shunned or seemed to scorn it. Twice she had been sought in marriage, once by the Keeper of the Tower, one Edric Elhalyn, and more recently by her cousin, Valentine Hastur, the same man who had come to her home in the hills so very long ago. This gentleman, close kin to the Hastur-lords of Thendara and Carcosa, had first asked her to marry him in her second year in the Tower. At that time she had refused him, pleading the recentness of her widowhood. Now, on an evening late in summer, some eighteen years after she had first come to the city, he renewed his suit.

He found her in the garden of her town house, sitting on a rustic bench there, her fingers busy with needlework. The dog Jewel was at her feet, but she raised her head and growled softly as he approached her mistress.

"Quiet; good girl," Erminie chided the dog gently. "I should think you would know my cousin well enough by now; he has been here often enough. Lie down, Jewel," she added sternly, and the dog subsided into a floppy rust-colored heap at her feet.

Valentine Hastur said, "I am only glad you have so faithful a friend, since you have no other protector. If I have my way, she will know me better still," he added with a meaningful smile.

Erminie looked into the deep gray eyes of the man who sat beside her. His hair was now woven through with silver, but otherwise he was unchanged—the same man who had offered her support and affection for nearly two decades. She sighed. "Cousin—Val, I am grateful to you as always; but I think you will know why I must still say no."

"No, I'm damned if I do," Lord Valentine said fervently, "I know you cannot still be in mourning for the old duke though that may be what you would have people believe."

Jewel rubbed against Erminie's knees and whined, demanding the attention she felt was being denied her. Erminie petted her distractedly.

"Valentine, you know I care for you," the woman said, "and it is true, I mourn no longer for Rascard; though he was a good husband and a kind father to my children. But at the moment, I do not quite feel free to marry because of my son."

"In Avarra's name, kinswoman," Valentine Hastur demanded, "how could it affect your son's fortunes other than well, should his mother marry into the Hastur kindred? Suppose he became Hastur rather than Hammerfell, or I swore to devote myself to restoring him to his proper rank and inheritance; what then?"

"When first I came to Thendara, I owed my very life to you; and that of my child." Valentine waved that aside.

"It would be a poor reward for your kindness to

end by entangling you in this old unsettled blood feud," Erminie answered.

"It was no more than owing to kin," he said. "And it is I who am everlastingly in your debt, my dear. But how can you still speak of this old feud as unsettled, Erminie, when there are no living men of the line of Hammerfell save for your son, who was but a year old when his father and all his household died in the burning of the keep?"

"Nevertheless, until my son is restored to his inheritance, I cannot enter into any other alliance," Erminie said. "I swore when I married his father that I would devote myself to the well-being of the line of Hammerfell. And I will not forswear that pledge, nor will I draw others into it with me."

"A promise to the dead holds no force," protested Valentine, quite beside himself. "I am living, and I think you owe more to me than to the dead."

Erminie smiled affectionately at Valentine.

"My dear kinsman, I owe you much indeed," she said. For when she had first come to Thendara—half starved, penniless, in rags—he had taken her into his home, and managed to do it without compromising her reputation. At that time he had been married to a noble lady of the MacAran kindred. Valentine and his lady had fed and clothed her and her child, found her this very house where she still lived, and chosen her for the Tower, from which she had achieved her present high place in the society of Thendara. All this was between them as he stood looking into her sad eyes. It was the Hastur whose eyes dropped first.

"Forgive me, my dear Erminie, you owe me nothing; I said so before, and I meant it. If anything, the debt is mine, that for all these years I have been privileged with your friendship and your good will. I remember, too, that my wife loved you well; I think it would not profane her memory if I claimed you in marriage."

"I loved her, too," said Erminie, "and if I thought of marriage I could ask no better than you, my dear friend. It is not easy to forget all you have been to me, and to my son as well. But I have pledged that till he is restored—"

Valentine Hastur frowned and looked up through the boughs of the tree beneath which they sat, trying to sort his feelings. Alastair of Hammerfell was, he felt, a spoiled and worthless youngster, worthy neither of his high position nor of his mother's solicitude; but it would be no use whatever to say this to the boy's mother. Since he was all she had, she could see not the slightest fault in him, and clung to him with a passionate partisanship which nothing could tarnish. And Valentine knew he had done wrong to remind her of her son; for Erminie knew that Valentine, kindly as he always was, did not love the boy.

The year before, Alastair had incurred a heavy fine for a third offense of driving his carriage recklessly inside the city walls. This was an offense all too common for young men his age, and, unfortunately, young men tended to think it a point of honor to defy the laws pertaining to safety in riding or driving. These young fops who thought of themselves as ornaments to society were, Valentine thought, a disgrace to their kinsfolk; but he knew that was a belief common to men of his own age. He wondered if he was simply getting old.

At her feet the dog stirred and raised her head,

and Erminie said with relief, "That can hardly be Alastair so early; I did not hear his horse in the street. Who can it be? Someone Jewel knows, surely—"

"It is your kinsman Edric," said Valentine Hastur, looking toward the garden gate. "I should go—"

"No, cousin; if it is Edric, it will be nothing but business, you may be sure, and if he doesn't wish to speak before you, he will not hesitate to send you away," Erminie said, laughing. Edric was the Keeper of the first circle of matrix workers in Thendara Tower and close kin to both Erminie and Valentine.

Edric strode into the garden, and made a chilly but civil bow to Valentine Hastur.

"Cousin," he said formally.

Erminie gave him a formal curtsy. "Welcome, cousin; this is a strange hour for a family visit."

"I have a favor to ask of you," Edric said wasting no time in his characteristic, brusque manner, "A family affair, really. You know, I am sure, that my daughter Floria has been in training as a monitor at Neskaya Tower, away from the city?"

"Yes, I remember; how does she?"

"Very well, cousin, but it seems there is no permanent place for her at Neskaya," Edric said. "However, Kendra Leynier is pregnant, and she is returning to her husband till the child is born, which would make a place for Floria in the third circle at Thendara. But until we are certain, Floria must live here in Thendara, and as my most suitable female kin, I wanted to ask you to chaperone her in society." Floria's mother had died when she was very young; she, too, had been a close kinswoman of Erminie's.

Erminie asked, "How old is Floria now?"

"Seventeen; marriageable, but she wishes to work first for a few years in the Tower," Edric said.

Grown so quickly, thought Erminie. *It seemed like yesterday that Floria and Alastair were children playing in this very garden.*

"I would be *delighted,*" Erminie said.

"Are you attending *Dom* Gavin Delleray's concert tonight?" asked Edric.

"Yes," said Erminie. "*Dom* Gavin is a close friend of my son's. They studied music together when Alastair was younger. I think Gavin was always a good influence on him."

"Then perhaps you will join me—and Floria—in our box at the theater?"

"I wish we could," Erminie said, "but I have subscribed to a box myself for this season; partly because of Gavin's concert tonight." Her tone became nostalgic. "Oh, Edric, I find it so hard to think of Floria as seventeen; when last I saw her she was but eleven, in short frocks with curls in her hair. I remember Alastair used to tease her dreadfully—chase her around the garden with spiders and snakes, until I'd try to stop it by calling them both in for supper; but even then he'd keep on teasing her by stealing all her cakes and sweets; he had many a spanking from his nurse for such behavior."

"Well, Floria has grown a great deal; I doubt her cousin will recognize her," Edric said. "It's hard to remember what a little hoyden she used to be, but I think your ladylike example will still do her a great deal of good."

"I hope so," said Erminie. "I was very young when Alastair was born; not much older than Floria is now. That is the way in the mountains, but I wonder if it is not a mistake—how can one so young be a wise mother, and don't children suffer the lack of a mature parent?"

"I would not necessarily say that," Edric said. "I think you have been a fine mother, and I do not think ill of Alastair. In fact, when Floria is older—" he broke off, then continued. "I was only sorry to see you burdened with children when you were but a child yourself. I would rather see a young girl carefree—"

"Yes, I know," said Erminie. "My kinsmen did not want me to marry Rascard; yet I have never been sorry I did. I have nothing but good to say of him, and I am glad I had my son while I was young enough to enjoy having a baby around the house." She thought with the usual pain of her other son who had died in the burning of Hammerfell. But it was so long ago. Maybe she should marry Valentine after all while she was still young enough to have other children. Valentine picked up the thought—which she had not thought to shield—and smiled warmly at her. She lowered her eyes.

"Be that as it may," Edric said, and Erminie wondered if he, too, had picked up the thought—it was not to be imagined that he would disapprove of a marriage into the powerful and prominent Hastur clan, "I shall welcome you to our box at the theater at intermission tonight. Floria will be happy to see you again—you were always her favorite kinswoman, because you were still so young and playful."

"I hope I am still young enough to be more of an elder sister and friend to her than a chaperone," Erminie said. "I envied her mother—I have always wanted a daughter."

Once again she knew that Valentine picked up the thought which this time she had quite deliberately failed to shield. As Edric turned to leave, she touched his arm, "Edric, there is another matter—a dream I had again, last night. I have had it so often—"

"The same dream, about Alastair?"

"I am not sure it *was* Alastair," Erminie with confusion said. "I was in the Tower, in the circle, and Alastair came in—I *think* it was Alastair," she repeated uncertainly. "Only he—you know how meticulously he always dresses—in my dream he was poorly dressed in the mountain style—such clothing as his father might have worn. And he spoke to me through the starstone—" her voice faltered; she touched the matrix jewel that hung at her breast.

Edric said, "You have had this dream before—"

"All this year," Erminie said. "It seems like some vision of the future, and yet—it was you who tested Alastair—"

"True; and I told you then, as I tell you again now; Alastair has but little *laran*, not enough to be worth the trouble of training," Edric said. "Certainly not enough for a Tower worker; but your dream tells me that you have not yet accepted my decision. Does it mean as much as that to you, Erminie?"

"I am not sure this dream is as simple as that," she said, "for when I woke, my starstone was glowing as if it had been touched—"

"I cannot see what else it *could* mean," said Edric thoughtfully.

Before any more could be said, the dog stirred again and bounded toward the gate. Erminie rose, "It is my son returning; I should go and greet him."

Valentine looked up at her. "You are too protective of him, my dear."

"No doubt you are right," Erminie said, "but I cannot forget that night when I lost my other son because I let them out of my sight for only a few minutes. I know it has been a long time, but I am still fearful whenever he is beyond my eyes' reach."

"I cannot fault you for being a careful mother," Valentine said, "but I beg you to remember that he is no longer a child; he must in the very course of nature cease to need his mother's constant concern. And if he is to recover his heritage, he must begin to strive for himself. But you know, Erminie, that I think it might be far better to let this feud burn itself out for lack of fuel—to wait for another generation."

"You will have no luck with that line of reasoning, cousin," interrupted Edric, "I have said all this to her before. She will not hear sense."

"And let my son live always in exile, a landless man?" she countered indignantly. To Valentine she seemed very beautiful, with her eyes glowing with determination; he only wished the subject were more worthy. "Should I let my husband lie restless in his grave with his ghost unavenged haunting the ruins of Hammerfell?"

Shocked, Valentine asked, "Do you truly *believe* that, kinswoman—that the dead keep their grudges and old grievances against the living?"

But he could see in her eyes that she *did* believe this, and could not imagine how to change her mind.

The dog sprang up and bounded across the garden, coming back with prancing leaps and frisking around the feet of the tall young man.

"Mother," he said, "I knew not that you were entertaining guests." He bowed gracefully to her, and inclined his head respectfully to the Hastur-lord, and then to Lord Edric. "Good evening, sir. Good evening, cousin."

"Not guests, but our kinsmen," said Erminie. "Will you remain and dine with us? Both of you?"

"It would be a pleasure; unfortunately, I am expected elsewhere," Valentine said in civil excuse, and took his leave, bowing over Erminie's hand.

Edric hesitated, then said, "I think not tonight; but I will see you at the concert later this evening."

Erminie watched him go, standing with her arm round her tall son's waist.

"What did he want with you, Mother? Is that man sniffing round to get you to marry him?"

"Would that displease you so much, my son—if I were to marry again?"

"You cannot expect me to be pleased," said Alastair, "if my mother marries some lowlander to whom Hammerfell is less than nothing. When we are restored, and you are again in our rightful place at Hammerfell—then if he would like to come wooing, I will consider what answer I will give him."

Erminie smiled gently, "I am a Tower technician, my son; I do not need the permission of any guardian to marry. You cannot even make the excuse that I have not yet arrived at years of discretion.

"Oh, come, Mother, you're still young and pretty—"

"I am truly glad you think so, my son; but even so, if I wish to marry, I may consult with you, but I shall not ask your leave." Her voice was very gentle and held no trace of reproach, but the young man lowered his eyes and blushed anyway.

"Among our people in the mountains, men show

more courtesy; they come properly to a woman's male kinsmen and ask leave to pay court to her."

Well, she could not blame him; she had brought him up to the habits and customs of their mountain kinsmen, and bade him never forget that he was Duke of Hammerfell. If this was what he now thought himself, it was the product of her own teaching.

"Night is falling; we should go in," she said.

"The dew is falling; shall I fetch your shawl, Mother?"

"I am not yet so old as that!" she said, exasperated, as he took her arm. "Whatever you think of him, my son, Valentine said one thing which made sense."

"And what was that, Mother?"

"He said that you were a man, and that if you wished to recover Hammerfell, you would somehow have to recover it for yourself."

Alastair nodded. He said, "This has been much on my mind, Mother, these last three years. Yet I hardly know where to start. I cannot, after all, ride to Storn Heights and ask old Lord Storn, or whoever sits in his place these days, to give me the keys. Yet if these Hastur-lords truly value justice as they say, it occurs to me that they might be willing to lend me armed men to recapture it; or at least they might be willing to make public acknowledgment that Hammerfell is mine and Storn holds it unlawfully. Do you think our kinsman Valentine could get me an audience with the king?"

"I am quite sure of it," Erminie said; she was glad to know that her son had been thinking on the matter. So far there was not much of a plan; but if he was willing to seek counsel of older and wiser heads, at least that was a good beginning.

"Surely you remember we have a concert to attend this evening, Mother?"

"Of course," she replied. But for some reason, she did not wish to mention why this evening's plans had particular significance for her.

As Erminie went to her rooms to summon her lady-companion to dress her for the concert, she felt a curious foreboding, as if this evening would be fateful, and she could not imagine why.

When she was dressed in a gown of rust-colored satin that set off her shining hair to perfection, a garland of green jewels at her slender throat, she went down to join her son.

"How fine you look tonight, Mother," he said. "I was afraid you would insist on wearing your Tower robes; but you have dressed as is fitting to our station and I am proud of you."

"Are you, indeed? Then I am glad of the trouble I have taken to dress tonight." Alastair himself was wearing a laced tunic and knee breeches of gold satin, set off with dark yellow sleeves and black lacings; around his neck he wore a pendant of gleaming carved amber. His red hair was curled elaborately just above his shoulders; he looked so much like her childhood playmate Alaric that even after so many years, Erminie felt a lump rise in her throat. Well, he was, after all, Alaric's half-brother; this tie to her long-dead kinsman was among the reasons, though not the primary one, which had impelled her to marry Rascard of Hammerfell.

"You, too, are handsome tonight, my dear son," she said, and thought, *It will not be long that he is content to escort his mother to such events; I should enjoy his companionship while I still have it.* Alastair went to summon his mother a sedan chair, the commonest public conveyance in the streets of Thendara, and rode beside her chair toward the palatial building which had been constructed last year for concerts and such performances in the great public market of Thendara.

The great square was crowded with sedan chairs, mostly the drab black public conveyances, but a few richly hung and decorated brilliantly with embroidered or jeweled coats of arms.

Alastair, giving his horse to one of the grooms of the public stable, assisted his mother to alight, and said, "We should have our own chair, Mother; you should not have to summon a common chair whenever you wish to go abroad; we should have one made with the arms of Hammerfell. It would be much more fitting to the dignity of your position— folk would look at it and know that you were Duchess of Hammerfell."

"What, *I*?" Erminie could not help laughing at the thought, but then she saw her son's face and realized that she had hurt his feelings.

"I need no such dignities, my boy. It is quite enough for me to be a Tower worker, a technician; do you even know what that means?" she asked with a touch of aggravation.

And again she remembered her dream; why, if he was all but devoid of *laran*, should she see him again and again in dreams that way? Was Valentine right? Was she keeping him too close to her skirts—unhealthily close? But no, she had encouraged him to live his own life, and saw little of him from one week's beginning to the next. She recalled the time a year ago, when he had told her he had been refused for Tower training; it was only then that Erminie had told him he had been born with a twin brother who had perished in the flames that burned Hammerfell, and that he was evidently the twin with lesser ability. He had said then with anger that he could not regret having lost a brother "who robbed me of my share of an ability which means so much to you, Mother."

"You should not begrudge your brother that," she had told him, "since the title of Duke and Heirship of Hammerfell came to you who were first-born, he needed to have something special as well." Then she drew his attention for the first time to the small and inconspicuous tattoo of Hammerfell which marked his shoulder.

"This was set here to distinguish you from your twin; it proclaims you everywhere as the rightly born Heir to the Great House and estate of Hammerfell, true Duke of that line," she had told him.

The group of brightly dressed nobles made their way through the crowd thronging the square. Erminie, as a Tower technician, was known to most of them, and the young Duke of Hammerfell was well-known, too. There were bows and curtsies, and the commoners surrounding the square hoping for entrance to the performance—for, by long custom, none of the common seats could be sold until all the nobles were placed—watched the high-born gentry, and called out to them.

As one of the young women passed, Alastair tugged unobtrusively at his mother's sleeve.

"Mother, do you see the fair-haired young woman in the white robe?" he whispered, and Erminie sought with her eyes for the girl he pointed out.

71

"I *do* know her, she said softly in surpise.

"You *do?*" " He was equally surprised; he had no idea who she was, but knew that he *had* to meet her—she was the loveliest girl he had ever seen.

"Why, yes; and so do you, my son; she is your cousin Floria. When you were children, you played together almost every day."

"Floria!" he said in astonishment, "I remember chasing her around the garden with a snake, and teasing her—I would never have known her! She is beautiful!"

"It was for that Edric came to the house today," Erminie said. "He wishes me to chaperone her during Council season."

"I would willingly assume that task myself!" Alastair said, laughing. "I have heard that the plainest girls grow up to be the most beautiful! But my cousin Floria!" He looked stunned, completely disbelieving.

"She is the daughter of our Keeper and thus is not allowed to work within his circle; she went to Neskaya for training, but now she has returned to her father's house, awaiting a place in one of the other circles here."

"If she were a milkmaid, or a silk-weaver, I would still think her the most beautiful woman I have ever known," he declared. "Floria," he repeated the name almost reverently. "I doubt that Cassilda of the legends, who was loved by Hastur, could have been any more beautiful than she."

"She is young still, but in a year or two Edric will probably be entertaining offers for her hand."

"Hmm," Alastair murmured. "I must be the luckiest man alive! She is available, kin to us, and she has *laran.* Do you think she will remember me, Mother? Do you think I have a chance?"

The mellow tone of a chime, the warning signal that they should seek their seats, interrupted his musings, and mother and son passed under the arched entrance and through the great doors. In the box seat on the first balcony which she had reserved for this performance, they took two of the upholstered chairs and Alastair dutifully draped his mother with her fur-lined cloak and adjusted a padded footstool under her feet before looking around the ring of boxes, seeking the young woman on whom his fancy had alighted.

"There, I see her," he whispered. "In the box decorated with the Elhalyn coat of arms." Then he murmured in surprise, "I see the royal box is occupied, too." King Aidan was not known to be fond of music, and the royal box was seldom occupied these days.

"No doubt it is Queen Antonella," said Erminie. "It was her generous gift and love of music which rebuilt this house after the fire last year. She is old, very fat, and now quite deaf as well; but she can still enjoy the high tones of her favorite singers."

"I heard a story about that," Alastair interrupted, "when I was singing with the Mountain Choir last year; they said she had commissioned *Dom* Gavin Delleray to write a cantata for sopranos and violins only, since her hearing loss was fairly selective; she can hear high notes better than low ones."

"So I hear tell," said Erminie, looking over toward the royal box, where the elderly queen, very short and stout in an unbecoming dress of a singularly unlovely shade of blue, sat munching candied fruit, her lame leg propped up on a footstool. Despite her age, she was accompanied in the box by an elderly woman in the dress of a chaperone, and Alastair smothered a snicker.

At her age the lady can hardly need a chaperone," he whispered, stifling laughter in his sleeve.

"Oh, *hush!*" implored Erminie. "No doubt the kind old lady is giving a treat to one of her ladies-in-waiting who loves music."

Alastair had noticed that Floria Elhalyn was accompanied in her box only by her father, dispensing with any form of female companionship. He asked, "At the first intermission, will you introduce me?"

"Certainly, my dear boy; it will be a pleasure," Erminie promised, and they settled back to the ripple of applause that greeted the orchestra and choral singers. The nobles all having been seated, the commoners surged into the lower hall, and the performance began.

The cantata was a fine one, featuring as conductor and chief performer the young composer himself, *Dom* Gavin Delleray, a handsome young man who sang several solo pieces for bass voice, interspersed with choral works. Erminie listened, thinking that if he would apply himself, Alastair could certainly sing as well as *Dom* Gavin himself.

She looked, when Alastair was not watching, toward Edric Elhalyn's box; he smiled at her and nodded, an obvious confirmation of his earlier invitation for herself and her companion to join him at intermission. The girl, too, caught the older woman's eye and smiled in the friendliest manner, and Erminie thought perhaps Floria had noticed that her son was looking at her.

It was to be expected, of course, at his age, that her son's interest would be caught by first one young woman and then another; it was only surprising that it had not happened before this.

From time to time, while the young bass soloist was performing, she glanced at the form of the old queen in the box, staring straight before her with a look of rapt attention (or was it only shortsightedness?) and Erminie, thinking of what her son had said, wondered how much of the music the elderly queen could actually hear.

The music ended, and there was a round of applause for the popular young composer—he was the same age as Alastair; they had been inseparable during much of their childhood and adolescence. To her surprise, Queen Antonella led the applause, and unpinned a spray of flowers from her dress, weighted with a handsome jewel, which she flung to the stage. This began a veritable shower of flowers, nosegays, and jewels; Gavin gathered them up, beaming with delight, and smiled and bowed to his royal patron.

Alastair chuckled softly.

"Why, I never heard that Queen Antonella was as fond of music as that—nor yet that she had an eye for pretty young men," he murmured.

"Alastair I'm surprised at you," Erminie chided. "You know very well that his mother was the queen's favorite cousin, and that Gavin is like a son to her, since the royal couple has the ill fortune to be childless." She saw Alastair's derisive frown subside, but even without using telepathy she knew he was saving up this tidbit to tease his friend.

As the applause began to dwindle, there was an exodus from boxes and stalls, young couples and family groups going out into the hallways to stretch their legs, or briefly outside for fresh air, or down to the elegant bars in the lower part of the house for cold or hot drinks or other refreshments.

"I should really go and congratulate Gavin ..." said Alastair guiltily. It was clear he was still thinking of Floria.

"I am sure that he will be happy to see you," Erminie said. "But first, remember, I promised to present you to Lord Elhalyn and his daughter."

Alastair's eyes brightened as he followed his mother along the corridor between the boxes and the outer hall. Many lackeys were hustling back and forth with drinks and other refreshments, for in the concert hall anything could be had from a mug of beer or a plate of sweet cakes to a beautifully catered dinner to be served in the private room behind each box. The crowded corridor was filled with the good smell of these refreshments, and the busy sound of people enjoying themselves; from the auditorium came the faraway sound of the orchestra readying themselves and tuning their instruments for the second part of the concert.

Erminie tapped lightly at the door of the Elhalyn box. Lord Edric rose to greet her, with a smile of welcome, and bowed gracefully over her hand, just as if they had not parted less than three hours ago.

"Greetings, kinswoman," he said. "Come join us. A glass of wine?"

"Thank you," she said, accepting the offered refreshment. "Floria, my dear, how lovely you have grown! You remember your cousin Alastair."

Alastair bowed over her hand.

"A very great pleasure, *damisela*," he said, smiling, "May I fetch you some refreshment? Or you, Mother?"

"Not at all, my boy," said Edric, indicating a table spread with a sumptuous array of cold meats, cakes, and fruits. "Please, help yourselves."

At his invitation, Alastair took a plate and filled it with a modest helping of fruits and cakes. A servant poured him a liberal glass of wine, and he sipped at it, never taking his eyes from Floria.

Floria herself seemed intrigued by Alastair. "Cousin, you are so changed! You were so cruel to me when we were children; I remembered you only as an obnoxious boy. But now you seem truly the Duke of Hammerfell! I could never understand the girls at Neskaya who thought the story of how you fled from your home as a child a romantic tale. Is it true that all your kinsmen perished in that fire? That seems tragic to me, not at all romantic."

"It's quite true, Lady Floria," said Alastair, thrilled by her interest. "At least that is what my mother has told me. My father died, and my twin brother. I have no other kin of the Hammerfell line; all my living kinsmen now are my mother's people."

"And you had a twin brother?"

"I do not remember him at all. My mother and I, so I am told, escaped only by fleeing into the woods with no one but our dog Jewel to guard us. But of course I can remember nothing of this; I was hardly old enough to walk."

Her eyes were wide as she looked at him.

"By contrast I have led such a quiet and peaceful life," she murmured. "And now you are grown, is Hammerfell yours?"

"Yes, if I can find a way to take it back," he said,

Marion Zimmer Bradley

and went on. "I am resolved to try and raise an army, if I can, and recapture it from our family's foes."

Her eyes widened, but she only looked at him demurely over her wineglass as she sipped.

"Father," she said softly, "Will you not—?" She looked at Lord Elhalyn pleadingly and as she had expected, he caught her thought and smiled.

"We are holding a dance for many of our young friends at the beginning of the next full moon," he said. "We should be very pleased if you would join the young people. The occasion is Floria's birthday, and it will be a simple and informal affair," he added. "You do not need to think of court costume or etiquette; an ordinary outfit and ordinary manners, no more."

"Just promise you won't chase me around the ballroom with a frog or a snake," Floria laughed.

"I wouldn't think of it," said Alastair, congratulating himself that Floria had asked her father to invite him. Not only was he enormously impressed by Floria's great beauty, but her high position and noble relatives made her a most valuable contact for his ambitions about Hammerfell. They *were* cousins, but she was of enormously more high kindred than his branch of the family. "I shall do my best to erase from your memory this unfortunate association of myself and snakes."

As Alastair and Floria renewed their aquaintanceship, Lord Edric said to Erminie, "I am pleased that our young people seem to enjoy one another's company. Now I remember; did Alastair not sing with a male quartet in Neskaya last year?"

"He did," Erminie said, "he is gifted in music."

"Gifted, indeed; you must be very proud of him," said Edric. "I'm afraid Valentine seems to think him a young good-for-nothing, one of these young fops who think of little save his appearance. Perhaps Valentine is too harsh on him."

"*I* think so," said Erminie, swallowing hard. "His father and brother died in the fall of Hammerfell. I have had to raise him alone—it hasn't been easy for him."

"I am troubled about the young people today," said Edric. "My four sons seem to care only for racing and gambling."

"Yes, I'm concerned for Alastair," Erminie said. "And I have a favor to ask of you, kinsman."

"Ask, and you know that if it is anything I can possibly grant, it is yours," Edric said. He smiled at her so intensely that for a moment the woman wished she had not asked.

But she had made the request, and after all it was a lawful thing which she meant to ask.

"Can you arrange an audience for my son with your kinsman King Aidan?"

"Nothing could be simpler; I once heard Aidan express an interest in the affairs of Hammerfell," Edric said. "Perhaps at this birthday gathering for Floria— it might be better if they could meet informally."

"I am grateful to you," Erminie said, declining a second glass of wine and nibbling delicately at a piece of fruit.

Meanwhile, aware of naught save each other's company, Floria asked Alastair, "Lord Hammerfell, do you know my brothers?"

"I believe I was once presented to your brother Gwynn."

"Oh, Gwynn is twelve years older than I, and I think he believes me so young I should still be in short frocks," she said with annoyance. "My favorite brother is Deric; he and I are but a year apart. He knows *you*," she said. "Do you ride a chestnut mare with a white blaze on her forehead?"

"I do," said Alastair. "She was a gift on my fifteenth birthday from my mother."

"My brother said you must have a good eye for horseflesh; that he has never seen a finer mare."

"It is my mother who should be complimented," Alastair said. "She chose the mare; but for her sake I thank your brother."

"You may thank him in person," Floria said, "for my brothers promised to join us here at intermission; none of them care much for music. I'm sure they have been visiting a tavern or perhaps a gambling-house. Do you not care for cards or gaming?"

"Not much," Alastair said, though the truth of the matter was that he could not afford much gambling except for the smallest stakes, which made it hardly worth the trouble. His income was very small, though his mother never grudged him enough money to keep up appearances.

At that moment four young men—the sons of Edric of Elhalyn—crowded all at once into the box, and surrounded the refreshment table. The tallest of them came quickly to Floria's side and demanded with a frown, "Who is this stranger you are talking to, sister? And why are you gossiping and flirting with strange young men?"

Floria said with a high color rising in her cheeks, "My brother Gwynn, Lord Alastair of Hammerfell; he is our cousin; I have known him since we were children, and we have been talking most correctly in the presence of both our parents; our father and his mother. You may ask either of them here if a single word has passed between us that is not perfectly suitable."

"That's right, Gwynn," said Lord Edric. "This lady is the Duchess of Hammerfell, an old friend and our kinswoman."

Gwynn bowed to Erminie. "Your pardon, ma'am. No offense intended."

Erminie smiled and said graciously, "None taken, kinsman; if I had a daughter, I could wish she would have brothers with such care for her behavior and reputation." But Alastair was glowering.

"It is for the lady Floria, and not you, sir, to say if my company is distasteful to her; and I'll thank you to mind your own affairs."

Gwynn all too eagerly picked up the glove, "Can you say it is *not* my affair when I see my sister conversing with some landless upstart in exile, whose old story of grievances is a joke from Dalereuth to Nevarsin?" Gwynn snapped. "When I came here to-night there was unrest in the city—hordes of displaced peasants in the streets, gangs of young toughs ready to make some gesture against aristocrats—but I'm sure you don't know or care—you were too busy telling your tired old story of Hammerfell . . . it might as well be cloud-cuckoo-land! You can call yourself what you will, but don't presume on some doubtful title in exile—there are a hundred such titles in Thendara. Lord of Cloudland Staircase, or of Zandru's Tenth Hell, I suppose. Such things may sound fine to young girls who know no better, but—"

"Look here, Gwynn," Lord Edric interrupted, "that's

enough—your lack of manners is appalling! I am not yet so old I cannot decide who is fit to be my guest or my friend. Apologize at once to Lady Erminie and Alastair!"

But Gwynn would not back down. "Father, don't you know that this Hammerfell affair is a joke all over the Hundred Kingdoms? If Hammerfell is his, why is he not with his people in the Hellers, rather than idling here in Thendara boring everyone in earshot—"

But this was quite enough for Alastair; he grabbed Gwynn's shirt front and pushed hard with his free hand on the young man's nose. "Listen, you! You keep your mouth off my family—"

Erminie cried out reproachfully, but her son was too angry to hear. Gwynn Elhalyn's face reddened furiously, and he shoved Alastair so hard that he stumbled over a piece of furniture and measured his length on the carpeted floor of the box. He jumped to his feet, grabbed Gwynn's shirt front again, and shoved him stumbling through the door of the box, reeling into a footman who was carrying a tray of glasses; the man went down in a crash of glassware, wine splashing everywhere. Alastair wiped his eyes, and snarled, plunging at Gwynn who had stumbled to his feet and had his *skean* out.

Lord Edric bellowed, thusting himself between them, grabbing Gwynn's dagger and restraining his son. "Damn it, I said that's enough, and I'll be obeyed! How dare you draw your dagger, boy, against your father's invited guests?"

Erminie interrupted tactfully, "Kinsman, the second cantata is about to begin; look, the soloists are taking their places on the stage. My son and I must take our leave."

"Yes, indeed," said Lord Edric almost thankfully. He nodded at Alastair, "We'll meet at Floria's ball—"

At that moment there was a disturbance in the passage; a group of poorly dressed young men, laughing and jeering, thrust their way into the box. Gwynn instantly grabbed the dagger from his father's hand, and Edric stepped protectively in front of Erminie. Alastair had his knife out and stepped toward the young men.

"Here, this is a private box; I'll thank you to leave," he said, but the foremost of the men sneered.

"How about that, then, cockerel? What god gave you this place that you can drive me out of it? I'm as good a man as yerself—you think you can throw me out?"

"I'll certainly do my best," said Alastair, and advanced on him, catching him by the shoulder. "Here, get out!" He marched the young man to the door, while the man, perhaps surprised that their intrusion was being protested at all, twisted around and grappled with him.

"Here, help me with this, cousin," Alastair called out, but Gwynn was protecting Floria. Over his shoulder he could see other boxes were being invaded; more young men, companions to the one he was shoving, had at once moved in on the refreshment table and were scooping up the rich foods by handfuls and stuffing them into pockets and sacks. He thought, hardly knowing he did so, *Can they really be hungry?*

As if his thought had reached the older people, Edric said quietly, "If you are hungry, young fellows, take what you want, and go. We have come here to listen to music; we do no harm to anyone."

The quiet words made most of the young intruders back off; they stuffed the refreshments into their pockets and hurried out into the halls again; but the one who was fighting with Alastair did not desist.

"You rich bloodsuckers think you can put us off with a few cakes? You've had our blood all these years—let's see the color of yours!" he cried, and suddenly there was a knife in his hand; he thrust at Alastair, who had not expected it, and was taken unaware. The knife sliced along his forearm, he cried out with pain and then whipped up his own knife, grabbing at a fold of his cloak to wrap round his arm. Erminie cried out in dismay;

"Guards! Guards!"

Abruptly, young Guardsmen in green and black cloaks filled the box; they seized the young man who was still staring numbly at the blood dripping from Alastair's blow.

"Are you all right, *vai dom*?" one of the Guardsmen asked. "There's a lot of this rabble in the city tonight; they turned over the queen's sedan chair."

"I'm all right," Alastair said, "I don't understand what he wanted—" He sank down on a chair, faint with the blood dripping from his arm.

"God knows," said the Guardsman, "I doubt he knows himself—do you, swine?" he demanded, giving the young man a rough shove. "How bad are you hurt, sir?"

Lord Edric caught up his own linen kerchief and thrust it at Alastair to stanch the blood from the small wound.

Alastair sat half-stunned, blinking at the sight of

the blood-drenched kerchief. "I'm not much hurt; let the fellow go. But if I ever catch sight of him again—"

Floria came and bent over Alastair. She said imperiously to the Guards, "I don't care what you do with him, but get him out of our sight." Then she reached out and drew the kerchief away. She said gently, "I am a monitor; let me see how deep it is." She raised her hand and passed it gently over his arm, without touching him. "It is not serious, but a small vein has been nicked." She took out her starstone and focused attentively on the wound; after a moment the blood oozed to a stop. "There, I think there is no real harm done."

"My boy, I am appalled that this should have happened in our box," Lord Edric asked. "What can I do to make amends?"

"It seems to be the common lot tonight," said Erminie, looking around the auditorium; the Guardsmen seemed to have the upper hand now, and all over the building, shabbily dressed invaders were being marshaled toward the doors.

One elderly man, as shabby as any of the invaders, was protesting loudly as the Guardsmen tried to force him toward the doors, "Here now, I wasn't one of those, I bought me ticket like anybody else! Do I need silk britches to listen to a concert, me lords? Is this the Hasturs' justice?"

Dom Gavin Delleray, standing at the edge of the stage, leaped down into the lower seats. He yelled, "Leave him alone, I know this man; he's my father's paxman!"

"Anything you say, me lord," said the Guardsman.

"Sorry, my man; but how's anyone to tell when he looks like that there riffraff!"

Erminie laid her hand on her son's arm, asking, "Shall I call a chair? Or do you want to remain for the rest of the concert?"

Alastair still had his hand in Floria's. He did not want to move. She was still regarding him with protective indignation.

"I don't think he should walk just yet," Floria said. "Gwynn, pour him some wine, if those ruffians have not drunk it all up. Sit down, cousin Erminie; you can listen to the concert just as well from here in our box."

The tumult was subsiding; the orchestra began to play an overture, and Erminie sat down next to Alastair. Through the music, she felt shaken; what was happening in the city she knew so well? The intruders had looked at her, and at her son, as if they were some kind of monsters; yet she was a simple, hardworking woman, and not even rich. What could they possibly have against her?

She saw Floria holding Alastair's hand, and without knowing why she was suddenly filled with foreboding. Yet Floria and Alastair were cousins, they had grown up together and were a suitable match. Why should it trouble her this way?

She lifted her eyes to the royal box. Queen Antonella, her lame leg still propped on its cushion, was placidly munching nut cake, as if there had been no interruption. Erminie began to laugh; she laughed so hard that she could not stop; there were angry stares from other boxes, and Edric came to her side, proffering smelling salts, a sip of wine; but she could not stop, though she tried, and at last Edric almost carried her into the anteroom behind the box, where she went on laughing till she began to cry, then lying in his arms, cried herself into collapse.

6

Conn of Hammerfell woke suddenly, crying out and clutching at his arm; he expected to find it covered with blood. He was confused by the darkness and silence, with no sound but heavy snow blowing against the shutters and the snores of sleeping men. In the small reddish eye of the fire he could see a cauldron swinging on a crane over the fireplace, a pleasant fruity smell steaming from it. Next to him Markos sat up, blinking in the dark.

"What is it, my boy?"

"Ah, the blood—" Conn muttered, confused, then, waking fully, said in surprise, "but there is nobody here—"

"Another dream?"

"But it all seemed so real," Conn said in a dazed, half-sleeping voice, "A dagger—we were fighting—the man forced his way in—there were people all round me, in such fine clothes as I have seen only in dreams, an old man who was a kinsman, and apologized to me—and a beautiful girl in a white robe, who—" he stopped and frowned, running his fingers along his forearm, as if surprised not to feel the wetness of blood there,"I don't know what it was she did, but she stopped the bleeding—" He lay back on the crude straw mattress, "Ah, she was beautiful—"

"Your dream-maiden again?" Markos laughed gently. "You have spoken of her before, but not recently. The same one? Was there more?"

"Oh, yes—music, and a man who mocked my heritage and picked a quarrel—and my . . . *mother*, and I know not what all—you know how dreams are always so confused—" he sighed, and Markos, reaching across from his straw pallet at Conn's side gripped the young man's hand in his gnarled old fingers.

"Hush—don't wake the men," he admonished, gesturing in the dark at the four or five men sleeping around them, "Sleep, lad. We have a long night and a longer day before us. No time to waste in fretting over dreams—if indeed it *was* a dream. Rest while you're able, they will not be here before midnight, at the earliest."

Conn said, "If they come. Listen to the storm outside. Devotion indeed, if they come out in *that*."

"They will come," said Markos confidently. "Try to sleep another hour or two if you can."

"But if it was not a dream, what could it have been?" Conn asked.

Markos said reluctantly, keeping his voice almost to a whisper, "You know there is *laran* in your family; your mother was a *leronis*—we must talk of this another time, and we will; but tonight there are other things to think of, with the men coming."

"I don't understand . . ." Conn began, but let the thought trail off, listening to the sound of wind and snow slamming against the shuttered window of the building. As he picked up his foster-father's emotion, he could sense that the old man was more troubled than he should have been by just a dream, even a recurring dream.

Except for the preliminary shock and pain of waking to feel himself stricken and bleeding, Conn himself had not taken it very seriously; he had had such dream-flashes of another life many times before this, though he rarely spoke of it to his foster-father; a life where he lived, not roughly in his little mountain village, always in hiding, his real name and identity known only to a few, but in a great city, surrounded by such luxuries as he found hard even to imagine. It troubled him deeply to realize that Markos seemed to think there was some level of reality to these all-too-familiar visions.

Markos was his earliest memory; try as he might, he could remember nothing else, nothing except images of fire deep in the back of his mind, that, and sometimes, a soothing voice that crooned to him in dreams. When Markos realized that Conn could almost remember the fire, he had told him his real name and the story of the burning of Hammerfell, and how his father and mother and his only brother had perished in that fire. When he was older, Markos had taken him to see the burned-out ghostly ruins that had once been the proud keep of Hammerfell, and impressed upon him that he was the only surviving man of Hammerfell kindred, and that the major duty of his life was to care for the abandoned clansmen of Hammerfell, and to recapture, rebuild, and restore his duchy.

Conn composed himself to sleep again; but the lovely face of the girl in white who had healed his dream-wound went down with him into the dark chasms of sleep. Was she a real woman, then? Markos had told him he had been born a telepath, gifted with the inherited psychic powers of his caste. Was it possible, then, that the girl existed somewhere in reality, that he had seen her through the very real power of the *laran* he had inherited? Or was his *laran* precognitive, was she someone predestined to come into his life?

More asleep than awake, conscious of roaring snow slamming against the shutters at the window, Conn drifted in fantasy with the beautiful girl at his side, till outside the half-ruined stone hut where they sheltered—not unlike the hut on the borders of Hammerfell where he had dwelt with Markos as far back as he could remember, alone except for a silent old woman who had cooked for them and cared for him when he was too young to be left alone during Markos's comings and goings—Conn heard through his dream the hoofbeats of riders approaching on the road, and before he could be summoned he woke and reached out to awaken Markos.

"It is time," he whispered. "They are coming."

"And there is the signal," Markos confirmed, as a rainbird hooted three times just outside. He struck a light and the other men began to stir, moving about and drawing on their boots.

Markos went to the door and hauled it open, the hinges creaking loudly enough to make Conn wince.

"I could hear those hinges creak if we were on the

far side of the Wall Around the World," he com-
plained. "Get an oilcan to them or the hills themselves will hear them like an alarm bell."

"Aye, m'lord," Markos assented—when they were
alone or among those who did not know Conn's true
identity, it was oftener "my lad" or "Master Conn,"
but since Conn's fifteenth birthday Markos had in-
variably addressed him respectfully by his title in the
presence of knowing others.

Half a dozen men, in full riding gear, crowded
into the room where they had slept. Despite the tiny
weather shielding anteroom, the icy wind and sleet
roared into the room with them, and the last in had
to struggle to slam out the biting storm.

In the dim light Markos moved to the center of
the men who had been sleeping on the floor, and
turned to the leader of the riders. "You're sure none
followed ye here?"

"If there's so much as an ice-rabbit stirring from
here to the Wall Around the World, I'll eat it raw,
fur and all," said the leader, a big burly man in a
leather jacket, with a fringe of reddish whiskers surrounding his face. "The woods are filled only with
snow and silence; I made sure of that."

"Are the men all well armed?" asked Conn. "Let
me see your weapons." Briefly he inspected the swords
and pikes shown to him, all old, some hardly better
than pitchforks; but bright, well-kept and free of
rust.

"Good, then we are ready. But you men must be
perished with the cold. Tarry a while, we have a hot
wine drink readied for you." He went to the fireplace and began to scoop up the steaming punch

into an assortment of clay mugs, holding out a cup to each man. "Drink this and we'll be off."

"One moment, my young lord," said Markos. "Before we ride, I have this for you." With an air of solemnity and mystery he went to the far corner of the room and rummaged there in an old chest. He turned and said, "Since that fire where Hammerfell perished, I have kept this hidden for you—your father's sword."

Conn nearly dropped the clay mug, but managed to thrust it unbroken into the hands of the man with the fringe of whiskers. He reached for the sword and gripped its hilt, visibly moved. He had nothing of his family; Markos had told him that everything of his father's had been destroyed in the fire. The men were all thrusting their mugs in the air. Whiskers shouted, "Aye, drink to our young duke!"

"Aye, may all the Gods bless him!" With noisy shouts they drank his health.

"My thanks to you, Farren—and to you all. May this night's work begin well the long task before us." Conn added, "There's an old story that the Gods bless those who work hardest before they ask for help." He sheathed the ancient sword—later he would study the runes engraved in it, try to gather from it something of those kinsmen who had borne it before him; but not now.

Farren said, "Our lives are at your disposal, my lord. But where do we ride tonight? Markos told us no more than that you had need of us, and so we came, in memory of your father. But surely you did not bring us out in a storm to drink your health— though this punch is excellent—and see you given the sword of Hammerfell."

"True," Conn said. "You are here now because I have heard a strange tale; that our old foeman, Ardrin of Storn, was burning out a village of our clansmen, tenants of Hammerfell, from the common land tonight."

"In a storm such as this? But why would he do so?"

"This is not the first time he has burned out tenants and thrust them homeless into the winter when they cannot fight, but must run to seek shelter from the elements," said Conn. "I hear he wishes to keep more beasts for wool and cloth on this land, since the beasts are of more profit to him than farming tenants growing their own food."

"Aye, that's true," said Farren, "he drove out my grandfather from a croft where he had lived fifty years, leaving the poor old man nothing to do but hobble to the lowland cities to find work as a warehouseman there, and lucky to get it. Now only woolies graze where my grandfather grew his crops."

"Storn is not the only one to follow that vicious practice," said Conn. "His own tenants—if they will put up with it—are not my affair. But I have sworn that Hammerfell men shall not be used so. I did not know about your grandfather, Farren; should I be victor over Storn and reclaim my lands, he shall have his home back as well; men so old and feeble should not have to toil and sweat for their porridge."

"In his name, I thank you," said Farren, bending to kiss his lord's hand, but Conn colored and held out his hand for a friendly handclasp instead.

"And now let us ride; Storn's men will strike in the night and burn the old folk out of their houses. But after tonight he shall know that Hammerfell lives and he shall not continue these crimes unchallenged."

One by one, they slipped out into the raging snow-storm, getting to their horses and mounting. It was Markos who led the way, Conn close behind him; the snow was blinding, and it was almost impossible to see where he was going. But he trusted Markos implicitly, and he knew the old man recognized every rock and tree of these mountains; he need only keep close behind his old servant's horse. So he rode, half closing his eyes to keep out the blinding sleet, and letting the horse find his own way, one hand just touching, with secret pride, the hilt of his father's sword.

He had not expected this; it somehow seemed a more important rite of passage than this night's raid. He had gone with Markos more than once to harry the Storns—in fact, money and animals seized from them had kept him and Markos all these years. It would never have occurred to Conn to think of himself, or of Markos, as a thief; before his birth, the Storns had stolen most of his father's property and when he was a year old, they had burned the small remainder.

He and Markos believed quite reasonably that since Storn had all of Hammerfell's property, a reasonable proportion of it should be diverted back to the support of its rightful owner.

But tonight Storn would learn who his enemy was and why he was being harassed.

The snow was so thick now that he could hardly hear the horse's hoofbeats; he gave the creature its head, knowing that if he tried to control it overmuch in this weather, the animal might lose its footing.

After a time Markos stopped, so abruptly that Conn almost rode his horse into the old man's.

Markos slid down and seized Conn's bridle.

"From here we walk," he whispered. "There may be some of his guards around, and they had better not see us."

"Oh. Right," he said, hearing what Markos did not say; the fewer he had to kill, the better for everyone. Storn's men were obeying orders and were not entirely responsible for what they must do—too much sympathy for the lordless Hammerfell tenants and they would share their fate. Neither Conn nor Markos had much taste for needless killing.

Silently, each man passed the whispered message to the one behind him, and the little party skirted the village, now leading their horses. Then the word ran to hold where they were, and be silent. Conn stood alone in the dark, feeling that his very breathing, the thumping of his heart must be audible to the people in the clustered cottages below.

But the cottages were almost all dark; only one of the ten or twelve had a light in the window. Conn wondered why—some oldster drowsing by the fire, a mother watching by a sick child, an elderly parent awaiting the return of a benighted traveler, a midwife at her work?

He waited, silent and motionless, the sword just loosened in its scabbard. *Tonight I am truly Hammerfell,* he thought. *Father, wherever you are, I hope you know I am caring for your people.*

Suddenly, from one of the cottages below, a wild yell rang out, and fire sprang up wildly through the storm-laden sky above the roofs; one of the buildings blazed up like a torch. There was screaming and confusion.

"*Now!*" Markos gave a terse command, and Conn's party hurled themselves onto their mounts and raced down the hill, screaming their outrage. Conn notched his bow at the dark armed figures slipping round the houses with other torches in their hands. An arrow flew; one of the torchbearers fell without a cry. Conn fitted another arrow. Now women and children and a few elderly and feeble men were coming out of the cottages, staggering, half asleep, crying out in confusion and in pain. Another of the cottages blazed up, and then Conn's party rode into the meleé, yelling like wild beasts and shooting arrows at the men of Storn who were burning out the village.

Conn bellowed at the top of his lungs, "Lord Storn! Are you here, or did you send your minions to do your dirty work and sit safe home by your own fireside this night? What do you say, Lord Storn?"

A long delay, with only the crackling of flames and the wailing of terrified children; then a stern voice called out.

"I am Rupert of Storn; who dares take me to task for what I must do? These wretched folk have been told again and again to vacate their houses; I do not do this unprovoked. Who challenges my right to do as I will on my own lands?"

"These are not Storn lands," yelled Conn, "they are the rightful lands of Hammerfell! I am Conn, Duke of Hammerfell, and you may do your dirty work all you will at Storn, if your folk will allow it, but touch *my* tenants at your peril! Fine work this for a man—warring on women and little children still unbreeched! Aye, and a few old gaffers! How brave are the men of Storn, when there are no menfolk to say them nay or protect the women and babes!"

A long silence. Then a reply came.

"I had heard that the wolf cubs of Hammerfell died in the fire that wiped out that accursed line. What upstart makes this lying claim?"

Markos whispered in Conn's ear, "Rupert is Storn's nephew and heir."

"Come forth if you dare," retorted Conn, "and I will prove to you that I am Hammerfell, prove it on your worthless carcass!"

"I do not fight with imposters and unknown bandits," replied Rupert's voice from the darkness. "Ride away as you came and cease to meddle with my people. These lands are mine and no nameless bandit shall inter—" The words choked off in a yell of pain and ended in a horrible spluttering sound; it was followed by a horrified screech of despair and rage. Farren's arrow, winging noiselessly out of the dark, had torn out Rupert's throat.

Markos shouted, "Now will ye come out and fight like men?"

There was a terse low-voiced command and Conn's men rushed at the Storn party in the shadows; the fight was bloody and brief. Conn cut down someone who rushed at him with a pike, fought briefly with a second man who seemed to melt away in front of him, then Markos gripped his arm in a grasp of iron and dragged him away.

"On to your horse; they've had enough, and no more heart for their dirty work this night. See, they're loading Rupert, or what's left of him, on the horse ... no more; they're gone," Markos said. And as Conn, breathing hard and feeling faintly sick, let

Markos urge him into his saddle, the women and children, wearing the nightgear in which they had turned out of their beds, crowded round his horse in the snow.

"Is it really the young duke?"

"Hammerfell's come back to us!"

"Our own young prince."

They crowded close, kissing his hands, weeping, pleading.

"Now those bandits of Storn won't be able to turn us away . . ." one old lady said, holding up a torch she had snatched from one of Storn's vanished men. "You're the image of your father, dear lad—my lord," she amended quickly.

Conn stammered, "My people—I thank you for your welcome. I pledge to you—from this day there'll be no more burnings if I can prevent it. And no more war on women and babies."

"Aye," Markos muttered when at least they rode away silently into the night, "the hawk's loosed now from the block. From this day, lad—" he broke off, "No, you're no lad now—my lord, from this night they'll know there's a Hammerfell in these woods. I'd say you'd blooded your father's sword wi' honor this night."

And Conn knew he had taken up a challenge in a just cause. It was for this that he had lived in hiding all these years with Markos; it was for this that he had been born.

7

On the night of the full moons, Edric Elhalyn celebrated the eighteenth birthday of his youngest daughter Floria, at the Thendara palace of the Elhalyns. Among the guests were King Aidan and Queen Antonella, and as Edric had promised, during a break in the dancing, he came to where Floria and young Alastair of Hammerfell were seated together, talking and quietly sipping a cold drink.

"I trust you are enjoying yourself, my dear," he said to his daughter.

"Oh, yes, Father! It is the most beautiful party ever. . . ."

"I am afraid I must interrupt you for the space of a dance or two. Alastair, as I promised you, I spoke to King Aidan—His Grace is eager to meet you. Please come with me."

Alastair made his apologies to Floria, then rose and followed Lord Elhalyn across the room through the dancing couples and into an adjacent chamber, elegantly fitted with dark woods and hung with silken panels.

Seated in one of the elaborately upholstered chairs was a surprisingly small white-haired man; he was richly dressed and seemed bent with age, but the eyes he raised to them were focused and keen. He said, in a voice unexpectedly deep and strong, "Young Hammerfell?"

"Majesty," said Alastair, bowing low.

"Never mind that," said King Aidan Hastur, holding out his hand and waving Alastair to take a seat, "I know your mother; a charming lady; I have heard much about her from my cousin Valentine. He is, I think, eager to be your stepfather, young man, but he could not tell me what it is I really wish to know— about this blood feud which has all but wiped out both of these two mountain kingdoms. What can you tell me? How and when did it begin?"

"I do not know, sir," Alastair said. It was hot in the room, and he began to feel sweat trickling down inside his silken tunic. "My mother speaks of it but little; she said my father himself was not sure of its true cause and origin. I know only that my father and brother died when the armies of Storn burned Hammerfell over our heads."

"And even the street-singers in Thendara know that much," King Aidan said. "Some of these mountain lords have grown too arrogant for their own good; this challenges the peace we have won at such a price beyond the Kadarin. They think the Aldarans their overlords, and we are still at war with the Aldarans."

He scowled and considered, "Tell me, young man;

101

if I should help you to recover Hammerfell, would you be willing to be faithful vassal and lord under the Hasturs and fight for me if need came against the Aldarans?" As Alastair was about to speak, King Aidan interrupted, "No, don't answer at once; go home and think about it." He added: "Then come and tell me what you have decided. I need loyal men in the Hellers; otherwise, the Domains will be torn with war as they were in Varzil's day. And that would not be good for any of us. So go back to the party now, and in two days or three, when you have thought this through, come back and see me." He nodded and smiled to him pleasantly, then averted his eyes, an obvious indication that the audience had come to an end.

Lord Edric touched his shoulder; Alastair backed away, turned, and followed the older man out of the room. *Go away and think,* the king had said, but could there be any question what he should do? His first and only duty was the recovery and rebuilding of his home and his clan. If the price of that was loyalty to the Hastur kings, surely he could pledge that much.

Or could he? Was he giving up power which rightfully belonged to Hammerfell and to the mountain lords of the Hellers? Could he truly trust Aidan or any Hastur king? Or would the price paid be too high for royal favor and King Aidan's help in recovering his lands?

When he returned to where he had been talking with Floria, she was gone; across the room he could see the flash of the glittering gems in her pale hair. She was dancing a ring-dance with a dozen other girls and young men; absurdly he felt angry and jealous. She could have waited for him.

It was not long before she came back, rosy and flushed from the exercise, and he could hardly keep himself from pulling her into his arms. Being a telepath, of course, she caught the impulse to which he did not give way, and blushed, smiling a smile so radiant that he might as well have kissed her. She whispered, "What happened, Alastair?"

He said, almost whispering, "I spoke with the king, and he has promised me his aid to recover Hammerfell." He did not mention his part of the bargain.

She cried out, sharing his joy, "Oh, how wonderful!" And all through the room heads turned to look at her. She blushed again, and laughed a little.

"Well, whatever may come of it, we have made ourselves conspicuous; thanks be to Evanda we are under my own father's roof," she said practically. "Or there would be a scandal from here to—to Hammerfell."

"Floria," he said, "surely you know that when I am restored, the first thing I shall do is to speak to your father—"

"I know it," she said, almost in a whisper, "and I am as eager for that day as you." And for just a few seconds she was in his arms, kissing his lips so lightly that a minute afterward he hardly knew if it had happened or if he had dreamed it.

She let him go and reluctantly he came back to the ordinary world.

"We had better dance," she said. "Quite enough people are looking at us already."

His doubts and qualms had evaporated; with Floria as the reward he felt ready to pledge to whatever King Aidan wanted.

"I suppose so," he said. "I do not want your brother

picking another quarrel with me; one feud at a time is enough."

"Oh, he would not; not when you are a guest beneath our father's roof," Floria assured him, but Alastair looked skeptical; he had forced a quarrel when Alastair was a guest in their father's box at the concert hall, so why not beneath his father's roof?

They moved out on the dance floor, his fingers just touching the silk at her waist.

Far to the north, Conn of Hammerfell all but cried out, disoriented. The woman's face, the touch of his hands, the warmth of her body under the silk, the almost-memory of her lips fleetingly against his own ... he overflowed with emotion. His dream-woman again, and the blazing lights, the richly clad people whose like he had never seen ... what had come over him? What had happened to him, that this lovely woman companioned him so closely now night and day?

Alastair blinked, and Floria asked gently, "What is it?"

"I hardly know—I was dizzy for a moment," he said, "dizzied with *you,* no doubt—but for a moment it seemed I was far from here, in a place I have never seen."

"But you are a telepath, surely; perhaps you picked up something from someone who is to be part of your life; if not now, sometime in the future," she said.

"But I am *not* a telepath, not much," he said. "I have not even enough *laran* to be worth training, so my mother has told me—what makes you think that?"

"Your red hair; it is usually a mark of *laran.*"

"Not in my case," he said, "for I was born a twin; and my brother, so my mother said, was the one with *laran*." He saw the troubled look on her face and asked, "Does it mean so much to you?"

"Only—it is one more thing we might have shared," she said, "but I love just as you are." She blushed and said, "But you must think me bold, to speak so frankly before it has been settled between our parents. . . ."

"I could never think anything but good of you," he said fervently, "and I know that my mother will welcome you as a daughter."

The music came to an end, and he said, "I should go and tell my mother of my good fortune—*our* good fortune. Another thing," he asked, suddenly reminded by his mention of his mother, "do you know of a good dog breeder in the city?"

"A—dog breeder?" she asked, wondering what he meant by the sudden change in direction.

"Yes; my mother's dog is very old now. I want to find her a puppy so that when Jewel goes at last where all good dogs must go, Mother will not be left alone—especially now I shall have to be out of the city a great deal."

"What a good idea!" Floria exclaimed, involuntarily warmed by his care for his mother's happiness. "Yes; I know where my brother Nicolo buys his hunting dogs; tell him I sent you and he will find you a good house pet for your mother." And she thought, *See how kind and good he is, to be so thoughtful of his mother. He will surely be good to his wife as well.*

He asked, hesitating, "Will you ride with me tomorrow?"

She smiled at him and said, "I should like it very

much; but I cannot. I have been in the city for five tendays awaiting a place in the Tower; and I have finally been asked to be monitor in Renata Aillard's circle, and I must go tomorrow to be tested.

Through his disappointment Alastair felt curiosity; although his mother had been a Tower worker since his childhood, he knew really very little about it.

"I did not know women were allowed to be Keepers," he said.

"They are not," Floria said. "Renata is an *emmasca;* born so. Her mother is of Hastur blood, and many of that line are born *emmasca*, man or woman as they may choose. It is sad; but it opens to her the work of a Keeper and perhaps some day real women may be allowed such work. It is very dangerous for women; I think I would rather not attempt it myself."

"I would not have you run into danger," Alastair said fervently.

And she said, "I shall be finished, and know if I am accepted for the circle by noon; then, if you wish, we shall go and choose a puppy for your mother."

"Accepted? But I thought you already had a place in the circle—"

"Yes; but it is very important for all the workers in a circle to be acceptable to one another; if there is anyone in the circle who feels he or she cannot work with me, then I shall have to wait again for a place. I have met Renata and I like her very much; and I think I am acceptable to her. But tomorrow I shall be tested to see if the others can work with me."

"If there is anyone who dares to refuse you, I will declare war on him!" said Alastair, only half in jest, and beneath the joking tone she sensed his seriousness and took his hands in hers.

"No," she said. "You do not understand these things, since you are not a trained telepath. Please promise me that you will not do anything rash or foolish."

The music had ended, and they moved to the edge of the dancing floor. She said, "Now I must dance with my other guests—though I would rather stay with you."

"Oh, why must we do what others desire just because it is the custom? I am sick to death of the 'proper way to do this' and the 'proper way to do that'!"

"Oh, Alastair, don't talk like that! I have been taught that we were not sent here to do our own will, but to do our duty to our people and our family. You are Duke of Hammerfell; a day may well come when—as is right—your duty to Hammerfell may have to come before our pledges to one another."

"Never!" he vowed.

"Don't say that! A private man may make such pledges, but a prince or a duke, a lord with responsibilities, may not." Inwardly she felt troubled, but thought: *He is young, he has had too little training for his post; he was educated in exile, not schooled to the responsibility of his birth.*

"It is only that I cannot bear to leave you," he said. "Please stay with me."

"My dear, I *cannot.* Please understand."

"Whatever you say," he said morosely and gave her his arm, conducting her silently to her kinswomen—among whom, he noticed with an instant of awe, was Queen Antonella, smiling a bland and vacant smile.

The queen said, in the curiously strident voice of the hard-of-hearing, "At last; we have been waiting for you, my dear. But I think I do not know your young escort."

"He is the son of the Duchess of Hammerfell; Erminie, Second Technician in Edric of Elhalyn's circle," said Floria in her gentle voice, so softly that Alastair wondered how the deaf old lady could hear. Then he remembered that she was surely a telepath and could understand what Floria said, though not in spoken words.

"Hammerfell," she said in her rusty voice, nodding blandly to him. "A pleasure, young man; your mother is a fine woman; I know her well."

Alastair felt gratified; recognition in one evening first from the king, now from the queen was more than he had hoped for. A young man Alastair did not know came up and claimed Floria for a dance, and Alastair, bowing to Queen Antonella, who returned the salutation most graciously, went in search of his mother.

He found Erminie in the conservatory examining the profuse flowers; she turned as he came in and said, "My dear boy, why are you not dancing?"

"I have had enough of dancing for one evening," he said. "When the moon has set, who cares to look at the stars?"

"Come, come," Erminie said. "Your hostess has other duties."

He said irritably, "Floria has already lectured me on that, Mother, do not *you* start."

"Then she did well," Erminie said, but sensing that he had much to say to her, asked, "What is it, Alastair?"

"I had an audience with the king, Mother—but I cannot say much of it here in public."

"You wish to leave at once? As you wish," she said and beckoned to a servant. "Summon a chair for us, please."

On the way, Alastair poured out all his emotions to his mother. "And, Mother, I asked Floria if she would look favorably on me when I was restored to my own—"

"And what answer did she give you?"

Alastair almost whispered, "She kissed me and said that day could not come too soon."

"I am so glad for you; she is a lovely girl," Erminie said, wondering why, if all this were true, he looked so pensive.

But, since Alastair was not a developed telepath, she read him wrong, thinking that perhaps Alastair had pressed the girl for an immediate pledge, or even immediate marriage and Floria had quite properly refused him.

"Now tell me every word that His Grace said to you," she demanded, and settled down to hear him.

8

The village of Lowerhammer was not much more than a cluster of stone houses at the center of a dozen farms; a poor place, but it was harvest time, and the village's largest barn had been cleared and converted into a dance hall. It was crowded with raucous revelers and lit with a festive array of lanterns; pipers and harpers played a lively dance tune. All along one wall a row of trestles were spread with planks, and every mug and glass in the village was lined up there around jugs of cider and beer, along with benches for the elders, while at the center a ring of young men circled to the left around a ring of young girls stepping to the right.

Conn was in the circle; when the music came to an end, as expected, he held out his hands to the girl with whom the circle had brought him face to face and led her toward the refreshment table. He filled her a mug, and another for himself.

It was hot in the barn; beyond a rough wooden bulkhead there were still horses and dairy animals and four or five hearty young men were guarding these doors to make certain that no torches or candles were carried where there was hay or straw. The fear of fire always overshadowed country festivals, especially at this season before the fall rains had drenched the resin-trees.

Conn sipped the rough cider, smiling woodenly at the girl he had partnered in the dance. Why at this moment did he see, as if *through* her, another woman—one he saw at almost every turning, one who was with him at work during the day, and in dreams at night—the stranger dressed in brilliant satins; a woman with fair hair, dressed elaborately in jeweled braids?

"Conn," Lilla said, "what is it? You are a thousand leagues away; are you dancing on the green moon?"

He laughed. "No, but I was daydreaming of a place far from here," he confessed. "I don't know why; there is no place *better* than here—especially at a harvest ball." But he knew he was lying; next to the woman in his dream, Lilla looked like the rough-handed farm girl that she was, and this place no more than a travesty of the brilliantly lighted palace of his daydream. Were these bright scenes he saw as if in dreams the reality, and these rustic festivities the dream? He felt confused, and rather than pursue the thought, turned to his cider.

"Do you want to dance again?"

"No, I am too hot," she said. "Let's sit here for a few minutes."

They found a bench at the end of the barn, near the wooden bulkheads; behind them he could hear the soft stamping of the animals, everything near him was dear and familiar. The talk around him was of harvest and weather, the familiar realities of everyday life; but for some reason they now seemed alien, as if suddenly everyone were talking in a strange language. Only Lilla at his side seemed solid and real; he took her hand, and put his free arm around her waist. She leaned back against his shoulder; she had braided fresh field flowers into her hair and some crudely dyed red ribbons. Her hair was dark, curling coarsely around her red cheeks; she was plump and soft against him, and his hands strayed into the softness under her shawl. She did not protest, only sighing a little when he bent to kiss her, pulling her face around to his.

He whispered to her, and she came compliantly into the darkness at the end of the long barn. Part of the game was to elude the young men who made sure that no fire was carried into the area of stored grain, but they wanted no lights. Surrounded by the fresh sweetness of the hay, with clover flowers adding to the scent, Conn held her tightly and kissed her again and again; after a little he murmured to her, and Lilla moved with him farther into the darkness. They were standing pressed together, his head buried in her breasts, his hands fumbling blindly with the laces, when he heard someone call his name.

"Conn?" It was Markos's voice; Conn turned angrily to see the old man, a fire-shielded lantern in his hand. He held it up to look into the girl's face. "Ah, Lilla; your mother wants ye, girl."

Rebelliously, Lilla looked round; she could just see her mother, small and dark in a striped gown, gossiping with half a dozen other women. But Markos's scowl was too forbidding and she chose not to argue. Reluctantly she let go of Conn's hand, her own fingers quickly tightening the laces of her bodice.

Conn said, "Don't go, Lilla; we'll dance again."

"No such thing; ye're wanted, young master," Markos said deferentially but with a sternness Conn had never dared to resist. He followed Markos sullenly out of the barn and once outside, turned to demand, "Well, what is it?"

"Look, the sky's dark; there will be rain before dawn," said Markos.

"And for this you interrupted us? You overstep yourself, foster-father."

"I think not; what's more important to a landlord than a farmer's weather?" Markos said. "Besides, it's my business to be sure ye remember who you are, Master Conn. Can ye deny that in another quarter hour, you'd have had the girl in the hay?"

"And so what if I did, and what's that to you? I'm no gelding; do you expect—"

"I expect you to do right by whoever you take," Markos said. "There's no harm in dancing, but as for more—you're Hammerfell; you couldn't marry the girl or even do what's right for her child if anything came of it."

"Am I to live all my life womanless because of our family's ill luck?" Conn demanded.

"By no means, lad; once Hammerfell's yours again, you can sue for any princess in the Hundred Kingdoms," Markos said, "but don't let some farm girl trap you now. You can do better for yourself than your cowman's daughter—and the girl deserves better of you than to be taken lightly at a festival," he added. "I've never heard but that she's a good girl and deserves a husband who can respect her, not to be tumbled by a young lord who has nothing more for her. Your family's always been honorable with women. Your father, may the Gods be good to his memory, was the soul of propriety. You wouldn't want it said that you were just a young lecher, good for nothing but to lure women into dark corners."

Conn hung his head, knowing that everything Markos said was true, but still angry at the interruption and aching with frustration.

"You talk like a *cristoforo*," he said sullenly.

Markos shrugged. "You could do worse. At least wi' their creed you'd never have anything to regret."

"Or to rejoice," Conn muttered. "You've disgraced me, Markos, hauling me away from a dance like a naughty boy to be sent home to bed."

"No," said Markos. "Ye don't believe me now, boy, but I've *kept* you from disgrace. Look here—" he indicated the dancing farmers, who had struck up another tune; Conn's eyes followed Lilla, who had been swept into another dance. "Use your head, lad," Markos urged softly. "Every mother in the village knows who you are; don't you suppose any one of them would be glad to lure you into her family, and not be above baiting the trap with her daughter?"

"What a view you have of women!" said Conn in disgust. "Do you really think they are so scheming? You never said this to me before—"

"Nay, I didna' " said Markos, exaggerating the rough country accent. "Till the other night, no one knew you as anyone but *my* son; now they know who you really are, and you *are* Duke of Hammerfell—"

"And with that and a silver *sekal*, I can buy a cup o' cider," Conn said. "I see little benefit in that yet—"

"Gi' yourself time, youngster; once there were armies at Hammerfell, and they haven't all turned in their swords for ploughs," Markos said. "They'll gather when the time comes again, and it won't be all that long now. Just have patience." They were moving gradually along the village street until they reached the small cottage where he lodged with Markos. An old man—a bent veteran with one arm—who had waited on them for much of his life, came and took Markos's cloak and Conn's and hung them up.

"Will ye sup, masters?"

"Nay, Rufus, we ate and drank at the festival," said Markos. "Get to bed, old friend. There's naught moving tonight."

"Good thing, too," grunted old Rufus. "We had a watch on the pass, in case Storn had his greedy eye on Hammerfell harvests; but there's not so much as a bush-jumper stirring on the hills."

"Good," Markos said, and went to the water bucket, dipping himself out a drink. "There'll be rain before dawn, I think; good it held off till the bluegrain harvest was stored." He bent to unlace his boots, saying, without looking at his foster-son, "I was sorry to tear you away so abruptly, but it seemed to me the time to take action. I should perhaps have spoken before; but while you were just a lad, it seemed unnecessary. Even so, honor demanded—"

"I understand," said Conn roughly. "It doesn't matter. Just as well we got home before *that*—" And as he spoke, outside there was a great rush of wind and a sudden roaring as the heavens opened and violent heavy rain sluiced downward, blotting out all other sound.

"Aye, the poor girls will have their harvest finery

spoiled," said Markos. But Conn was not listening; the stone walls of the cottage had faded away, and a blaze of light drenched his eyes. The rough bench beneath him was a brocaded chair, and before him a small, white-haired man, elegantly dressed, with piercing gray eyes, looked straight at him and demanded, *If I should give you men and arms to recover Hammerfell, would you then swear to be faithful vassal to the Hastur kings? We need faithful men there beyond the Kadarin . . .*

"Conn!"

It was Markos shaking his arm.

"Where were you? Far from here, I could tell—was it your dream-maiden again?"

Conn blinked at the sudden darkness of the crude lantern and firelight after the brilliance dazzling him.

"Not this time," he said, "though I could tell she was near. No, Markos; I spoke with King—" he fumbled for the name, "King Aidan in Thendara, and he pledged me arms and men for Hammerfell—"

"Merciful Avarra," muttered the old man, "what sort of dream—"

"No dream, foster-father; it *couldn't* have been a dream. I saw him as I see you, but more clearly in the light, and I heard his voice. Oh, Markos, if only I knew if my *laran* is that of foretelling the future! For if it is so, I should go at once to Thendara, and seek out King Aidan—"

"I know not," said Markos. "I know not what *laran* was in your mother's line—it might well be that."

Markos watched Conn carefully, puzzled by this recurrence of the "dream." For the first time in many years, it crossed his mind: *Was it possible that somehow the Duchess of Hammerfell had survived, and had kept alive the cause of Hammerfell in Thendara?*

*Or even, perhaps, that Conn's brother had somehow
survived that night of fire and disaster?* No, surely not;
this could not account for Conn's visions; still Conn,
he remembered, had always had an unusually strong
link with his twin. . . .

Conn urged, "Should I not go to Thendara and
speak with King Aidan Hastur—?"

"It's not so easy as that, to drop onto a king's
doorstep," said Markos, "but your mother had Hastur
kinsmen and for her sake no doubt they'd speak for
you wi' the king."

*Should I tell him that I suspect his mother—or even his
elder brother—might live?* Markos wondered. *No; it
wouldn't be fair to the boy, to let him wonder about that all
the way to Thendara—there's enough on his mind—*

"Yes," he said with resignation. "It seems you must
certainly go to Thendara, and find out what they
know there of Hammerfell and what can be done to
aid our people. It is also time we tried to approach
your mother's kin for possible aid they could offer
us themselves." He paused for a moment before
continuing. "I must also add, my boy, that it is time
you spoke with someone more knowing of the ways
of *laran*—these 'episodes' are becoming too frequent,
and I worry about your welfare."

Conn could not help but agree.

Conn rode southward through the soft rain, which
blurred the outlines of the hills. As he passed through
the southern reaches of the old realm of Hammerfell,
and into the kingdom of Asturias, it seemed that all
the Hundred Kingdoms were at his feet. There had
once been a saying that many a smaller king in the
Hundred Kingdoms could stand on a hill and see

117

from border to border of his kingdom; and now as he passed from little kingdom to little kingdom, border after border, Conn could see that it was true. To the south, he had been told, lay the Hastur Domains, where during long wars in the past the brilliant King Regis IV had at last reunited many of these miniature Kingdoms under a single rule.

He crossed the Kadarin River into the foothills, and came to Neskaya, said to be the oldest city in the world. There he spent the night, guesting with a lowland family for whom Markos had written him an introduction. They paid him honor and introduced him to all their sons and daughters; he was not too young and naive to understand that this homage was paid not to him but to his heritage and title; but it was still a heady drink for a boy of his age. He was given to understand that he would be welcome there almost indefinitely, but he kindly declined—his mission pressed him on.

And on sunset of the third day he passed the cloud lake of Hali with its curious fish and the shining ruins of the great Tower which had once stood there and which would forever remain unrebuilt as a memorial to the great folly of waging war with *laran*. Conn was not sure he understood the reasoning behind this; if there was so powerful a weapon surely the most merciful thing to do in a time of war was to use it at once and bring the conflict to a quick end before there could be additional deaths, but he could see that if such a weapon fell into the hands of the wrong side, it would surely be disaster. And when he thought it over a little more, he realized that even the wisest might not be able to tell which cause was the most righteous.

118

He slept that night in the shadow of the ruins, and if there were ghosts, they did not trouble his sleep.

At a travel shelter that morning he washed, combed his red hair, and changed into the clean suit in his saddlebags. He ate the last of his food, but that did not trouble him; he had always hunted for provender, and now he was well supplied with money by his modest standards, and knew he would be soon getting into more populated areas where he could buy both food and drink. Like a child looking forward to a treat, he was eager to see the big city.

Soon after midmorning he became aware that he was entering the environs of the city. The roads were wider and smoother, the buildings older and larger; most of them had a look of having been inhabited for a long time. He had been proud of his fine new suit; but although it was well sewn from sturdy cloth, by taking note of the other youths his age he saw in the streets he soon realized that in it he looked like a country bumpkin, for no one seemed to be wearing such clothing but a few elderly farmers, with mud on their boots.

What do I care? I am not, after all, going to dance at the king's midsummer ball! But to himself he confessed that he *did* care, after all. He had had no great wish to come to the city, but if the roads of his fate led him there, he would prefer to look like a gentleman.

It was toward noon and the red sun high in the sky when he sighted from afar the walls of the old city of Thendara, and not more than an hour later, he rode into the city proper, dominated by the old castle of the Hastur-lords.

At first he was content to ride through the streets looking around; later he found himself a meal in a cheap tavern. In the tavern someone came through and waved carelessly to him; Conn had never seen the man before and wondered if it was merely friendliness to a stranger or if the man had mistaken him for someone else.

When he had finished his meal and paid his score, he inquired for the house of Valentine Hastur as Markos had advised, and was directed there. As he rode through the streets, he wondered again if he were being mistaken for someone else, as once or twice a man waved in a friendly fashion as one would to an acquaintance.

He found Valentine Hastur's house easily enough from the instructions he had been given; but hesitated before he approached the door. At this hour of the day the lord might indeed be out and about his business. No, he reassured himself; the man was a great nobleman, not a farmer; he had no fields to plough nor flocks to tend, and anyone who had business with him would probably seek him at his house; he would be as likely to be home as not.

He ascended the steps, and when a servant answered the door, he asked courteously if this were the home of the lord Valentine Hastur.

"It is, if that's any of your business," the man said with a look of ill-concealed scorn at Conn's appearance and the country fashion of his clothing.

"Say to Lord Valentine Hastur," Conn said firmly, "that the Duke of Hammerfell, a relation of his from the far Hellers, asks for audience with him."

The man looked surprised—as well he might, thought Conn—but he ushered Conn into an anteroom and went to deliver the message, and after a time Conn heard a firm step approaching the room—

obviously, he thought, the step of the master of the house.

A tall, slim man with red hair going sandy in age, Valentine Hastur strode into the room, his hand extended in welcome.

"Alastair, my dear fellow," he said, "I had not expected to see you at this hour. But what is this? I had not thought you would be seen at home, not to mention in the street in such an outfit! And have you and the young lady set the date yet? My cousin told me but yesterday that he was just waiting for you to come and talk to him." At this point Conn frowned; it was all too evident that the Hastur-lord was not speaking to him, but to someone for whom he had mistaken him. Valentine Hastur strode along the hall, and did not notice the look; but rambled on amiably, "And how is the little dog working out? Did your mother like the creature? If she did not, she is hard to please. Well, what can I do for you?" Only then did he turn to look again at Conn.

Then he stopped. "Wait a moment . . . *you're* not Alastair!" Valentine was dumbfounded. "But you certainly resemble him! Just who *are* you, lad?"

Conn said firmly, "I don't understand this. I am grateful for your welcome, sir; but who do you *think* I am?"

Valentine Hastur said slowly, "I thought, of course, that you were Alastair of Hammerfell—the young duke. I—well, I thought you a young man I've known since you—he—was in baby clothes, and your mother my closest friend. But—"

"That's not possible," Conn said. But this friendliness could not help but make some impression on him. "Sir, I beg your pardon. I am Conn of Hammer-

121

fell, and I am grateful to you for your welcome, kinsman, but—"

Lord Valentine looked displeased—*no*, Conn thought, *puzzled*. Then slowly his face brightened.

"*Conn* ... of course ... the brother, the *twin* brother—but I was always told you died in the burning of Hammerfell."

"No," Conn said. "It was *my* twin who died—with my mother, sir. I give you my solemn word I am Duke of Hammerfell and the only man living who can lay claim to that title."

"No, you are mistaken," said Valentine Hastur gently. "I see now that there has been a dreadful mistake; your mother and brother live, my boy, but they believe it was *you* who perished. I assure you, the Duchess and Duke of Hammerfell are very much alive."

"You are joking, surely," said Conn, feeling light-headed.

"No; Zandru seize me if I would jest on such a matter," said Lord Valentine fiercely. "Now I begin to understand. Your mother, my boy, has lived for many years with the sad belief that her son died in the fall of Hammerfell; I gather you *are* the other twin?"

"I believed that they both died in the burning of Hammerfell," said Conn, shocked. "My brother is known to you, sir?"

"As well as I know my own sons," said Lord Valentine, looking searchingly at Conn. "Now I look closely at you, I can see little differences; your walk is somewhat different than his, and your eyes are set a little differently in your face. But you are very much like him indeed." Valentine's face was lit with excite-

122

ment, "Tell me why you have come to Thendara, then, Conn—if I may call you so, as a kinsman."

He stepped forward then and took the younger man into a kinsman's embrace, saying, "Welcome to my house and my home, my dear boy."

Conn blinked; to find an affectionate kinsman, where he had expected to find a stranger, was a shock, though not an unpleasant one.

"You spoke of my mother—she is living near here, then?"

"To be sure; I dined at her house but last night," said Lord Valentine, "and even before you tell me why you came here to Thendara, I would suggest that you go and make your presence known to her. With your permission, I would like to go with you and be the first to give her this news."

"Yes," said Conn, visibly shaken, "I certainly must first see my mother."

Valentine went to his desk, seated himself and scribbled a few hasty lines; then summoned a servant, and said to him, "Take this message at once to the Duchess of Hammerfell, and say to her that I shall be there within the hour. But we must give her time to ready herself to receive guests; let me at least offer you a little cold meat and bread; you have traveled a long way and we can eat before we ride."

Conn, however, could eat but little. As they rode together through the streets, Lord Valentine said, "This is a joyous day for me; I am truly eager to see your mother's face when first she looks upon you. She has long mourned you as dead. Why did you never come in search of her before now? Where have you lived?"

"In hiding, on my father's lands, believing myself

the last of Hammerfell's line," said Conn, "with no living kin but my father's old paxman Markos."

"I remember old Markos," said Valentine. "Your mother believed that he, too, had perished; he must be very old indeed, now."

"He is, but he is strong and hearty for such an old man," said Conn. "He has been like a father to me, and more than many kinsmen."

"And why have you come here now?" asked Valentine.

"To appeal for justice from the Hastur king," Conn said, "not for my people alone; but all through the Hellers. The lords of Storn are not content with destroying my family and my line, but they are trying to starve or kill my clansmen and tenants by burning them out and driving them from lands they have farmed for generations—so that they can use the land for grazing, sheep being more profitable and less troublesome than tenant farmers."

Valentine Hastur looked troubled. He said, "I do not know if King Aidan can or will do anything about that, my boy. It is a nobleman's privilege to do as he likes with his own lands."

"And where, then, are people to go? Are they to starve or die for the convenience of a noble lord? Are they not more important than sheep?"

"Oh, I agree with you," Lord Valentine said. "I have set myself firmly against any such thing on Hastur lands. Nevertheless Aidan will most probably not interfere—in fact, cannot by law interfere with his nobles, or he would not long hold his throne."

This gave Conn much to think about, and he fell silent, deeply troubled. When they arrived at the house where Erminie had lived for many years, they passed through the gate, and Conn said, bemused, "I *know* this place; but I thought it was nothing but a dream."

As they passed into the courtyard, an old dog came stiffly into the paved space, and lifted her head in a sharp inquiring bark.

"I have known her for years," Valentine said ruefully, "yet to her I am always a stranger. Here, Jewel. Good girl, it's all right, you silly creature—"

The dog sniffed at Conn's knees, then in a perfect frenzy of wagging her tail, jumped stiffly around him. Erminie, coming through the door at the far end, said, "Jewel, behave yourself, old girl! What—" and, raising her eyes, she looked straight at Conn— then crumpled, all but fainting, into a garden seat.

Valentine rushed to catch her, and after a moment she opened her eyes.

"I saw—did I see—"

"You were not dreaming," said Valentine firmly. "It was a shock to me, too, and I cannot imagine how it happened, but it is your other son, and he is alive. Conn, my boy, come here and prove to your mother that it is you and you are real."

Conn came and knelt beside her chair, and she clutched at his hands hard enough to hurt.

"How did it happen?" she demanded roughly, tears wetting her cheeks. "I searched for you and Markos in the wood all night."

"And he for you," said Conn. "I grew up on the tale of that search. I cannot, even now, understand how it could have happened."

"The important thing is that you are indeed living," said Erminie, and raised herself to kiss him. "There, Jewel, you recognize him, too? If I had not believed, Jewel would have convinced me; I used to leave you two with no other to guard you—she was as good as any nurse for looking after you."

"I think I remember," said Conn, letting the old dog swarm into his lap and hugging her close.

A series of sharp small yips came from the corner of the room and a furry half-grown puppy rushed at them, nipping Conn with her sharp small teeth. Conn laughed and playfully held the little dog away.

"No, you shall *not* make your lunch off my fingers, pup! Come now, be friendly," he coaxed, and Erminie said sharply, "Down, Copper!" Jewel barked her deep-throated bark, trying to push the puppy away, while Conn insisted laughingly, "So you don't like me as well as old Jewel, do you, puppy—Copper, is it? A fine name for a fine little dog."

They sat on the floor in a heap with the jumping, playful dogs, while from the door a voice Conn found as familiar as a dream, said, "I heard the dogs and came at once. Is all well, kinswoman?"

Floria came to pick up the puppy Copper, gently scolding her; Conn, unable to move, sat with his eyes fixed on the woman he never believed could be real.

"I dreamed of you," he said in a daze.

He was too untrained as a telepath, and therefore too unskilled, to hold back from the impulsive touch; for an instant he felt that his whole soul, his history, his being flowed out to embrace hers, and for just that instant he felt her impulsive response. Floria's eyes held his, and her hands went out to him; then, remembering that although she felt she knew Conn as well as she knew her own self, she had never actually set eyes on him before, startled and uneasy, she drew back, as was proper in the presence of a stranger.

She said shakily, "You are very like your brother."

And he replied, "I am beginning to believe that; so many people have said so. And Mother came near to fainting when she first looked on me."

"I had thought you dead for so many years," Erminie said, "and to recover a living son after half a lifetime—Alastair is eighteen and that was my age when you were born."

"When shall I meet my brother?" Conn asked eagerly.

Floria said, "He is putting away the horses; he will be here in a minute or two. We rode together this morning outside the city wall. Father allowed it because he said it was understood now that we should soon be married."

Conn heard this with a shock but knew he should have foreseen it; it was clear now that his flashes of city life—as well as his first sight of Floria—had come from the twin brother he had not known survived.

Erminie, who had observed the unspoken exchange between Conn and Floria, said to herself: *Oh, dear; what can possibly come of this?* But it was only a first encounter; and her newly-met son seemed to be a decent and honorable man; indeed, if Markos had brought him up, he could not be otherwise. He would hardly be the kind to approach his brother's promised wife, once he understood the situation. Yet, aware of the depths of Conn's feelings, she realized the heartache which lay ahead for him and wondered what she could do.

"And you came to Thendara without even knowing that we lived, Conn?"

"I should have known my twin brother lived, at least," he said, "for I have heard, from those who know more of *laran* than I, that the bond between twins is the strongest of all bonds; and for the last year or so, I have been plagued by images of places I have never been, and faces I have never seen. Do you know much about *laran* and the art of the starstone, Mother?"

"I have been a technician in Thendara Tower," she said, "for these eighteen years; though I have been thinking that when Floria is better trained and can take my place there, I may soon decide to leave the Tower and marry again."

Floria colored and said, "No, kinswoman, Alastair will not have it so."

Erminie said, "That's for you to say, child. It would be a pity if you left your work because of a man's selfishness."

"It's true we've had but little time to talk of it," Floria said. She raised her eyes again to Conn and asked, "And you, kinsman, you are a telepath; have you yet been trained in a Tower?"

"No," he said, "I have lived in the mountains and had no such opportunity; and I have had other things on my mind, such as defending my people from Storn's evil purposes."

Erminie realized that the conversation had strayed considerably from what she had intended to ask. She said, "Then Storn knows that you live?"

"Yes, and the feud's alive again, I'm sorry to say, Mother. For many years he thought that all our clan were dead."

"I thought—I hoped—that Storn believed us all dead, and therefore the feud would die out," Erminie said, "although I have sworn to help your brother regain our rightful lands."

"It might have died out, Mother, had I been content to lie hidden and let our people be abused," Conn said, "but I made it known to him not forty days since that if he continued his looting and burning, he would reckon with a Hammerfell." He explained the raid on Storn's burning-party.

"I cannot fault you for that, my son," said Erminie warmly, leaning over to embrace him, and it was at this moment that Alastair entered the garden. He saw the women sitting on the path with the dogs and Conn in his mother's arms, and instinctively knew at once what had happened.

To do him justice, his first emotion was one of warmth. He whistled to the dogs and they came, leaving the people on the floor unencumbered. Erminie sprang up at once, saying, "Oh, Alastair, the most wonderful thing has happened!"

"I met with Lord Valentine in the courtyard," he said, and smiled at Conn, his frank and charming smile.

"So you are my twin," he said musingly. "Welcome, little brother . . . you know that I am elder?"

"Yes," said Conn, thinking it rather odd that Alastair felt the need to bring that up before they had even become acquainted, "by twenty minutes or so."

"Twenty minutes or twenty years—it is all the same," Alastair said oddly, and embraced him.

"What do you in the city?"

"What I hope you will be doing in my place,"

Conn said. "I came to ask the aid of the Hastur king to recover our lands and protect our people."

"There again I am ahead of you," said Alastair, "for I have already spoken to King Aidan about this, and he *has* pledged his help." He smiled at Conn and the twins, like rough and refined mirror images, stared at each other.

"It was you, then!" Conn exclaimed. "I thought it was I who was to ask for his aid."

Alastair shrugged, not understanding what Conn's *laran* had conveyed to him.

"I am glad you have made yourself known to our mother," he said. "And to the Lady Floria, my promised wife; soon to be your sister-in-law."

And again, Conn thought, *why is he rubbing it into my face that he is my elder and will come ahead of me in all things? Well, he is truly Duke of Hammerfell, and while I presumed his death, I had every right to conduct myself as duke; but now that I know he lives, I must do my best to support him.* He bowed and said in his courtliest fashion, "My brother and my lord."

Alastair hugged him hard and said, "No need for such formalities between us, brother; time enough for that when I reign again at Hammerfell with you by my side." Then he smiled and shook his head, "But where did you get that clown's suit? We must have something fitting your station made for you at once; I shall send word to my tailor this afternoon."

Conn was rattled by this; did his brother have no manners *at all*? He said stiffly, "This suit is new and of good cloth; it would be a waste not to wear it."

"No need for waste; give it to the butler, it's fitting for his station," said Erminie in support of Alastair.

"It will do well enough for me in the Hellers," said

Conn, defensive but proud. "I am no city dandy!"

"But if you are to have audience with King Aidan—and he must know there are two of us," said Alastair more diplomatically, "you cannot go before him dressed like a farmer fresh from the turnip fields. I think you had better wear some of my clothes in the city; you're not too proud to borrow clothes from your own twin, are you, brother?"

At his disarming smile, Conn felt welcomed again and charmed; after all, it would take time to know his brother properly. He smiled at Alastair in turn and said, "All Gods forbid! Thank you—brother!"

Erminie got up and said, "Now come into the main room, Conn, and tell me everything about yourself . . . and perhaps we can find out how it happened that we did not recover one another until now! What has been happening all these years at Hammerfell? How fares Markos? Has he been good to you, my son? Floria, dear, you will stay with us and dine, of course. Come, my sons—" and she stopped and sighed, a sigh of pure but disbelieving pleasure. "How it fills my heart to say that again after all these years!" And, stretching a hand to each, she led them into the other room, followed by Floria and the dogs.

9

Little was talked of that summer in Thendara but the strange and romantic story of the loss and restoration of the second son of the Duchess of Hammerfell. Even Erminie got tired of repeating it, though she was proud of the attention given to her new-found son, and she grew so fond of Conn that there were times when she felt disloyal to Alastair who had been so kindly and thoughtful a companion for all those years.

Although it had been known for many years in Thendara that the widowed duchess did not much care to entertain, toward the end of the summer she gave a small dance to announce the formal handfasting of her son Alastair to Lady Floria.

Throughout that day, threatening clouds blew down from the Venza Mountains, and a little before sunset the rain started in earnest, battering down across the city with slamming force; people arrived dripping wet and great fires had to be lighted for them to dry a little before they could enjoy the lavishly-provided supper, and the dancing which was the best known feature of all Darkovan social occasions.

But damp clothing did not in any way dampen the spirit of the gathering. Alastair and Floria stood in the hall to welcome their guests, and Conn escorted and aided his mother. The dancing was at its height when Gavin Delleray arrived; he took Alastair into a kinsman's embrace, and claimed a kinsman's privilege, kissing Floria's cheek. Gavin was a plump and sturdy young man, dressed in the very height of the current fashion. Knee breeches of silk revealed stockings showing a fashionably plump leg, his brocaded coat was of flame-colored satin, and firestones adorned the high neck of his shirt. His hair was dressed, as was the fashion, in round curls to either side, so that it hardly resembled natural hair but could have been a stiff and artificial wig, dyed with streaks of bright rainbow colors. Alastair looked almost envious; he himself tried to follow fashion and strove for a dandified appearance, but he came nowhere near to Gavin in this brilliant plumage.

As Gavin put his damp cloak into a servant's hands, Alastair muttered to Conn, "I'll never be able to look as much in the mode as he does."

"And you should thank the Gods for it," Conn said forthrightly. "I think he looks a fool—like a dressed doll for a little girl's dollhouse."

"Between us, I agree with you, Conn," Floria whispered. "I would never think to dye my hair purple and have it done up with glue that way!"

When Gavin turned back to them with an ingenuous smile, Conn felt a little ashamed. For all his absurd elaboration of dress, Conn was fonder of Gavin than any other of Alastair's friends. Alastair teased Conn unmercifully about his countrified tastes, even after he had discarded his rustic suit, and wore as well-cut an outfit as Alastair's own, he could still not be persuaded to adorn his fingers with the fashionable rings, nor to wear jeweled and elaborately tied neckcloths. Ironically, Gavin, alone of the circle of Alastair's friends, had refrained from plaguing him about his refusal to follow fashions. Now he took Conn's hand warmly and said, "Good evening, cousin; I am glad you could be with us tonight. Floria, did my mother send word to Lady Erminie that the royal lady will be here this evening?"

"Yes, we have heard," Floria said, "but I fear she will not appreciate the entertainment; she is too deaf to enjoy the music much and too lame to dance."

"Oh, that's all right," Gavin said gaily. "She will play cards with the other old ladies, and kiss all the young girls; and if there are enough sweets—and Lady Erminie's chef is justly famous—she will not miss for entertainment." He raised his hands hesitantly to his hair. "I fear the dampness has got through my hood and my hair is wet; how does it look, friends?"

"Like a ball of feathers set up for the target at an archery contest," Conn teased. "If they begin shooting, you had better hide in a closet, or they'll aim at you." Gavin grinned widely, not in the least offended.

"Perfect! That's exactly how this hairdo is supposed to look, cousin." He went into the main room, bowed over Erminie's hand. "My lady."

"I'm glad you could be with us tonight, Gavin," said Erminie, smiling at her son's childhood friend with genuine affection. "Can we hear you sing this night?"

"Oh, to be sure," Gavin said, smiling. "But I'm hoping Alastair will give us a song as well."

Somewhat later, surrounded by his friends, Gavin took his place at the tall harp and played; then beckoned Alastair to his side, and after a brief conference in whispers, Alastair sang a melodious love song, gazing at Floria.

"Is that one of your songs, Gavin?" Floria asked.

"No, not this one; this is a folk song of Asturias. But it is clever of you to ask; many of the songs I have written are in the ancient mode of that country," he said. "And Alastair sings them better than I do. Do *you* sing, Conn?"

"Only a few songs of the hills," Conn said.

"Oh, do sing; I love the old country songs!" Gavin urged, but Conn smiled and refused.

Later when they began to dance, he also refused, "I know no dances but the country ones; you would be ashamed of me, brother; I would disgrace you before your fine friends."

"Floria will never forgive you if you do not dance with her," Alastair urged, but according to custom he led Floria out for the first of the couple dances. Gavin stood beside Conn, watching them as they moved away.

"I was not merely being polite when I asked you to sing," he said. "I never tire of the folk songs of the mountains; most of my music has been written in that idiom. If you do not want to sing in this company—and I don't blame you; except for Alastair himself there's not a man here who truly understands music—perhaps you'd come one day to my studio and sing for me there. It's possible you may know some songs I'm not familiar with."

"I'll think it over," Conn said, warily; he liked Gavin, but although he had as clear a voice as his brother, he had never been the performer.

At that moment there was a commotion in the street and a knock at the door. Erminie's chamberlain went and opened it, and stepped back in surprise; then, recovering his composure, announced, "His Grace Aidan Hastur of Elhalyn and Her Grace Queen Antonella."

The dancing stopped and all eyes turned to the door as the royal couple removed their cloaks. Conn at once recognized the man he had spoken to—or had it been his brother?—in his dream or vision. Queen Antonella was small and fat and hobbled with one leg shorter than the other in spite of a built-up shoe on that foot; King Aidan was small and white-haired and quite unimposing. All the same there was a respectful silence while Erminie came forward and bowed.

"My lady, welcome. My lord, this is an unexpected honor."

"Never mind all that," said the Hastur king genially. "I am here tonight simply as a friend. The story of your son has been much repeated; I have heard so much gossip, that I wanted to find out what *really* happened." He laughed loudly, putting them all at ease.

Alastair, with Floria on his arm, came forward, and Aidan beckoned to him. "Well, young man, have you thought about that matter of which we spoke?"

"I have, your Grace."

"Then come and talk with me about it," the king

requested, "and I would like to speak with your brother as well."

Alastair gestured to Conn. "Certainly, but I am the duke and the decision is ultimately mine, *vai dom*."

"Yes, of course," said Aidan peacefully, "but your brother *has* been living in those parts and can tell us most accurately what's going on there."

Meanwhile, Erminie signaled to the musicians to take up the music for dancing again, and ushered the queen inside.

"While the men talk, your Grace, will you come and take some refreshment?" she asked politely, offering Queen Antonella her arm. The elderly queen looked at Alastair and Conn. "Like as two pods on a featherpod tree, aren't they? Lucky Erminie, to have not one handsome son but two," she said, almost wistfully, and paused to smile at Gavin and stand on tiptoe to kiss him affectionately on the cheek.

"How tall you've grown," she said, and Erminie had to smile, for short as Gavin was, Queen Antonella was so small that next to the queen Gavin appeared to be quite a respectable height. She turned to King Aidan and said, "Hasn't he grown handsome? He really has dear Marcia's eyes, doesn't he?"

"I wish my mother had lived to hear you say so, kinswoman," said Gavin, bowing most deferentially over the old queen's hand. "And now, while my kinsmen speak with His Grace, will the Lady Floria honor me with a dance?"

Erminie nodded to Floria to dance with Gavin as she led Queen Antonella into the other room, while her sons went with the king into a small parlor off the large room which held the dancers.

Once they were settled by the fire, Alastair poured

out wine, which the king accepted, raising his glass silently. Then after a moment he said, "Well, shall we drink to the restoration of Hammerfell, then? Do you think you can pledge to be my faithful man in the mountains, Alastair?"

"I think so," Alastair said. "Does this mean you have decided to lend me armies and men, sire?"

"It's not quite that simple," Aidan said. "If I send an army unprovoked, then I am invading the country; but if there is an uprising there, then I can send troops to restore order. Your father—the old Duke of Hammerfell—he had soldiers; what happened to them when he died?"

It was Conn who answered, "Most of the men who served my father went back to their own lands after his death; they could not fight a leaderless war against Storn's men. But there are some who have remained close to us, in our service; like the men who join us when we raid Storn's men and attempt to keep him from burning out my tenants—"

"*Your* tenants?" Alastair asked softly. Conn seemed not to hear, but King Aidan raised his eyes and looked sharply at the twins, and Conn, who was a telepath, sensed that he was wondering if this rivalry could create trouble for them both. But the king did not voice his concern. "How many men are there, Conn?"

"Perhaps three dozen," Conn answered, "and some of them may have been the men of my father's personal guard—his household."

"And could you guess how many men are—in hiding, but ready to come out for a rising against Storn?"

Conn stopped to think it over.

"I really am not certain," he said at last. "There could not be fewer than two hundred; there might be as many as three hundred, but I am not certain there are more than that. With the men of my father's household—" at the back of his mind he heard the eerie echo, *My father's,* from Alastair, and it troubled him; he was growing almost hourly more conscious of his *laran,* "—there might be as many as three hundred and fifty, all told."

He added, "I should perhaps return to call them up, and find out how many we can be sure of."

"A good idea," said King Aidan, "for with fewer than three hundred you could hardly go out against Storn, who also has men and armies."

Alastair said curtly, "If anyone goes, brother, it should be me; after all it is *my* land—and they are *my* tenants." Conn sensed his sudden anger. *Who does he think he is! Does he think he can walk in after all my years of waiting and usurp my place?*

Conn felt his brother's wrath as if the words had been spoken aloud; and experienced, for his own part, a violent gust of anger, which he knew Alastair could not share. *Yes, what he says is true; he is the duke by birth. But to him it is only a title, an old story. I have lived with these men, shared their poverty and their sufferings . . . it is to me they turn when they seek help or leadership. Is it birth alone that can make a Duke of Hammerfell? Do the years I have served my people count for nothing?*

Although the words had come spontaneously and he knew Alastair could not hear them, impulsively he found himself crying out to the old king for an answer, though he knew that the Hastur-lord could not give him one—not, at least, at present. Aidan was looking at him sympathetically. Conn remembered, *I pledged to serve my brother loyally; I had not thought of this.*

The king said, consideringly, "Perhaps your brother is right, Alastair; the men know him, he has been living among them—"

"All the more reason they should get to know their true duke," Alastair exclaimed, and Aidan sighed.

"We will have to think it over," he temporized. "For the moment—Alastair of Hammerfell, will you be my true man in the lands beyond the Kadarin?"

Spontaneously, Alastair knelt before him, touched his lips to the hand Aidan extended.

"I swear it, my lord," he said, and a sense of loyalty and affection flooded through him for this king who was his kinsman and had promised him aid in the restoration of his lands. Conn watched without moving; but Aidan looked up at him and their eyes met. Aidan's thoughts were so clear to Conn he could hardly believe the king had not spoken aloud.

For life and death, I am your man, my lord.

I know. We have no need of spoken pledges, you and I.

Conn did not know why this love and loyalty had suddenly become so clear between them; before this night he had never in the flesh set eyes on the king; yet it seemed that he had known this man all his life and more, that he had served him since the beginning of time, that a bond as strong or stronger than the bond which bound him to his brother stretched unbroken between himself and Aidan Hastur. As Alastair rose, Conn knelt for a moment before the king; Aidan did not speak, but again, for a moment, their eyes met, and no more was necessary. Conn could feel in Aidan a pained puzzlement, and he knew the king regretted he could do nothing to overturn what now seemed to him a miscarriage of justice, that the wrong twin had been born eldest—

"So be it, sire," he said aloud. "I was born to my duty as you to yours."

Aidan said, "I think you had better go back to your dancing, my lads; even here there may be those who should not know what has been said and promised this night. But you should lose no time in getting to the hills, to rouse your clan." He carefully did not look at either of them when he said, "Your clan." For better or worse, he thought with a feeling very like despair, they would have to settle that between them, and he could not honorably take either one's part.

The king rose, gesturing them both to their feet, and they went out into the main room, Aidan holding back slightly. *It is just as well that the guests in general should not know that this conference has taken place.*

Conn, knowing that his twin had not enough *laran* to follow Aidan's thoughts, repeated this in a low voice to Alastair, who nodded, smiling, and said, "Oh. You're right, of course."

Floria came at once to join them.

"Now you *must* dance with me, Conn. It is a country dance, and you are sure to know it," she said eagerly, and dragged him into the ring. Conn, embarrassed, but feeling he could not refuse, joined in the dance. Abruptly he remembered dancing at the harvest festival with Lilla, and how different this was; then he remembered how Markos had dragged him away, and blushed.

They came to a stop at the end of the figure, and

Floria faced Conn. She was heated with dancing, and her emotions roiled within her. Under ordinary circumstances she could have stepped out on the terrace to cool herself a little, but the rain was blowing too hard into the courtyard. The old dog Jewel sat decorously by the door, and Floria pulled herself away absentmindedly to pat her and take a moment to slow her heart. Then she saw that Conn had stepped out into the rain; he looked troubled, and his eyes homed to hers, filling her with a strange deep-lying sorrow which was almost physical pain.

I have no right to comfort him, no right to touch him this way at all.

Nevertheless, she met his eyes—in itself a breach of decorum for a young girl in Thendara.

Decorum be damned. He is all but my brother!

He came toward her looking drawn and exhausted.

"What is it, my brother?" she asked him.

"I must go," he said. "By the king's word, I must return to Hammerfell—to summon what armies I have there."

"No!" He had not realized that Alastair was at his shoulder. "If anyone is to go, if the king intended anyone to go, I am the one, brother. I am Hammerfell; they are *my* armies, not yours; do you not understand that yet?"

"I understand, Alastair," Conn said, trying to control his temper "but what *you* do not understand—" He sighed. "I swear I have no intent to try and usurp your place, my brother. But," he fumbled to find words Alastair would understand, "I call these my men because I have lived among them all my life; they accept me, they know me—they do not even know you exist."

142

"Then they had better be learning," Alastair repeated. "After all—"

"You do not even know the *way* to Hammerfell," Conn said, interrupting in turn. "At the very least I should go and guide you—"

Floria broke in. "In this?" she asked, indicating the storm still raging outside, the pouring rain and the high winds battering the house.

"I will not melt into a puddle; I am not made of sugar candy. I have lived in the Hellers all my life, and I am not afraid of weather, Floria," Conn said.

"A few hours, after all, cannot matter," Floria protested. "Can it be so urgent that one of you must set forth in a storm, and in the middle of the night? And leave our handfasting undone? Alastair?"

"That at least should be completed," Alastair conceded with relief. "Let me go and find my mother and your father. It is for them to make the final decision on that." He strode away, leaving Floria and Conn standing together, regarding one another with frightened, troubled eyes.

Alastair walked through the crowd of holiday-clothed merrymakers, and spoke to Gavin Delleray at the tall harp. Gavin struck a chord and the crowd fell silent, while Erminie and Conn came to stand beside Alastair. All eyes turned to Floria, as her father took her arm and they joined the Hammerfells. Then Alastair spoke in his resonant singer's voice.

"My dear friends; I do not wish to interrupt the festivities, but I have learned that my presence is urgently required at Hammerfell; will you forgive me if we get on with the business which has brought us here tonight—Mother?"

Erminie took Floria's hand and frowned slightly at Alastair.

"I was aware of no messenger, my son," she said in an undertone.

"There was none," Alastair whispered back. "I will explain later—or Conn will tell you. But I would not go with the handfasting incomplete and Floria's pledge unspoken."

Conn looked faintly relieved. He moved to stand beside his brother, while Queen Antonella limped forward. From her stubby small finger, white and smooth, she drew a ring set with greenstones.

"A gift for the pledged bride," she said, thrust it on to Floria's finger—it was just a little too large— and stood on tiptoe to kiss the girl's rosy cheeks. "May you have much happiness, dear child."

"Thank you, your Grace," Floria murmured, "it is a lovely ring, and I shall cherish it as your gift."

Antonella smiled, and then a look of strain flitted across her face; she said, "Oh!" and her hand went to the lace at her throat; she stumbled and fell to her knees. Conn stooped quickly to raise her, but she was dead weight in his arms; she slid to the floor.

Instantly Erminie was at her side, King Aidan bending close; she opened her eyes and moaned, but it seemed that the queen's face had slipped all awry; her eye and mouth dragged down at the edge. She mumbled something; Erminie spoke reassuringly, holding the small pudgy figure on her arm.

"A stroke," she murmured to Aidan. "She is not young, and it might have happened at any time these many years."

"Yes; I feared it," the king said, and knelt by the stricken woman.

"It's all right, my dear; I'm here beside you. We'll take you home at once."

Her eyes slid shut and she seemed to sleep. Gavin Delleray rose quickly from her side and murmured, "I'll summon a chair."

"A litter," Aidan corrected, "I don't think she can sit."

"As your Grace wishes."

He went out into the rain, quickly returning, beckoning the footmen to open doors for the litter carriers. As if it were a million miles away, Conn noted distantly that the rain had made a wreck of Gavin's elaborate costume and coiffure, but he seemed not to notice. The littermen stooped, gently brushing King Aidan aside.

"By y'r leave, *vai dom*, we can lift her; it's our work, an' we're better at it than you. Easy, there; tuck the blanket round her legs. Now where do we carry her, me lord?" They had not recognized the king and it was probably just as well, Conn thought. Aidan gave quiet instructions and started out with them, walking beside the litter like any other elderly man worried about his suddenly ailing wife. He went to the king's side and asked, "May I summon your chair, sir? You'll get yourself drenched and catch your death of cold." Then he stopped, abashed; it wasn't his place to speak so to the king.

Aidan looked at him blankly. "No, dear boy, I'll stay with Antonella; she might be afraid if she called out and didn't hear a familiar voice near her. But thank you; now do go in out of the rain yourself, lad."

The rain was slackening somewhat, but Conn realized he was already soaked; he hurried back inside.

The porch was crowded with Erminie's guests taking their leave; the queen's collapse had quite effectively broken up the party.

Remaining in the hall were Alastair and Floria, still standing side by side before the fireplace, Floria looking down, stunned, at Antonella's ring on her hand; Erminie, moving dazed from the exodus off the porch; Gavin, even more drenched than Conn, rubbing his hair with a cloth a footman had brought him; Edric Elhalyn and Floria's brother Gwynn, looking troubled; and Valentine Hastur, who had stayed to see what he could do for Erminie in this sudden disaster.

"An evil omen for your handfasting," said Gavin, coming up to Alastair. "Will you continue?"

"We have no witnesses now, except our footmen," Erminie said, "and it would be an even worse omen, I think, to speak on over the queen's fallen body."

"I'm afraid you are right," said Edric. "That she should fall stricken just as she gave you a wedding gift, Floria!"

"I am not superstitious," said Floria. "I think we should go on with the handfasting—I do not think the royal lady would grudge us that. Even if this should be her last act of kindness—"

"All Gods forbid," said Erminie and Edric speaking almost together.

Conn thought of the kindly little old woman he had hardly seen, and of the king he had suddenly learned to love, who had called him "dear boy" even when so troubled, and sent him in out of the rain.

"I cannot think a handfasting at this moment would show respect," Edric said, and looked regretfully at his daughter. "But we will have all the more merrymaking at the wedding, which shall follow—" he looked at Erminie. "When? At Midsummer? Midwinter?"

"This coming Midwinter," Erminie said, "if it wins your approval, Alastair—Floria?" They both nodded. "Midwinter, then."

Alastair kissed Floria respectfully, such a kiss as a man might exchange with his promised wife in the presence of others. "May that day come soon when we shall be forever one," he said. Gavin came over and offered them congratulations.

"It seems a long time since Alastair and I used to chase you round the garden with spiders and snakes," he said, "but it was really only a few years. I think you much improved since those days, Floria; your jewels become you better than a striped pinafore. Lady—" he bowed to Erminie, "I am wet through; will you give me leave to go?"

Erminie started out of preoccupation, "Don't be foolish, Gavin; you are all but a son in this house. Go upstairs, and Conn or Alastair will find you something dry to put on, and then we will all go to the kitchen and have some hot soup or tea."

"Yes," said Alastair. "And I must set out before first light for Hammerfell."

"Mother," implored Conn, "tell him this is folly! He does not know the mountains, nor so much as the road to Hammerfell."

"Then the sooner I learn it, the better," said Alastair.

Conn had to admit that what he said was true but felt compelled to continue his protest.

"The men do not know you and will not obey you; they are used to me."

"Then they, too, must learn," said Alastair. "Come,

brother, this is my duty and it's time for me to start doing it; that I haven't done it before was wrong perhaps, but better now than never. And I want you to stay here and care for our mother. She has only just gotten you back; she should not lose you again so quickly."

Conn realized there was nothing more that he could say without giving the impression that he was indeed refusing to give up the right to the position which was in fact his brother's—or that he was reluctant to care for his mother, or to do the duty his brother and lord assigned him.

Erminie said, "I don't wish either of you to go; but I know you must, and also, Conn, I think Alastair is right; it is high time he took up his duty to his people. With Markos at his side there is no question the men will obey him, once they know who he is."

"I am sure you are right," Conn said. "You had better have my horse," he added, "she is mountain bred; that fine lowland mount of yours would stumble over the steep paths she must travel, and die of the cold on the first night. My horse may not be handsome, but she can carry you anywhere you must go."

"What! That rough-skinned brute? She is no better than a donkey," Alastair said lightly. "I wouldn't be seen on the beast."

"You'll find in the mountains, brother, that neither a man nor a horse is judged by his coat," Conn said, sick to death of this never ending argument he had with his brother. "The mare is shaggy for the weather she must endure; and those fine clothes of yours will be torn to bits by the briars along the mountain paths. I think after all I had better ride with you and guide you."

"By no means," said Alastair, but his thoughts were clear to Conn. *Markos still thinks of Conn as the duke and his lord; if Conn is there, I will never gain his total allegiance.*

Conn said softly, "You wrong our vassal and foster-father, Alastair; when he knows the truth—and sees the tattoo which he himself set on your shoulder as the mark of the rightful duke, his allegiance will be entirely yours."

Alastair hugged him impulsively. "If all the world were as honorable as you, my brother, it would frighten me less. But I cannot hide behind your strength and your honor; I must face my people on my own. Indulge me in this, brother."

"If this is what you feel you must do," Conn said, "all Gods forbid I should prevent you. Will you have my mountain-bred horse, though?"

"I am more than grateful for the offer," Alastair said with real warmth, "but I fear she cannot travel as fast as I should make my way."

Gavin Delleray came back into the room as he said this, wearing one of Conn's old coats which hung on him like a baggy tent. His hair had been roughly rubbed dry and was standing up in shaggy elflocks all over his head; a greater contrast to the perfect foppish appearance he had presented earlier would hardly have been possible. He said, "I would offer to go with you myself and guide you, my friend, if I knew the way any better than you. But if my services—here or in the Hellers—are any use to you, Alastair—"

Conn smiled at the thought of the slight, dandyish Gavin on the mountain roads. "If he will not accept me as a guide, nor the services of a twin brother, he would probably not accept yours either," he said almost ruefully, but then he thought: *Gavin, at least, is no threat to his power at Hammerfell.*

Alastair smiled and laid a hand on Conn's shoulder and on Gavin's. He said, "I think I should go alone; I must not need protection. But truly I thank you both for your offers." He turned to Erminie who approached them and said, "Mother, I need the fastest horse in our stables. In fact, what I truly need is a magical steed from the fairy tales you told me when I was a child. You bear magic, Mother; can you put it at my service now to bring me swiftly to Hammerfell?"

"All the magic at my command is yours, my son," Erminie said, and held out her hand to Edric Elhalyn. You may certainly have any horse in my stable; but I do agree that your brother's mountain-bred horse is best for you; I can more easily enhance a mount already suited to the nature of its task—maybe I can give you your magical steed after all. . . ."

Conn nodded, and Alastair climbed the stairs to the room which had been his when he was a small child. Several of his abandoned toys stood there, a few brilliantly carved toy soldiers, an old stuffed creature, more shapeless than a doll or a dog, made of wool, with which he had slept till he was seven years old; and, shoved into a corner beneath the window, his rocking horse.

He remembered riding many leagues on it when he was very small, clinging to its painted wooden neck; even now he could see where the paint had been worn away by the grip of his small sweaty hands. He looked at the toy soldiers and laughed, wishing his mother had it in mind to try and bring them to life and send them after him as armies. He did not doubt that she would if she could.

He remembered how often in his youth he would climb aboard the old rocking horse and head away northward—always northward—seeking, so he said—the way to Hammerfell. Once he had nearly set the house afire with a pan of coals from the nursery hearth, after which he had been strictly forbidden to make anything but toast on the proper toasting-rack, but otherwise he had not been punished, because his tearful excuse had been, "I was trying to make *clingfire*, and burn down old Lord Storn's house the way he burned ours down."

Quickly he changed out of his fine holiday suit, getting into a plainer suit of clothes, and went downstairs, throwing an old cloak over his shoulders. Turning his back forever on his childhood.

Downstairs, he found a startling change; the remains of the refreshments had been cleared away, and his mother had changed from her festival gown into an old technician's working robe, a simple long-sleeved tunic of pale green.

"Would there were more magic I could summon to go with you and guard your path, my son; but at least I can give you not only a magical mount, but a special guardian as well—Jewel shall go with you." They followed him into the stable-yard; the rain was dying down now to an occasional squall, Alastair could smell the freshness of the blowing wind, with ragged clouds showing occasional glimpses of one or the other of the moons.

Erminie beckoned to the old dog Jewel; she sat holding out her starstone and looked long into the dog's eyes, and Alastair had the curious sense that they were talking about him.

At last she said, "I thought at first to—I can give her human form if you wish; that is a simple enough magic; at least with a starstone. But she would be too old for a warrior, and it seems to me that in her natural form she would be more use as a guide. Even if I should change her to human shape, it would be only a seeming. She would still *be* a dog— she could not speak with you, and she would lose her keen hearing and sense of smell. At least as a dog, she can bite anyone who threatens you, while if she should do so as a human, it would—" Erminie hesitated and laughed. "It would be likely to provoke some remark."

"I should say so," said Alastair, bending to hug the old dog. "But does she know the way to Hammerfell?"

"You forget, my son, she was bred there; she can guide you there more dependably than any human guide. And she will warn you, too, if you promise me to listen to her."

"I am sure at least she would be more faithful and loyal than any other guide I might have," Alastair said, but secretly he wondered how his old dog could possibly warn him and how he would understand her if she did.

Erminie patted Jewel's head and said softly, "You love him just as much as I do; take care of him for me, my dear."

Jewel gazed up into Erminie's eyes so intently that Alastair was suddenly no longer skeptical; it was obvious to him that his mother and the dog were communicating more clearly than with words. He no longer doubted that when the time came she would communicate with him, too.

He was not at all sorry to know that the dog who had been part of his life since he was an infant too young to remember was to share this adventure with him. "Well, is she to ride behind me on my saddle?"

All the telepaths there—and even Alastair who was not, really—heard to their surprise what was almost a voice.

Where he can ride, I can follow, running at his heels.

"Well—if you can do that, old girl, let's get going," Alastair said, astonished, and clambered into the saddle of Conn's sturdy, but now subtly *different*, little mountain-bred horse; he gazed into Jewel's eyes and for a moment it seemed almost that he was speaking to the shadow of a woman warrior, like some of the Sisterhood of the Sword whom he had occasionally seen in town; almost a shadow hovering over Jewel. Did his mother's magic know no bounds? No matter— he must treat it as real. He straightened in his saddle, and bowed to his mother.

"All the Gods guard you, Mother."

"When will you come back, my son?"

"When my men—and my fate—will it," he said, and slowly walked the horse to the stable door. Once outside he dug his heels into the horse's flank; rough she might be, but she was a sturdy and a willing beast. Beneath his hand he felt her shudder, understanding, it almost seemed, the task before them.

They watched him ride through the little courtyard. Only Conn, who had been waiting in the hall, had the presence of mind to fling the huge spiked gate open; if he had not, it was clear that the horse, now with powers far beyond those of natural creatures, would have leaped clear over it.

The horse passed through, already galloping, the dog loping noiselessly with magically youthful strength at his heels. The sound of the galloping in the street outside died away quickly. Erminie stood looking out the open gate, tears streaming down her face.

Conn said under his breath, "Damn, I wish he had taken me with him. What will Markos say?"

Valentine Hastur said moodily, "You raised a stubborn son, Erminie."

"Why do you not say what you truly think?" she answered with spirit, "and call him headstrong and thoroughly spoiled? But with Jewel to guide him, and Markos to support him, he will do well enough, I am certain."

"Whether or no," Edric said, "he is gone, and the Gods must protect him, or not, as his fate demands."

They went into the house; but as the remaining kinfolk departed, Conn stayed in the courtyard, his eyes questing restlessly along the road taken by his brother, ever north toward the faraway peaks of Hammerfell.

10

Alastair clung to the neck of Conn's horse, still hardly believing in the mission which had called him away from everything he had ever known. The rapid galloping beneath him held a soothing rocking motion and he thought of childhood days when he had clung like this to the neck of his old rocking horse, rocking himself into a trance, frequently falling asleep on the horse's neck. He felt he could do so now, but if he did, he might wake to find this had all been no more than a bizarre dream and that he had fallen asleep at one of his mother's boring entertainments.

So swiftly he rode that before he knew it he had reached the gates of Thendara, and a voice challenged from the little guardhouse. "Who rides in the dark there, at this godforgotten hour when the city gates are shut and honest men within doors and abed?"

"As honest a man as yourself," said Alastair. "I am

Duke of Hammerfell, bound north on a mission that cannot wait for the daylight."

"So?"

"So open the gates, fellow; that's what you're here for, isn't it?"

"At this hour? Duke or no duke, these gates don't get opened till daybreak—not if you were the king himself."

"Let me speak to your sergeant, soldier."

"If I go an' wake up the sergeant, he'll only tell ye the same, Lord Hammerfell, and then he'll be angry wi' us both."

"I am not afraid of his anger, but I suppose you are," Alastair said. "It is a pity, but—Jewel, climb up behind me on my saddle."

He felt the old dog scramble up behind him, snuggling hard against his waist. He muttered, "Hang on—I mean, balance yourself, old girl."

Had he forgotten how high the city gates were—fifteen, twenty feet? In the dreamy sorcerous state he was in, it never occurred to him to doubt the horse's powers. He felt the horse gather herself together for the leap, shouted to Jewel, "Hold on tight!" and felt the world fall away beneath him as they went up and up—it seemed to him that they vaulted halfway to the shining moon and that he could see its greenish crescent fall away behind him . . . they fell for what seemed hours, then he felt the horse strike earth as gently as if she had cleared a log, no more. Jewel slid from the saddle and was running behind him again, her footfalls silent on the uneven paving of the road.

He knew he was far outside the city, without any very clear idea of how he had come so far, so fast.

156

He raced on into the darkness, knowing that his horse—or his mother's magic—was placing its feet unerringly with no possibility of a stumble.

Sometime before dawn he passed Hali, heard his horse's hooves ringing on the stones of Neskaya, and just as the dawn turned rosy in the east and the great crimson sun came up like a bloodshot eye, he saw the gleam of the River Kadarin flowing like molten metal before him. To his surprise, the mountain horse plunged into the flood and swam smoothly, well-trained muscles breasting the waves like a sea creature, scrambling up smoothly at the far bank and resuming her swift stride without visible pause or hesitation.

Behind him Alastair saw Jewel scramble from the water, running in a long, lean, effortless lope at the horse's heels. He had crossed the Kadarin—two days north of the city—within a single night!

Now they were past the country he knew; he had never come so far into the hills. For a moment he wished he had his brother to lead him; but Jewel was his appointed guide. Jewel! When had she last been fed? "Sorry, old girl," he said, "for a minute I'd forgotten about you." He stopped the horse in a wooded glen and dismounted, his knees trembling. Inside a saddlebag he did not remember filling, he found an assortment of cold meats and bread, and a flagon of wine. He shared the meats with Jewel, and drank some of the wine; he offered some to Jewel, too, but she snorted, running off to drink deeply at a spring, then came back and curled up at his side, her head in his lap. He thought of remounting; but realized that although his horse and dog seemed fine, not even winded, he was trembling with fatigue, every muscle shaking as if he had been in the saddle not for the scant few hours between midnight and dawn but for the two days and nights it should have taken him to ride so far normally. Jewel and the horse might be magically untiring, but he was not.

He had no blankets and he was cold. He wrapped himself in his cloak, and beckoned Jewel to curl up close for warmth; she shook herself, scratched for a moment, then curled down into his arms. Under his body the dead leaves crackled and felt damp, but he was too tired to care. Just as it crossed his mind that he was too wound-up and uncomfortable to sleep, sleep took him and he fell stunned into exhaustion. He slept till the light slanting down through the trees wakened him. Then he ate a little more meat and bread, drank the last of the wine, and turned to Jewel, "It's your turn to guide now, old girl. From here on, I'll follow you."

It was like a dream; although he did not really know where he was going, his moves seemed predetermined; he knew that whichever path he chose he would arrive at the appointed place. It seemed dangerous to abandon himself that way, but this *was* magic, and nothing he did could change the outcome of this fantastic journey, so he held back to let the dog take the lead.

Before long, it began to rain hard. Alastair was forced to dismount, and while blundering in the rain, he all but stumbled into a great net which hung from the tops of the thick overhanging trees; Jewel was barking and sniffing at the bait; the stark body of a rabbit-horn, stripped of antlers and tusks. But what had it been baited for? Then Jewel began barking, running about in little circles and whining. He raised his head to see a most astonishing creature. It was a little man—or so it seemed; not taller than four feet, face and body amply thatched by thick dark hair; gnarled and thick-bodied. He spoke in an ancient form of the mountain language.

"Who be you? And what be that?" he demanded, staring at Jewel. "You have spoilt my trap; what amends will you make?"

Alastair looked at the little creature, wondering if he were being confronted with some goblin out of legend. The little man seemed hardly aware of the heavy pouring rain. He was, however, wary of Jewel; he edged backward as she sniffed at his bare feet.

Alastair was dumbfounded, but he had, after all, been brought up on tales of the strange creatures, not all human, who dwelt in the lands across the Kadarin. Well, they had certainly lost no time in making themselves known to him!

"You are one of the Big Folk," said the little creature; perhaps you are harmless; but what is *that?*"

He indicated Jewel, with a strange look of misgiving; Alastair said, "I am Alastair, Duke of Hammerfell; and this is my dog Jewel."

"I do not know *dog,*" said the little man, "Is she—what kind of being is *dog*? Why does she not speak?"

"Because she cannot; it is not her nature," said Alastair. He did not suppose he would have much luck trying to explain *pet;* but something of the concept must have been clear to the little man, who said, "Oh, I see; she is like my tame cricket, and she thinks some danger threatens her master; tell her, if you can, that no danger threatens either of you."

"It's all right, old girl," Alastair said, though he

was not altogether sure of that. Jewel whined a little, but subsided. Alastair mustered his courage and asked, "Who are *you*?"

The little man answered, "I am Adastor-Leskin, of the Nest of Shiroh; what is *that*?" With frank curiosity he pointed at Alastair's horse. Alastair could not be sure the little man did not mean to rob him, but he explained what a horse was as best he could, and the little man appeared delighted.

"How many strange things I am seeing today! I will be the envy of all my clan! Still there is the matter of a trap between us; you have broken mine; what amends will you make?"

Alastair had decided to abandon himself to whatever strange fate had brought this adventure to him.

"I cannot mend your trap," he said, "I do not have the proper tools, and I do not understand the art of its making,"

"I would not ask it," said the little man. "Do as I would ask of a traveler of my own kind who inadvertently trespassed; give me of your best riddle."

"Are we to stand in the rain and tell riddles?"

"Oh," said the stranger, "yes, I had heard that the cold and the rain even of a summer shower like this can inconvenience your kind. Come, then, and shelter in the Nest of my tribe."

So saying, he put his feet on the lowest of a series of slats nailed—or somehow fastened—to the lower branches of a great tree;

"Can you follow this road?" he asked.

Alastair hesitated; his quest beckoned him, yet it would be impolite and impolitic not to make amends to this man and his kind. He climbed, not much liking the feel of the tree-ladder, or the sight of the

forest floor increasingly far below him, but resolved
not to reveal his fear to the little being, who climbed
as if he had been born to it—which, reflected Alastair,
he probably had.

Up the equivalent of several stories they went, and
then stepped off the ladder on to a rather wide, well-
floored road, thickly planked, which ran through the
tree. Here at last they entered a wide aperture which
led into a dark room, quite spacious, roughly furnished with a couple of low cushions of loosely woven
cloth. The little man sank down on one of these
cushions, gestured Alastair to another rather like it.
It felt soft, and rustled when he moved; it must have
been stuffed with dried grass, for it gave off a sweet
scent. Adastor leaned over and seizing a long, har-
dened stick, poked a fire into life, which gave off just
enough light that Alastair could see around the room.

"Now," he demanded, "some riddles; when we sit
around the fire at night playing at riddles, I will
have a new one for my people!"

Alastair, his mind a complete blank, could only
ask, "What kind of riddle would you have? I do not
know which kind of riddles are suitable to your game."

The wide eyes of the little man—Alastair decided
they must be very strange eyes indeed if they could
see much in this room—shone in the dark.

"Why," he demanded, "do the birds fly south?"

Alastair said, "If you were asking for information
other than the obvious reasons of weather prefer-
ence, I would say only that they do it for reasons no
man outside their kind understands. What answer
would you give?"

Adastor giggled unmistakably. He said, "Because
it's too far for them to walk."

"Oh," Alastair groaned, "*that* kind of riddle. Well—" he searched his mind and could think only of one from his childhood; "Why does the ice-rabbit cross the—er—path?"

"To get to the other side?" guessed the little man. Alastair shook his head and Adastor's face fell. *"Wrong?"* He sighed, "I should have known it could not be so simple! Meanwhile I have been remiss— you are my guest; let me offer you refreshment."

"I thank you," said Alastair, though he could not keep back fears that he would be invited to dine on raw rabbit-horn; he was not sure that even for politeness' sake he could bring himself to do that. After all, this was what the little man used for bait in his trap.

But what the little man brought him, after rummaging at the far end of the room, was a beautifully woven plate of reeds, done in several colors, which held a surprisingly beautiful arrangement of different colored berries. Alastair sampled them, thanking Adastor with real pleasure. The man demanded, "Tell me now the answer to your riddle; I am certain that as your people are bigger than mine, so your brains are bigger than ours, and your minds more subtle. Why *does* the ice-rabbit cross the path?"

"Because it's too long to walk around," replied Alastair sheepishly.

He was not prepared for Adastor's virtual collapse; he had heard the little man giggle, so he knew he had a sense of humor—which could have told him of the acceptability of his riddle—but Adastor fell over, evidently taken aback by the childish old joke.

"Too far to walk around!" he guffawed, and collapsed again. "Too far—oh, that is very good, very good indeed! Tell me another!"

"I have no time," Alastair said with perfect truthfulness, "I must be on my way; I am sorry for your trap, but I have fulfilled my promise, and must be about my business."

"The trap is of no consequence," replied the little man. "Adastor and the whole Nest of Shiroh is grateful to you, for you have enriched me with a riddle, and with new ideas, and new thoughts; I will guide you back to *dog*, and *horse*, and while you go on your way, I will contemplate my new ideas. Come."

The return, with Alastair laboriously clambering down the tree trunk while Adastor scampered like a monkey, was definitely difficult. Alastair climbed slowly and carefully, with no small measure of fear, while Adastor, close behind him, and obviously at ease, snickered at intervals, *"Too far to walk around!"*

It was with definite relief that Alastair set his feet on the ground, and felt Jewel clambering all over him and sniffing as she welcomed him. The horse, like a good mountain pony, had not strayed. He turned to take leave of the little man;

"I am sorry I inadvertently broke your trap," he said, "Believe me, it was an accident."

"That is all right; while I fix it, I shall contemplate my new riddle," said the little man, almost graciously, "I wish your friend, *dog*, could talk; now *her* riddles would no doubt be even more worth hearing. I bid you farewell, my big friend. You are always welcome with your riddles in the Nest of my people."

So saying he moved away, seeming to melt into the trees, leaving Alastair to be slobbered over by Jewel and wondering if the whole little adventure had been a bizarre dream.

"Well, old girl, I suppose we must be on our way," he said. "I wish if we had to meet someone—or some*thing*—it had been something that could guide us to Hammerfell. I guess it's up to you, then."

She sniffed the ground, then raised her head almost challengingly to look back at him.

He said aloud, feeling foolish, "Yes, old girl; take us to Hammerfell by the quickest way you know." He clambered into his saddle again, as Jewel put her muzzle to the ground and looked back at him with a faint questioning bark.

"It's no good asking me, old girl; I haven't the faintest idea which way we ought to be going," he said. "You're going to have to take us to Hammerfell, if you can; Mother said you could guide me, and I've got to trust you to do it." Jewel lowered her muzzle again, and began running along the road; he clucked to the horse, who trotted easily after her, with the long stride that ate up the distance.

Soon the way grew very steep, as they followed the road into the hills, and began to climb almost upright along a stream bed that dashed its way down from the heights. It was hardly a road at all, now, not much better than a goat track. Nevertheless, the mountain horse and the old dog went swiftly upward. Alastair began to look down into incredibly deep valleys filled with mist and the tops of trees far below, from which now and again wisps of smoke rose curling from little villages in the valleys.

All the rest of the day he rode without encountering a single other rider. The sun reached its height and began to decline. He had no idea where he was now, letting the magic take him where it would; in the early twilight he paused to eat the last of the bread and share the meat from his saddlebag with Jewel, who ate her portion hungrily.

He was so weary from the swift unyielding ride that his legs trembled and he felt that if he sat longer in the saddle he would fall; again he found a soft nest of long grasses and curled up in it, Jewel in his arms. He woke in the night and she was gone, but from somewhere came a soft hunting call and the sound of small animals in the woods; she came back after a time licking her jaws, and curled up again at his feet. In the dark he heard her chewing something and wondered what she had found to eat, then decided he didn't really want to know. He patted her rough hair and fell asleep again.

Waking in the early morning light, he washed his face in a cold mountain spring and climbed again into the saddle. Was it only his fancy or did the horse move more slowly now? Any normal beast would have been exhausted—or dead—after this unsparing journey.

The roads were even worse now, if possible, and there were times when Jewel had to find the way through thickets overgrown with briars and thorns. The horse breasted them uninjured, but in some places there was no road at all, and Alastair, scratched by thorns, though he wrapped himself in his cloak, wished he had accepted Conn's offer of suitable clothing for these hills. Fear and doubt gnawed at Alastair. He had no way of knowing where they were going, on the right or wrong road. And when they actually came to Hammerfell, if they ever *did*, would he even know? And what then? How would he find his way to Markos? And how would he know him when he found him? Could he rely on more of the magic which had borne him along so far? And it was once again growing dark; soon they would surely be unable to find their way.

He was contemplating a search for a good place to spend a third night among the forests when they suddenly entered upon a well-surfaced road running almost parallel to the course they had been pursuing. It was not the first such road they had crossed, but always before Jewel had taken a different path; now she began to run along the road with abandon, and it was all his horse could do to keep up with her.

Before long the road turned upward again and Alastair looked up at the heights. On the ridge against the skyline, like the broken teeth of an ancient skull, stood a blackened ruin. Jewel whined softly and ran a little way upward toward the ruin, then turned back, whimpering, toward Alastair; and abruptly he understood. He had ordered Jewel to take him to Hammerfell—but Hammerfell wasn't there any more, at least not the Hammerfell the old dog had known.

Alastair got down off his horse and shakily walked through the posts that were all that was left of the ruined gates. A flash of unusually brilliant memory, unexpected—for he did not know how he remembered —showed him the castle of Hammerfell as once it had risen against the sky, gray and unbroken; and his mother and father, standing on a green lawn with flowers, and old Jewel, only a clumsy puppy then, frisking at his mother's feet.

Well, there was nothing here; looking at the clumsy remnants of fallen stone which were all that remained of the bastion of his ancestors, he felt suddenly empty and sick. He had come all this way, with magical strength—for *this*? Rationally, he knew that he must take up the quest again, find Markos somewhere—good sense told him the man could not be so far away that he could not be found. But emotionally he felt as shattered as the ruin around him. He felt weak, a bag of sawdust punctured and with all the sawdust running out, like his old stuffed toy in the nursery. He stood in the ruins of his ancestral home, and all he could think was, *I should have let Conn come,* he *would have known what to do.*

What *would* he do? Alastair tried to clear his head and pull himself together—he should not have been surprised, he had known for a long time that the place was in ruins; *in fact, my first memory is of its burning.*

He could not stand here in the ruins and feel sorry for himself; he must find Markos, so that he could at least begin to do what King Aidan had sent him to do . . . to discover what army was here awaiting Hammerfell to retake his lands and castle. *Although,* he thought bitterly, *there's not enough here of the castle to be worth retaking.*

There was an old saying in Thendara: *the longest journey begins with a single step.* And there was, he thought ruefully, one good thing about being disillusioned like this; anything he did would have to be a step in the right direction, since from where Hammerfell was now, things could only improve.

He reached for the reins of his horse and climbed aboard; down below he could see a few lines of smoke which must surely be a village, and there he was likely to find someone—in the very shadow of the burned castle, they were likely to be Hammerfell tenants, those who owed, or once had owed, loyalty to Hammerfell.

The downward path seemed steeper than the upper; he had to hold the horse to a slow pace, and at the edge of the village—a cluster of small cottages built of the local pinkish stone—he paused, looking about for any sign of an inn or even a tavern. One building, a little larger than the others, displayed a sign with three leaves and a crown; he walked his horse toward it and tied up the creature at the rail. Conn's horse, under whatever magic had brought it here so quickly, probably would not wander; but there was no point in making it look like anything but an ordinary horse.

Inside there was a small taproom, with the usual taproom smells, uninhabited at this hour of the day except by a couple of very old gaffers, dozing in the chimney corner, and a chunky woman behind the bar, in cap and apron.

"M'lord," she said, raising her eyes pertly enough that for a moment Alastair wondered—she spoke as if she knew him. But, of course, it would be Conn she knew.

"Can I get something to eat at this hour? And something for my dog—"

"There's a roast haunch of mutton; not too tender—it was an old critter—but it'll serve—and some dog-bread," she said, looking puzzled. "Wine?"

"For me; not for the dog, I think."

"No," she said, "though once I knew a man train his dog to drink wine an' he went around laying wagers on it; but I'll give her a bowl of beer if you like; it's good for them, or so the dog breeders say, especially if she's a bitch nursing pups."

"No pups," Alastair said, "but dog-bread and a bowl of beer for her, then. The roast'll do me well enough, or whatever you have." He could hardly expect to find elegant fare at a place like this. He collected his plate and sat down in a corner. The wine was not very good; when Jewel's bowl of beer came, he called the woman to bring him some for himself. It was a good rich country brew, very filling and warming. He drank it off, ate the tough roasted meat hungrily and shared the well-roasted skin and the bones with the dog. As he was eating, he heard noises outside the door, and a group of women, clad in crimson tunics, each with a long golden hoop earring in her ear, came in.

"Ho, Dorcas," one of them called. "We're wanting bread and beer for six."

They were all armed; and Alastair saw a litter standing outside, well-veiled, like one he might see in Thendara; obviously it was intended to conceal a well-brought up and well-chaperoned lady.

One of the litter bearers saw Alastair and raised a hand in greeting, but the barwoman said in an undertone—but not so low that Alastair did not hear—"No; I thought the same when he came in, but he speaks like a lowlander." She assembled six plates of bread and six mugs of beer. "And the Lady Lenisa; would she like something? The wine's quite good, even though it's not good enough for—" she jerked her elbow at Alastair.

Alastair opened his mouth to protest; he was not accustomed to having anyone question his taste, especially one making no effort to conceal her opinion. Then he shut it again; if he was only an unregarded outsider, his tastes would not be worth anything and he had already been noticed.

Outside the door the curtains of the litter opened and a pretty girl of fourteen or so, richly dressed in lowland silks of a lilac hue, got down from the litter and came into the barroom. She looked around for the woman who was evidently the head of her escort.

"Little lady," said the woman reprovingly, "you shouldn't come in here; I commanded wine for you—"

"I'd rather have a bowl of porridge," said the girl mutinously. "I'm cramped with sitting inside the litter, and I'm sick for some fresh air."

"Porridge you shall have, as fast as Dorcas can boil it," said the swordswoman, "can't she, Dorcas? But your grandfather will throw a fit if you are seen here in Hammerfell country."

"Aye, that he will," said the woman next to her, "Lord Storn wouldn't approve of you traveling here at all . . . but the road is smoother this way—"

"Oh, *Hammerfell!*" said the girl in a pettish voice, "I have heard all my life that there were no living Hammerfells—"

"Aye, and so your grandfather believed till a moon or so ago," said the swordwoman, "when the young duke killed your father—so get back in your litter like a good girl, before someone sees you and carries messages, and you wind up in the grave beside him."

The girl came and wound her arms coaxingly around the swordswoman. "Dear Dame Jarmilla," she murmured, "let me ride with you and not be stifled inside the litter. I'm not afraid of Hammerfells old or young, and since I haven't set eyes on my father since I was three years old, you can't truly expect me to grieve for him."

"What a way to talk," the woman—Dame Jarmilla?—replied, "Your grandfather would—"

"I'm tired of hearing what my grandfather would do; he must be given to fits, then," said the girl Lenisa. "If you think I'm afraid of Hammerfells—" she broke off, having noticed Jewel lying under the table.

"Oh, what a dear," she said, kneeling down beside her and extending her hand for the dog to sniff. "Well, what a fine old girl you are, then."

Jewel condescended to let the girl pat her on the ruff of long pale hair, lighter copper than the rest, round her neck. Lenisa raised her eyes to Alastair and looked full into them.

"What is her name?" she asked.

"Jewel," said Alastair honestly, before he realized that if this girl was, as she seemed to be, a granddaughter of Lord Storn, then she might well have heard that such a dog was the property of the Duchess of Hammerfell—but then again, they wouldn't be likely to remember the name of a puppy thought dead these eighteen years. At any rate, Alastair did not intend his identity to remain secret for long.

The girl was a Storn; this meant she was his deadliest enemy. Yet she was just a pretty fair-haired girl, her hair tied back in a long braid, her blue eyes meeting his in a frank and open way no girl in Thendara would ever have looked at him.

He had heard tales of the boldness of mountain girls. Yet the blue eyes seemed innocent and even ingenuous; she was patting the dog affectionately.

"Lady Lenisa—" he began, but at that moment he heard the clatter of a horse outside on the road; then the sounds of another horse being tied up at the rail outside. Jewel pricked up her ears, with a short, sharp bark of recognition, and bounded toward the tall old man who came in; he looked round, and saw Alastair where he sat, then frowned slightly at the array of swordswomen and made a signal to Alastair to remain where he was.

The senior swordswoman, the one Lenisa had addressed as Dame Jarmilla, came to Lenisa and tugged at her collar. "Get up *at once*," she said in a taut voice. "Such behavior, sitting on the floor among strangers—"

"Oh, Jewel doesn't know what a stranger is—do you, girl?" Lenisa crooned, still holding out her hands to coax the dog back from the newcomer's feet. Dame Jarmilla pulled her up by main force and thrust her out through the door, though the girl was still complaining that she hadn't had her porridge and that she didn't want to ride in the litter anyhow. The protests were cut off abruptly as the old swordswoman pushed her inside and yanked the curtains shut.

Alastair was still staring after the girl. How lovely she was! How fresh and innocent! The man who had entered was bending over Jewel in delighted disbelief while she sniffed at his feet with apparent joy, barking in short little barks, demanding attention. He smiled at Alastair and said, "Bad luck, this day of all days, that Storn's girl chose to breakfast here with her ladies."

"Storn's girl?"

"The Lady Lenisa, Rupert's daughter, the old man's great-niece, but she calls him grandfather," the old man said. "The dog remembered me, but I don't suppose you do, lad? Though I recognize you well."

He said with wonder, "There's only one man on earth whose face could be so familiar, yet so new—my boy. We thought you dead!"

"You must be Markos," said Alastair. "My brother sent me; we must talk—" he noticed the woman Dorcas at the bar staring at them and amended, "privately, I think. Where can we go?"

"My place," said Markos. "Come along." Alastair paused only to leave some money on the bar, untie his horse, and lead her through the village street to a small cottage at the far end.

"Tie her in back," Markos said. "Conn's horse, I see. Half the county would recognize her; there'd be news of a stranger here all over the county in half a day, an' we don't need that. Bad luck that Storn's girl saw you, but I hear she's a spoiled bratty little thing, and doesn't care for anything much outside herself."

"I would hardly say that," Alastair protested. "She seemed—" and stopped; he had seen the girl only for a few minutes and knew nothing about her. In any case she was the granddaughter of his sworn enemy and part of the feud which had destroyed his family; he had no business thinking about her in this way.

Markos led the way inside. The interior was clean enough; bare except for a fireplace with a few pots hanging on the edge, a couple of rough chairs, and a table formed by laying planks over a couple of trestles. The far end of the table was covered with a piece of white cloth, and on this cloth were two silver goblets, blazoned with the arms of Hammerfell. Markos, following his glance, said curtly, "Aye; I found them in the ashes a few days after the fire; kept them here in memory of my lord and lady. . . .

My *lady*—then she must be alive as well! I can hardly believe my eyes—Alastair, is it truly you?

Alastair unlaced the top of his shirt and drew the fabric aside to display the tattoo the old man had put there himself long years ago. Markos bowed silently.

"My lord duke," he said deferentially. "You had better tell me what happened. How did Conn find you? Did you see King Aidan?"

Alastair nodded and began to tell Markos about his reunion with his brother and his audience with the king.

11

After Alastair departed, Conn moped about the town house in a way that troubled Erminie. She was ready to lavish on her son all the love she would have given him all those lost years, but he was far too grown-up for much display of affection. Now that Alastair was gone and they were alone, she realized poignantly that he was essentially a stranger to her. About all she could do was to question him about his favorite meals and give instructions to her housekeeper to provide them. It pleased her that he spent a good deal of his time in training the puppy Copper, and that he seemed to have a sure hand with such training. This made her think of his father. Rascard had insisted that he had little *laran*—Erminie wondered if his skill with horses and dogs was a type of *laran* not fully known to her.

"You should go to the Tower for testing, my dear son," she told him one morning. "Your brother has little *laran*, which means that you, as his twin, probably have more than your share; indeed I was sure of that while you were still a child."

Conn knew very little of *laran*, and had never handled a starstone; but when Erminie brought him one, he managed to key it so quickly and naturally that his mother was delighted; it was as if he had handled one every day of his life.

"Perhaps you will find your true work and mission in the Tower, Conn, when your brother is duke at Hammerfell," she hazarded. "You will not wish to be a hanger-on, little more than his steward or *coridom*. That would hardly be a fitting use of your talents." At this, his brow darkened and she almost wished she had not spoken. After all, he, like Alastair, had grown up believing himself lone survivor and rightful Duke of Hammerfell. If he were jealous or resentful of his brother, he could hardly be blamed.

But to her great relief all he said was, "Whatever happens, I shall want to remain with my people; Markos taught me that I was responsible for them. Even if I am not their duke, they know me and they trust me. They may call me what they will. *Coridom* is in its own way as honorable a title as duke."

"Even so," Erminie answered, "you have so much *laran* that it must be trained; an untrained telepath is a menace to himself and everyone around him."

Conn knew too well the truth in his mother's words. "Markos said as much when I was growing up," Conn agreed. "But Alastair? He has *none*?"

"Not enough to be worth the trouble of training," Erminie replied. "Though I sometimes think his skill with horses and dogs may well be a variation of the old MacAran Gift. There were MacArans in your father's mother's family."

She walked to the sideboard and pulled out a scroll to show him. Conn was astonished to see she had produced a written record of his ancestors for the last eight or ten generations; he studied it with interest, saying with a laugh, "I did not know they kept studbooks like this except on horses, Mother! And is it written down here how many of my father's people fell to this feud with Storn?"

"Yes," she said sadly, and showed him the markings which indicated that the ancestor in question had met a violent death as a result of the ancient feud.

At last he said, "I have lived and breathed this feud since I was able to button my own breeks; but I never knew till now just how much those bastards of Storn owed me; I thought only of a father and two older brothers. Now I see how many of my kin have fallen to Storn—" He broke off and stared into space.

"There are better things in life than vengeance, my son," she said.

"Are there?" he asked, and seemed to look straight through her; for a moment the increasingly familiar face of her son was again that of a total stranger and she wondered if she would ever know or understand this complex, quiet man who was her youngest.

But, concealing the chill she felt, she went on briskly, "As for your *laran*—I have enough skill in testing to know that you have an unusually strong talent for handling a matrix; and the access to that sort of technology can only be properly trained within a Tower. Fortunately, I have friends in most of the Towers; your cousin Edric Elhalyn is Keeper here at

Thendara Tower, and my kinsman Valentine was once a technician; either of them can teach you much, but for a time you should go and live within the walls of a Tower where you will be protected from the dangers of your emerging powers. I will speak at once to Valentine. Fortunately there will be no need to wait until the season when the monitors ride forth to test all the children of the Domains; I can speak to them and have you admitted at once. Without training, your full talent must yet be unborn, and you are old for such a transition."

Conn was a little confused at the speed with which this had all happened, but he was not at all averse to the idea, and also he was curious (as was every outsider in the Domains) about what went on within a Tower. He felt pleased and gratified to realize that he was one of the elect who could qualify to find out.

Once accepted for training, Erminie told him, he would be required to live among the Tower members.

"But you know everything about it, Mother; why can't you and Floria teach me?"

"It's not customary," Erminie said. "A mother does not teach a grown son, or a father his grown daughter; it's simply not done."

"Why not?"

"I don't know; it may go back to customs of the old days," Erminie said. "Whatever the reason, it's simply *not done*—and it's a taboo I wouldn't feel comfortable breaking. I will leave your training to our kinsmen, and later to a Tower. But Floria can teach you some things, if she will. I will ask, if you like," she added, sensing without words that Conn might be too shy to ask this kind of favor of a woman. "She will be here perhaps tonight, and if not, I see her, or her father, every day or two; I'll make an opportunity to ask her."

Later that day, as Conn and Erminie took the little dog on her training leash through the streets, Conn said, "I wonder if my brother has reached Hammerfell?"

"I should think perhaps so," Erminie said, "though I do not know what the roads are like now. You can find out with your *laran* if you wish."

Conn thought that over; he had shared his brother's experiences many times, but never purposefully. He did not know if he wanted to knowingly intrude on his brother's thoughts; he was not yet accustomed to the idea. Still, if his mother suggested it, and Alastair had been brought up taking this for granted —he would consider it. He turned his attention to Copper, running her through the standard training exercises of "Walk at heel," "Sit," and "Stay." He had always had a certain affinity for working with animals, and this was not the first puppy he had trained. Now it had been suggested to him, he thought it *was* possible that the intense affinity he felt for the little dog was some variety of what Erminie called *laran;* he had never thought of that, but believed it simply an acquired skill, like his ability to ride, or to fence. Was there *nothing*, then, which was his own? Did everything that he knew or could do, stem from this inheritance, a gift of the mysterious Comyn who had bred these skills into his line as he would breed horses for racing, or dogs for good temper? He felt very small, and inclined to resent them.

Conn and the dog were walking a little ahead of Erminie in a remote street where there would be few people about and plenty of room to put Copper through her basic exercises. The little bitch was tractable and easy to teach; she went obediently through each exercise, fortified by much petting, many kind words and a few tidbits of dried meats from the kitchen. Conn was winding up the training by letting Copper run hard on her leash, the sprint helping to clear the confused emotions he felt, when they entered a quiet street where one of the larger town houses was in the final stages of construction. He pulled Copper back to a walk, waiting for Erminie to catch up.

There they saw a robed group, the crimson-garbed Keeper at one edge of the circle, two green-robed technicians and a blue-robed mechanic, with a tall white-clad woman at the center whom Conn already recognized as a monitor. A few hangers-about in the street were watching, mostly young children or idle day laborers. A green-cloaked City Guard stood by, but Conn was not sure whether he was in his official function to keep order or whether he, too, was simply exercising a free citizen's right to gawk at any interesting thing in the street.

Copper interrupted the proceedings by rushing forward, barking joyously to welcome an old friend; Conn recognized the white-clad monitor as Floria, and felt the familiar yet shameful rush of love he always felt in the presence of his brother's betrothed. She briefly patted the young dog, then admonished her, "Good girl, go lie down, I can't play with you now!"

"Here, sir," said the Guardsman sharply. "You get that there dog away out of here; there's work being done." Then, noticing and recognizing Erminie, he added in a respectful tone, "Is it your dog, *domna?*

Sorry, but you'll have to keep her quiet or take her away."

"It's all right," Floria said. "I know the pup; she won't disturb me, not from over there."

Erminie spoke sharply to Copper, who sank down between her feet and lay there as quietly as a painted plaster model of a dog. The Keeper, a slight veiled person—Conn was not even sure whether man or woman—although women as Keepers, he knew, were very rare, so that the Keeper was probably a man of very effeminate appearance or an *emmasca*—stood by patiently waiting as the interruptions were disposed of, then with a flick of the head gathered the circle together again. Conn could see—and feel—the strands binding them together, the invisible bonds that wove between the circle of telepaths, artificially linked by the matrix crystals.

And although he had never seen or felt anything like it before, he had no doubt or hesitation about what was happening. Without knowing how he did it, or even being aware that he was doing it, he touched Floria's mind. Although she was totally pre-occupied, with a minute fragment of her conscious-ness, it seemed to Conn that she recognized and made him welcome, as she might wordlessly have summoned him into a room where she was playing some musical instrument and bidden him sit and listen quietly.

He sensed with just a fragment of his own con-sciousness that his mother was there also, likewise relegated to watching from the sidelines. Even the puppy Copper seemed somehow part of this closely gathered intimacy. He felt comfortable, welcomed, accepted—never had he felt half so welcome or accepted, though not one of them even raised their eyes to see Conn, or paid the faintest attention to him; by their outward demeanor, not one of them acknowledged he was there.

The Keeper, having joined them together in some manner that Conn was not yet able to understand fully, somehow directed their attention to a heap of building materials at the edge of the street, then gathered their strength—at this point Conn wholly lost track of what was happening—his perception blurred into blue glare as if his starstone were a crystal before—or inside—his eyes. The huge pile of building materials began to rise in the air. Though it was only a loosely piled heap of shingles, they did not slip or slide on one another, but somehow clung as if they were all glued together one to the others. Into the air the pile rose, higher and higher, and Conn felt the Keeper aiming it so that, within a few seconds, the great heap was balanced on the flat part of the roof, where the workers, without any fuss at all, began pulling it apart and laying the shingles to nail them into their proper places. The taut concentrated circle then seemed to drop apart like the shingles themselves. Floria said to the Keeper in a low voice, "Any more?"

"No." The Keeper responded. "Not until the pavings in the castle court are ready to be laid. That was the last, and we'd have done it last night except for the rain. We'll have to set the glass in the conservatory in a few days; but no hurry about all that once the roof's on. I talked to Martin Delleray yesterday; the paving can't be put in till they have a gardener come and see about the shrubbery. He'll let us know in good time."

182

"This part of the city is growing fast; we'll have more streets to put in next spring when the snows melt."

One of the technicians grumbled, "I don't like construction work; and there is talk in the city that we are taking away honest work from woodworkers and builders."

"No such thing," said the Keeper, "when we can do in half a day what it would take all manner of heavy equipment to do; and how's it to be moved into this part of town? As much as people grumble they would be grumbling more, never doubt it, if we weren't here to do this work."

"More likely someone grudges our fees," said the other technician. "There's hardly a paving laid here by hand, or a pane of glass set. Lifting materials with ropes and pulleys not only wastes energies, but endangers the passersby."

This was a facet of *laran* which had never occurred, even briefly, to Conn. *I wonder if this is how we can rebuild Hammerfell?* It had never occurred to him but that it would take a crew of stoneworkers countless years to raise the burned-out shell of his castle from the ruins; with *laran* workers, like this, Hammerfell might rise again in less time than he had ever believed possible. While he was thinking it over, Floria raised her eyes and smiled at him and his mother. She beckoned to Copper, who burst from her obedient silence and hurled herself at Floria, licking her hands.

"And what a good, quiet dog you are," Floria said, caressing her. "Erminie, you have trained her as well as Jewel; soon she will be well-trained enough to lie at our feet in the circle itself! Good dog, good, good dog," she repeated to the puppy, petting and stroking her, while Copper licked her hands lovingly.

"Conn is training this one," Erminie said, "and I brought him here to observe the more public work of a matrix circle; he knows little about *laran*, because of his upbringing. But he's ready for training— and after that for a place in a circle, at least for a time."

The Keeper, raising a pallid face dominated by large luminous eyes, turned to Conn with a questioning gaze. "I touched you when we were actually within the circle; are you certain you have had no training before this? I thought perhaps you might have worked in the mountains with the people at Tramontana."

Conn repeated his denial. "None whatever; before I came to Thendara I never had a starstone in my hands."

"Sometimes the kind with natural gifts make the best matrix workers," the Keeper said, and thrust out a bony hand to shake Conn's. "I shall be happy to welcome you among us. I am Renata of Thendara."

Conn knew that this kind of address was limited to Keepers, and it was a shock to find a woman—even though, he supposed, the Keeper was not really a woman but an *emmasca*—among them.

Erminie said with a deprecating laugh, "Well, I failed with Alastair, my older son; he had not the potential. So I suppose I deserve all the more success with this one."

"Without a doubt," said Renata gently, "I can tell that after training he will be a credit to us. Since he cannot work in your circle, Erminie, I will welcome him to mine."

Conn was surprised to see his mother color with pleasure. "Thank you, Renata; that is gracious of you."

Floria, still standing beside Conn, said softly, "Will you come to us in the Tower, then? It will be a pleasure to help with your training, brother-in-law."

"The pleasure, I assure you, will be mine," said Conn, and turned to hide the flush he felt heating his face.

As they walked together, following the members of the circle who had turned down a street which would bring them back toward the Tower, she turned to him and said, "It has been a busy season . . ."

"It has indeed," Conn murmured. His life had changed so radically in a few short tendays, more than he could ever have believed possible."

Although his name had not been mentioned, Alastair was in their thoughts and they both fell silent; it was as if he were there, standing between them. Conn's thoughts darkened, and Floria seemed to withdraw as they followed the little party of matrix workers some steps ahead.

She said aloud, "I wonder what Alastair is doing now?"

"Since he rode off on my horse?" said Conn with a forced laugh. "You are a telepath; can't you reach him?"

She said, lowering her eyes, "Not really; a glimpse, no more. Perhaps if we were lovers . . . but even then it would not be easy at such distance. You are his twin . . . that is the strongest bond."

"Then, if you wish, I will search," said Conn. "Though I have never before consciously sought him." He laid a hand on the starstone his mother had given him, which hung in a small silken bag tied on a ribbon round his neck. He had had so many glimpses of Alastair without any such help, he never doubted that he could see Alastair now.

When it came, it was nothing like the dreamlike pictures he had so many times caught of his twin. Did the starstone act as an amplifier? He did not know; but all round him were the familiar tall trees, the smell of evergreens, the sighing winds and skies of his whole life before this. And another smell which filled the heart of any mountain-bred man with dread and panic: *fire!* Somewhere near his twin, and within Alastair's perceptions, fire raged in the Hellers.

Standing in the quiet street of Thendara, Conn discovered his heart was pounding so hard he could feel the blood racing in his veins. What was burning? And where? It was not here, though the smell of fire and burning leaves made him feel dizzy and sick.

Erminie, turning, knew at once what they were attempting. Under ordinary circumstances she would have paid no attention, allowing the young people to do as they would. But Conn's pale face was too frightened. She came quickly back toward the two young people. They had come through the streets to where the Tower loomed only a little way away.

Erminie laid her hand so lightly on Conn's wrist that she attracted his attention with the least possible interruption or shock. She said quietly, "Inside the Tower it will be simpler to finish what you have begun—and with less danger, Conn, for either of you."

It had never occurred to Conn that what he had done so often, without even owning a starstone, could be in any way dangerous, either for him or Alastair.

But the strangeness, this new sense of urgency and danger, disarmed him; he said quite meekly that he would be glad of a cup of wine, and came inside with them.

The wine was brought and poured, but as Conn sipped at it he had the most fearful sense of urgency; he wished that all these people would go away and let him get back to the search for his brother.

He took no part in the light social cross talk and banter which accompanied the drinking; he drank off the wine when it was put in this hand, almost without tasting it. He was unconscious of Renata drawing them all together again through the matrix; he was too new to this to have developed the detachment which protected the matrix worker from dangerous emotional involvement in what he was doing. He was already too emotionally involved; it was his brother, his land, his people. . . .

The Keeper Renata, who understood this interplay of stresses better than anybody alive, watched with a detached sadness, but made no effort to alter his natural approach; when he was better trained, he would have a more balanced and less passionate method of working, but for that skill, Conn would have to sacrifice some of his youthful intensity.

Floria gestured to Conn. "Link with me; together I am sure we can find him."

Again, gently, the broken link reforged. Surprisingly, what Conn saw first was the face of his foster-father Markos, and through his eyes looked on Alastair. The smell of smoke and fire was physically distant but seemed somehow to dominate their every thought as it dominated the countryside with the immanence of any violence of nature. No more to be

187

ignored than a tornado or a tidal wave, it licked constantly around the edges of their thoughts, nibbling away at confidence and courage.

Alastair, he knew, was angry.

"What is this that you are telling me? That I must go, after all these years of blood feud, and fight to save the property of this man who killed my father and so many of my ancestors? Why? Isn't it better for all of us if it burns him out and be damned to him?"

Markos stared. "I am ashamed of you," he said sharply. "What upbringing did you have that you can say that?" he demanded. Conn, too, felt ashamed of his twin for such ignorance, unbelievable in any mountain man. Fire-truce was the first fact of life in forested country. All other considerations, whether kinship's dues or blood feud, all were suspended during the forest-fire season in the Hellers.

Then Conn remembered; *how could he have expected Alastair to know?*

Markos answered as Conn would have, and Conn somehow felt responsible for all that he had neglected to explain to his twin.

"Tomorrow your own slopes may be burning and you will need to know that Storn—or anyone else who may be present—will help to defend you. As you should know."

He added in a more conciliatory tone, "You're weary and you have ridden a long way. Time enough when you've slept a bit and eaten something."

Markos led him through a door into an inner room roughly furnished. Conn knew the place well; he had lived there with Markos since he was fourteen years old.

At this point Conn dropped out of the rapport. The faces of Markos and Alastair died out in a blue flare as of the matrix jewel and he stood up, saying aloud, "It is ill done to spy on him without his knowledge; he is safe with Markos, then."

He looked up into Erminie's stricken eyes. "Your son is safe, Mother. No," he added, as she reached out to him, "I understand—he was the one brought up in your lap, not I; it is only natural that you fear for him."

"That seems very sad to me," said Erminie. "My greatest wish all these years was to have you both in my care."

Conn came and gave her a rough hug.

"Oh, I know now what I missed, and I wonder if my brother truly appreciated it. But if there is trouble up north, I should be gone—Markos will need me! Alastair—" he broke off; he could not say to his mother that he did not think her favorite son was fit to take his place at Hammerfell. But his hand, almost without thought, touched the hilt of his father's sword, and he knew Floria, at least, was still reading his thoughts. He reached out to break that rapport and met her eyes. Instantly she lowered her gaze, but the shock of intense emotion was palpable in the room full of telepaths.

Dear Gods, he thought, *what shall I do? This is the woman of my dreams; I loved her before ever I set eyes on her, and now I have found her, she is all but my brother's wife; of all women in this world, she is the one forbidden to me.*

He could not look at her, and as he raised his eyes, he realized that the Keeper was looking at him. The *emmasca*, safely insulated and removed both by high office and sexlessness from this most painful of all human problems, was regarding him with sad, wise eyes.

12

Work on the fire-lines was making Alastair reconsider his mental picture of hell. At the minute, the thought of being in one of Zandru's frozen upper hells was rather appealing. Sweat drenched his hair and clothes, the skin on his face felt as though it was being slow-roasted, and his mouth and throat were dry and burning. And though he wasn't as much of a dandy as some people might think, all his life he *had* been encouraged to consider his appearance as an indication of his position and title. Now he was unhappily aware that his clothes were never going to be the same again. Even if the damage being done to them by flying sparks was carefully mended, he would look as disreputable as the old man working to his right.

The peasants here certainly do seem to be tough, though. He must be old enough to be my grandfather, but he's still going strong while I'd like to curl up and die. Of course, peasants aren't as sensitive as I am.

Jewel was curled up at the end of the fire-line; he sensed the extra call of loyalty it was demanding to keep her there. She was unwilling to take her eyes off him or go out of earshot despite the fear she must be feeling. He should have made the effort to send the old dog away from the fire-line to a place where she would not be so acutely troubled.

A slim figure in an old, shabby tartan dress and a broad-brimmed lilac sunbonnet came up to the old man and handed him a waterskin. He handed her his shovel to hold as he rinsed his mouth and took a quick drink. Then she handed him back the shovel, took back the waterskin, and continued down the line toward Alastair. Her eyes widened as she recognized him; one of her escort had evidently told her who he was.

She kept her voice low. "I am astonished to find you here, my Lord Hammerfell!"

She might well say that, thought Alastair; he was somewhat astonished to find himself here.

"*Damisela*—" He gave her his most courtly bow. "What can you possibly be doing here? Of all places in the Domains this is the last for a lady."

"I suppose you think a lady will not burn if the fire gets out of hand? Anyone could tell that you are a foolish lowlander!" she flared angrily. "*Everyone* here turns out on fire-watch—men and women, commoner and noble!"

"I haven't seen old Lord Storn risking his precious neck," Alastair growled.

"That's because you haven't bothered to look in the right direction—he's standing less than a dozen feet from you!" Lenisa indicated the old man with an outflung arm.

Alastair gaped in shock. That old man, Lord Storn? That stooped old fellow, could he truly be the bogeyman of Alastair's childhood? Why, he looked as if a sudden gust of high wind would blow him away! He didn't seem terrifying at all!

Lenisa's gesture had attracted Storn's attention; he flung down his shovel and headed toward them with a grim expression on his face.

"This idiotically dressed young dandy annoying you, girl?"

Lenisa hastily shook her head. "No, Grandfather."

"Give the fellow his water, then, and get about your work. Don't hold up the line! You know how important it is to keep water coming regularly to everyone—do you want the men farther down collapsing on the lines?"

"No, sir, of course not," she said meekly, and raising her eyes briefly to Alastair, passed on down the line with her bucket. Alastair stood for a moment watching her, until the man next to him nudged him in the elbow and he resumed his work with the hoe, scraping at the firebreak in the leaf-strewn forest floor.

Storn's granddaughter. Nothing like the old man that he could see, "idiotically dressed," indeed. Yet this woman and he were forever separated, and if only because of that she had the lure of the forbidden. He reminded himself sternly that he was a man promised in marriage . . . promised to Floria, who waited for him in Thendara, and therefore not to be eyeing other women—especially not a woman with whose family *his* family had been at blood feud for the last four generations! He tried to put Lenisa firmly out of his mind, to think only of Floria in

Thendara; he wondered how she and his mother fared in his absence, even wondered what being a telepath was like—able to summon up in his mind an instant communication with an absent loved one.

The thought troubled him; he was not sure he would want that. If he were now in communication with Floria, would she watch him flirting with the Storn girl, and think him faithless? Would she read his mind and be troubled by the images of Lenisa? He found himself trying to explain in his mind to her, and broke off, troubled by the knowledge that Conn, his twin brother, was mentally linked to him and would know his innermost thoughts. He would never be able to lie to Conn nor persuade his brother of his good intentions or his worth. . . .

What was it like, to live like that, with all one's innermost thoughts and desires exposed to any number of people?

It frightened him. He had been open to Conn; his brother knew him perhaps better than he knew himself, and that was a frightening thing. But even more terrifying was the realization that his brother knew the worst of which he was capable. . . .

He tried to bring Floria's image before his mind, and failed; he saw only Lenisa's flirtatious little smile.

He turned off his thoughts with an effort and put all his attention to the work he was doing on the firebreak. Out of the corner of his eye he noticed that the old man, Lord Storn, was keeping pace with the younger men, doing his share and more of the hard manual work. When the girl Lenisa came round again with her water pail—this time, he noticed gratefully that the pail was steaming and decided it must be some sort of herb tea—Lenisa stopped beside her grandfather, and Alastair could just hear what she said.

"This is foolish, Grandsire; you are not strong enough for this kind of work at your age."

"That's ridiculous, girl; I've been doing this work all my life, and I'm not about to stop now! Get about your own business, and don't presume to try and give orders to me."

At his glare, most girls would have been annihilated, but Lenisa went on, arguing, "What good do you think it will do to anyone if you collapse from the heat and have to be carried away? Will that not be a fine example to all our men?"

"What do you want me to do?" he growled. "I have taken my place on the lines every summer, man and boy, for seventy years."

"Then don't you think you have done a lifetime's share, Grandfather? No one alive would think less of you if you went back to the camp and did lighter work there."

"I'll ask no man to do what I'll not do myself, Granddaughter. Go on and do your own work and let me tend to mine."

Against his will, Alastair felt a grudging admiration for the stubborn old man. When Lenisa came to him and held out the pail, he hoisted it to his lips and drank thirstily; this time it contained, as he had believed, a warm herb tea of some sort with a strong fruity flavor, exceptionally thirst-quenching against the charred taste at the back of his throat.

He returned the pail and thanked her.

"Does your grandfather always work on the lines with his men?"

"He has done so as long as I can remember, and

well before, so our people say," she replied. "But now he is really too old; I wish I could get him to go back to the camp. His heart is not really very strong."

"That may very well be true; but I admire the heart which bids him work beside his men," Alastair said with honest admiration, and she smiled.

"So you do not think my poor old grandfather is really an ogre, then, Lord Hammerfell?"

Her tone was mischievous; Alastair gestured to her to lower her voice. Fire-truce might be the law in the mountains and the noblemen such as Lord Storn might very well keep it, but he did not trust all these strangers; if they knew who he was, he might well be mobbed.

"It would do your grandsire's heart no good to know his oldest enemy was here!"

She said proudly, "Did you believe that my grandsire would dishonor the fire-truce, our oldest law?"

"Only before I saw him; surely you must know that gossip and hearsay could make a monster of Saint Valentine of the Snows himself," Alastair said, but privately he was sure he wasn't going to give Lord Storn a chance, one way or the other. "And hearsay has had much to say of Lord Storn."

"And most of it good, I must believe," said the girl. "But have you had enough to drink? I must be about my work or he will scold me again."

Unwillingly he relinquished the bucket, and bent again to his work. He was not used to manual labor; his back ached and there seemed to be a separate toothache in every muscle of his arms and legs. His hands, even protected by heavy leather gauntlets, were beginning to feel as if they were being skinned alive and he wondered if he would be eaten raw or

196

cooked. He supposed it depended on how near they got to the fire. He cast a glance at the sky and the merciless burning sun. If only some clouds would build up; his shirt was sticking to his aching back. It was only a little after noon and he felt as if it would be forever till supper time.

If the girl had offered Alastair an easier job at the camp he would have jumped at the chance. He glanced wistfully after the girl's lilac sunbonnet, now retreating down the long line of men.

They had plenty of manual workers; was every single strong back so valuable? Of course, out here among these mountain types it was perhaps some kind of pride or proof of manhood that kept them at it, even old Lord Storn who certainly in any rational society would have been recognized as being long past such work. In Thendara they would have made some kind of distinction between nobles and commoners, but from his brother Conn he knew there were few distinctions of that kind in the Hellers. Well, just let them offer him an alternative, *he* certainly didn't feel the need to prove his manhood! He leaned on his hoe, sighing as he straightened his aching back. Why the devil had he come here anyhow? Above him he could hear a strange, almost mechanical whine, an unexpected sound. A ragged cheer went up from the fire-lines as a small airship appeared among the trees, maneuvering carefully to keep out of the eddying smoke. Alastair had heard of matrix-powered gliders in these hills, carrying fire-fighting chemicals; but he had never actually seen a heavier-than-air vehicle. It droned out of sight and the man next to him muttered. "*Leroni* from the Tower, coming to help us."

"They are bringing fire-fighting chemicals?"

"Thass right. Very good of 'em—if we could ever be sure they han't started the damn' fire themselves with their *clingfire* or some such deviltry!"

"More likely it was lightning did it," Alastair said, but the man looked skeptical.

"Oh, sure. But why are there more fires now than in my granfer's time, you tell me that, can ye?"

Alastair hadn't the faintest idea. He could only say, "Since I wasn't alive in your grandfather's time, I don't know that there *are* more fires now; and what's more, I don't think *you* do, either," and bent again to his work.

This was no place for the Duke of Hammerfell. If he had known that taking his place as Duke of Hammerfell would mean grubbing away in the dirt, Conn could have come in his place, and welcome!

Oh, well. Grimly he stared up at the sky, imagining it covered with softening clouds. Cooling clouds, gray and damp, blotting the scorching sun and bringing rain—blissful rain! There *was* a cloud to the south, small, fluffy; he imagined it growing, spreading quickly over the sky, swirling and darkening, moving closer. . . .

It *was* growing and spreading, a cool breeze springing up in its wake as it grew darker and heavier. Alastair felt astonished and delighted; *did I somehow do that?* He experimented briefly until he was sure he was right, somehow his own thoughts controlled and built the cloud higher and higher, till its fantastic castles and pinnacles covered more than half the sky!

Was this a new *laran* for which they had not thought to test him? He had no way of knowing. The cloud had cooled him substantially; dutifully he bent again over his hoe before it occurred to him to wonder: *Could I make it rain? Could I put out this fire and save us all a lot of trouble?* The trouble was, though he could visualize the cloud building higher and darker, he really had no knowledge of what made a cloud decide it was full enough to rain. He should have paid more attention to his mother when she had tried to tell him something more about the simpler uses of *laran*. *What a pity I cannot get into Conn's mind as I understand he can get into mine, and learn more of this art from him.*

So much time had been consumed by his effort at cloud-minding that the girls and boys who had been set to carrying water were again making their rounds. Among them he saw Lenisa, this time at a considerable distance, and he wondered if she had been moved to a different line. It was at that moment he realized he was jealous of the man who would receive water from her hands . . . more jealous than he was of Conn in Thendara with Floria. *Of course, my brother Conn knows so little of city life that he would not even notice—far less seduce—any woman if he thought she belonged to someone else.*

For just a moment, Alastair's scorn of his brother flagged. *Is that really something to sneer at, that Conn is honorable? But should I then be bound by his country-bumpkin sense of morality?*

The sky was now so dark with clouds that a damp wind had sprung up. Alastair had stripped to the waist for the work on the lines, and now he shivered and reached for the shirt he had tied round his waist. It was damp with sweat—no; they were drops of rain, large and sloppy and far apart as yet . . . but he imaged them dropping down smoothly faster and faster. . . .

Another cheer went up from the fire-lines as it began to rain hard and fast, causing clouds of steam to rise along the edge of the burning forest. Alastair laid down his hoe and gazed at the sky with relief and satisfaction.

"Look out!" someone yelled. Raising his eyes, startled, he could see a burned-through tree beginning to tilt and topple; and to his horror, Lenisa was hauling her water pail within a few yards of it. Even before he knew what he was doing, Alastair was streaking along the firebreak; he flung himself at the girl, tackling her and shoving her out of the path of the falling tree. . . .

But not quite far enough. The tree crashed down with a great sound like the end of the world, taking a crowd of smaller trees and underbrush with it. Lenisa and Alastair were crushed to the ground beneath it; he thrust the girl in his arms as far as he could out of the tree's path and felt her body beneath his as the world collapsed on top of his head. The last sound he heard was Jewel's frantic howling.

13

Conn had seen the fire from afar, with no particular wish to intrude on Alastair. Somehow, sooner or later, Alastair must make his own peace with Markos and with the people of Hammerfell. If the people of Hammerfell saw him accepting his duty among them, including fire-watch duty, which Conn himself had done regularly since he was nine years old, they would certainly accept him all the sooner.

But danger of death broke all barriers; Alastair's panic as he saw the falling tree and snatched Lenisa from its path broke into Conn's mind as if he himself had been in the path of the burning treetop crashing down; the stifling holocaust of the flaming forest and the cracking smash of the falling giant—even Jewel's frenzied howls—roared through his brain as if it were all here in his mother's quiet room. He leaped to his feet, for an instant unaware that the pounding of his heart, the rush of adrenalin through

Marion Zimmer Bradley

all his limbs, had no reality for his own body and brain.

He was cognizant only of danger; desperate terror and danger; and not until several harrowing moments had passed was he once again aware that he was alone in the falling twilight, hearing only the sounds of the quiet streets of Thendara outside; a dog barking somewhere in the distance, the faraway rumble of a cart. Suddenly Alastair was gone—dead or unconscious, that fierce situation wiped from Conn's awareness.

Conn mopped unexpected sweat from his face. What had happened to his brother?

Sternly as he had judged him at times, his heroism had endangered his life; had it actually *taken* his life, then? Cautiously, Conn sought in his mind for the broken rapport with Alastair, and found pain and darkness . . . but at least the pain meant Alastair had survived, perhaps gravely hurt, but he still lived.

On the floor the young dog Copper whined restlessly; perhaps, Conn thought, she, too, had picked up something from her absent master, or had she only picked up Conn's own disturbance and distress?

"It's all right, girl," he said, patting the puppy's silky head. "It's all right, then. Calm down." Copper's huge dark eyes looked up at him beseechingly, and he thought, *Yes, I must somehow go to him; one way or the other, Markos will need me there.*

He was accustomed to making his own decisions; he flung clothing into a saddlebag, and made his way to the kitchens for food for the journey before it occurred to him that he was living as a guest in his mother's house and he really should—if not actually ask her leave—at least inform her of his plans.

He left the saddlebag half packed and went in search of Erminie. But as he traversed the hall, the outside door of the house opened and Gavin Delleray came in, looking like a brightly plumed bird, the leather of his boots dyed crimson, to match the coloring of the tips of his curls and the ribbons in his shirt cuffs. He looked at Conn and could tell that something was wrong. "Good morning, dear friend, what's the matter? Have you had news of Alastair, then?"

Conn, who was in no mood to waste time on pleasantries, said curtly, "There's fire in the hills, and he's been hurt—perhaps killed."

The aspect of a young dandy slid off Gavin's face like a mask. He said quickly, "You should speak with your mother at once about it; she will be able to find out if he still lives."

Conn had not thought of that; he was still too new to the life of the *laran*-gifted. He found that his voice was shaking as he said, "Will you come? I cannot bear to face her if I should cause her to learn of Alastair's death—"

"Of course," said Gavin.

Together they went in search of Erminie, and found her in her sewing room. She looked up, smiling to her son, but when she saw he did not respond, her look turned to one of frightened foreboding.

"Conn, what's the matter? And you—Gavin, what are you doing here? You know you are always welcome, but to see you here at this hour—"

"I came only to ask for news, at first," Gavin said, "but I found Conn in this state—"

"I must go at once to Hammerfell, Mother; Alastair

has been hurt—near killed, I suspect—on the fire-lines."

Her face went white.

"Hurt? How did you know?"

"I have been in contact with him before this; strong emotion—fear or pain—will do it," he said, explaining what she knew already as swiftly as she asked the question. "I saw him hit in the fall of a burning tree!"

"Merciful Avarra," Erminie whispered. Snatching out her starstone, she bent over it and in a moment looked up with relief. "No; I do not think he is dead. Badly hurt, perhaps, even unconscious, but not dead. He is beyond my reach; I should send for Edric—or for Renata—who will be able to reach the people in the Tower at Tramontana; they will know what is happening in the hills. All the Keepers can reach one another."

"Send for Floria, too, kinswoman," said Gavin. "She would want to know what is happening to her promised husband."

"Yes, of course," said Erminie, bending over her starstone. After a moment she looked up and said, "They will come."

Conn said, "I do not like this delay; I feel I should go to him at once."

Erminie shook her head firmly. "There can be no such haste as that; better, if you must go, to go knowing exactly what is happening. Otherwise you could ride into a trap set by Storn—as your brother did, long before you were born."

"If there is any question of that," Gavin said, "he shall not ride alone into danger; I swear I will be at his side for life or death."

Erminie embraced Gavin, so moved that she had no words; she stood clinging to them both until Copper pricked up her head and barked; there were steps in the hall, and Floria came in, with Renata in her crimson robes, and a little behind them, Edric Elhalyn.

"I came as soon as I knew you wanted me, kinswoman," he said, going quickly to Erminie.

Renata said in the husky and sexless voice of the *emmasca*, "Tell us what has happened, my dear."

Conn explained swiftly; Edric frowned. He said, "Word of this should be sent to King Aidan at once."

Renata frowned and said, "By no means; His Grace has enough troubles of his own at this moment, and no thought to spare for those of Hammerfell."

"Is Antonella dead, then?" Gavin asked. "I heard she was mending."

"Till last night, that was true," said Floria. "Last night they sent for me to monitor her; another blood vessel in her brain has burst. She will not die, but she cannot speak, and her whole right side is paralyzed."

"Ah, poor lady," Renata said. "She is good to everyone, and Aidan will sorely miss her; at least he must stay with her as long as his presence can still give her any comfort."

"I should remain with her, too," Floria said. "Perhaps vigilance and constant monitoring might prevent another stroke—which would most probably mean death."

"Then it is I who should go to her," Renata said. "At this time I think your place is here, Floria, with your promised husband's mother—" but it was directly at Conn that she looked, "and I think your father will agree. Erminie needs you, and I will remain with Her Grace. I was a monitor before I was Keeper—"

"And your skills are immeasurably greater than mine," added Floria, relieved and grateful.

Conn felt torn, too, between his brother's danger and the king he had begun to love. His voice was irritable. "Then, in the name of all the Gods there are, let us know at once what is happening with my brother."

He looked at Floria; she raised her eyes to his and neither of them dared acknowledge the thought that hung between them.

I wish my brother no harm. I swear it; but if he is no longer between us—

And her answering thought: *I think maybe I only loved Alastair because it was through him I saw you. . . .*

One way or another, Conn knew, he and Floria could no longer ignore their feelings. But first, they must care for Alastair.

Even before Renata could raise or uncover the starstone, the outer house door opened and Valentine Hastur came in. "Ah, Renata, I hoped to find you here. You are needed; go at once to His Grace, I will look after the Lady Erminie and her sons—after all, they are to be my stepsons."

Renata nodded briskly and hurried out. Erminie blushed, then looked up briefly and smiled at Valentine.

I am so glad you are here, kinsman; you always come when I am most in need.

Conn thought: *I am glad for her; she was married to my father almost before she had put away her dolls, and has lived alone all these years, thinking only of my brother's welfare. It is time she had someone to think first of her happiness.*

The starstone blazed in Edric's hand; swiftly he drew them together into the circle. At once, Conn felt the presences of another circle, and knew without being told that they were the assembled workers of the faraway Tower at Tramontana.

Welcome, kinsmen; the fire is contained and we have leisure to greet you now. In Conn's mind was a picture of the timberlands burned over, one village made all but uninhabitable—a village on Storn lands, not his own—and the shelters set up for the homeless, food and clothing distributed.

What of my son? It was Erminie who formed the question, and her mind went out seeking him, Conn immediately present in the search.

He is recovering, but in Storn's hands—pledged as a guest, under the laws of hospitality which he holds sacred, the faraway Keeper reassured Erminie at once. *No harm will come to him, and his wounds are not mortal, we assure you.*

"If Alastair is wounded, Markos—and my people—will need me," Conn said. "Mother, give me leave to depart. I am already packed, but you must let me have a good, strong horse. My old pony has gone with Alastair. I must go as swiftly as I can."

"Take whatever you need," said she. "Any horse in the stables is at your service. I shall follow at my best speed; but you can ride faster alone."

"*We* will follow," Floria said firmly. "I'm coming, too."

"I shall ride with Conn," said Gavin.

Conn turned to Gavin and his mother, "Why need either of you come? Mother, you should remain here in safety, and Gavin, you should stay to care for her. I know your good will, my friend, but you do not know the mountain roads, and one can still travel faster than two."

"If Alastair is hurt, he will need me," Erminie said firmly. "And you will be busy on the king's business, raising the armies he spoke of. I know the road to Hammerfell as well as you. But you must go as quickly as you possibly can."

"Then, Gavin, you must stay and escort my mother and Floria if they feel they must come; this would be the best service you could possibly do me, my friend," Conn entreated, taking Gavin's hands in his.

Floria said in a low voice, "I feel I should go with *you*, Conn. This is between you and me—and Alastair."

"You are right," he acknowledged, "but you dare not. Stay with my mother. She will need you."

Erminie followed Conn to his room, where he finished thrusting a change of clothing into the saddlebag, fetched bread and cold meat from the kitchen, and saddled a good horse. She stood watching him at the gate as he rode away.

Copper scrambled through the gate after him, hauling Erminie bodily after her. Erminie tried to hold the dog, then, resigned, let go her collar, whispering, "Take good care of him, girl." She stood and watched her second son ride away into the mountains that had already swallowed up her first. Then she went into the house, sent a message to the Tower that she must have a leave of absence from her work, and arranged matters with her servants, preparing to leave at first light in the morning. The time had come to return to the heritage she had abandoned twenty years before.

She slept but ill, and woke in the morning to

discover Floria already in the kitchen preparing travel bags.

"I did not wish to wake you," the younger woman said, "but we should begin our journey as soon as possible."

"But, my dear," Erminie protested, "it is not right that we should both be absent from the Tower at once."

"Nonsense," Floria said. "Now and especially at this season there is little work to be done. There is another monitor who can take my place in the circle if the circle bothers to gather at all, and two young trainees to work in the relays if there is need. To stay here when I am needed elsewhere would simply be cowardice—using my work in the Tower as an excuse." She hesitated, "But if it is simply that you do not want my company. . . ."

"No, not at all," Erminie said. "I have no taste for long journeys alone; I would be more than glad of company. But—"

"Alastair is gone, and he is my promised husband," Floria said. "And Conn is gone—" she stopped, unable to form the words, but Erminie knew what she would have said and motioned her to silence.

"Even the dogs are gone," she said, trying to make a joke of it. "Why should we stay here alone? But I do not know—have you ever ridden so far?"

"No," Floria confessed, "but I am a good rider; I will try not to hold you back. And Gavin has pledged to ride with us."

"By your leave—" Gavin Delleray came into the room and at the sight of him, Erminie had to laugh.

"You are welcome to escort me, my dear lad; but

not in that outfit! Go and borrow some sound, sensible riding clothes from Conn's room—"

"As you will," Gavin said lightly, "though I confess I had hoped to bring the latest fashions into the hills where no one knows anything of the proper cut of a coat." He went, and quickly came back attired in a leather tunic and riding breeches, a pair of Conn's boots laced halfway to his knee.

"I can only hope none of my court friends see me in this ridge-rider's getup," he grumbled. "I would never live it down."

"It is a long journey, and not an easy one unless you are mountain born," Erminie warned. But Floria and Gavin were undaunted, so she led the way to the stables. Floria had brought her best horse, and the women changed into riding skirts and heavy cloaks— for, though it was warm in the city streets, Erminie knew it would be bitterly cold in the higher country to the north—and rode away toward the north gate of the city.

The first day's ride was mellow and sunny, and they slept at a quiet inn, supping well on cooked food to spare their dried journey bread and travel provisions. They were glad of Gavin's company; like any minstrel, he insisted on singing to them before they slept. The next morning was cold and gray and before they had ridden an hour it began to rain hard.

As they rode north in the rain they were silent, each woman wrapped in her own thoughts; Floria thought sorrowfully of her promised husband, lying hurt or dead in Storn's castle, and guiltily longed for Conn; Erminie sadly relived the long-dormant memories of her marriage, and without really intending it, found herself envying the young woman's intense love—something she, married so young to an older man, kind as he was, had never known. She had not really missed it till now when she witnessed—sadly secondhand—what young passion could be. She was fond of Valentine, but she knew that a second marriage at her age was likely to bring companionship, even happiness—but hardly this kind of love.

Gavin rode with them, not really knowing why he had insisted on sharing this adventure. Alastair was a kinsman and an old friend, and he had quickly become fond of Conn, but this was not reason enough to thrust himself uninvited into this kind of danger. He told himself that he might find material for a ballad in the story of the twin heirs to Hammerfell, and finally resolved that it must be simply the workings of fate. He had never believed in fate, but he felt inexplicably compelled to join this desperate mission and could think of no other explanation.

The rain grew heavier and colder as they crossed the mountain pass and went higher into the hills. By late afternoon of the third day it was mixed with snow, driving needles of sleet into their faces, and the horses found it heavy going on the trails that lay icy underfoot.

The paths were so slippery, and the narrow roads so confusing, that Erminie was hardly able to find her way along the road she had traveled but once, and then in the opposite direction. Toward evening she began to fear that they were lost, and found herself reaching out telepathically for Conn, to verify which way he had gone, which of the confusing narrow trails was the road. But Conn was not alert for her touch and she had to reach through the overworld, in search of some traveler who might be going the same way and knew the right road. This was not, strictly speaking, ethical for a trained telepath, but Erminie could think of no other way to avoid wholly losing herself, Gavin, and Floria in the unfamiliar woods.

Eventually they found themselves in a small mountain village; there was, she discovered, no inn, but one of the villagers agreed to furnish them a bed and supper, at an extortionate price, and offered them a guide to the next village in the morning. Erminie agreed, for want of any available alternative, though she was troubled; she lay awake half the night, while Floria slept beside her, fearing that the "hospitable" villagers might be thieves who would attack and rob them, or worse, during the night. But she finally succumbed to sleep and woke at the first light, untouched, with all her possessions intact, and more than a little ashamed of her suspicions. She remembered that her husband and her son had both lived all their lives among mountain people, and that while there were doubtless villains among them—Lord Storn for instance—most of them were certainly decent, honorable people.

Another weary day of riding, with the village guide who set them on their path with instructions as to how to reach both Hammerfell and Castle Storn, brought them within one or two long days' travel to Hammerfell. At twilight of the fifth day, they came to a fork in the road marked by a cluster of trees which Erminie recognized as a landmark; the left path led upward to Hammerfell, the right-hand fork to the castle of Storn Heights, which could actually be seen, a little horn of stone, over the crest of the mountain beyond.

Here Erminie hesitated; she was not certain whether she ought to travel to her own place at Hammerfell (which she had last seen in ruins) and seek out allies, or whether she should go directly to Storn and demand to nurse her injured son.

She broached her confusion to Floria, who said, "Conn did say that he had been living with Markos, Lady Erminie; I think you would do better to seek shelter there."

"But with Alastair in Storn's hands—" Erminie protested, "He may not be safe—"

"Have we not always been told that fire-truce is sacred to the mountain people?" Floria protested, "and Alastair was injured on Storn lands, during the fire; Storn could not do other than care for him honorably."

"I have no reason to trust in the honor of Lord Storn," Erminie said.

"All the more reason, then, not to trust yourself to him unannounced," said Floria. Erminie could see the good sense of that, and they turned toward Hammerfell. They had ridden only a little way when the sound of approaching riders fell on their ears. Without the slightest notion of who might be approaching, Erminie and Floria guided their horses off the road and into the thicket of bushes. Then Erminie heard a familiar bark, and then a human voice she knew, although she had not heard it in half a lifetime.

"My lady Duchess?"

"Can it possibly be you, Markos, my old friend?"

"Yes, and I myself, Mother," Conn called, and

with an audible sigh of relief, Erminie rode onto the road, and fell almost fainting into Markos's arms. Having ascertained that his mother was safe, Conn gave Gavin a friendly hug, then hesitantly embraced Floria, too.

"You really should not have come," he scolded. "You would have been safer in Thendara, what with Alastair in Storn's hands, and seriously injured. . . ."

Breathing in the bracing mountain air, Erminie could not help remembering her old playfellow Alaric in Storn's castle, a captive, dying there. "How badly hurt is he? Has Storn made any threats?"

"Not yet," said Markos. "I dare say they will come later. My lady, I rejoice to see you alive and well. All these years I believed you dead—"

"And I you, old friend," said Erminie, taking her husband's old retainer's hand warmly. Then, impulsively, she leaned forward and kissed the old man's cheek. "I owe you much gratitude for caring for my son all these years, Markos."

"The gratitude is mine, lady; he has been the son I never had," Markos said. "But now we must find shelter for you. It is late, and the night's rain will soon turn into snow—I wish I could show you Hammerfell rebuilt as it should be, but I fear that day is yet to come. If we rebuilt it under Storn's very eyes, he would have known there were still Hammerfells in these hills. In the meantime, there is a blizzard coming and I have a home which is at my lady's service, and folk to look after you and the young *leronis*."

"What of the fire, and Alastair?"

"I think the fire is out," said Conn, slowly. "There has been so much rain, and I saw an airship which might have brought them help. There are *leroni* in Tramontana, Mother, and I think one of Storn's projects was to wheedle himself into their good graces, as if he were Comyn himself."

Erminie closed her eyes, focused on her starstone and extended her senses as far as she could. Silently calling on Floria to shield her, she scanned the countryside around as far as she could.

"The fire is out," she said at last, "the ground wet and steaming, a small patrol watching to make sure it does not blaze up again, and the men in the fire-camp bedded down for the night, to disperse to their homes in the morning, I suppose. But I see no sign of Alastair."

"He is not in the camp," said Conn. "He recovered consciousness a while ago—I felt his pain. He is sorely hurt, but not, I feel, in any immediate danger of death."

"Where is he, then?"

"He is within Storn Heights and, as far as I can tell, an honored guest," Conn said.

Both Floria and Erminie looked unsatisfied by this, but Conn said, "What alternative have we except to trust him, Mother? We cannot ride up to the castle and demand that Storn release him at once. That would indeed insult Storn's honor, and how do we know that Alastair is in any condition to be released?"

With that, Erminie had to be content.

"Very well," she said at last. "You said there is room in Markos's home to shelter us all for the night? Take us there, then; anything will be an improvement over the roads of the Hellers."

14

When Alastair first woke, he was sure that his nightmare of hell had finally claimed him. His body was bound in lines of burning pain; but after a few minutes of helpless struggle he slowly began to realize that he was wrapped in bandages, slick with smooth, strange-smelling ointments. He opened his eyes, and looked into Lenisa's troubled face.

Slowly, memory returned; the burning tree, his attempts to sweep her from its path . . . her face was reddened and flushed, one arm heavily bandaged, her hair burned away at the temples.

She saw his eyes rest on the unsightly burned patch, and said irritably, "Yes, it's ugly, but the *leronis* says it will grow back soon, that singeing is good for hair—that sometimes a hairdresser will singe hair-ends to make them grow faster."

"I don't care about that," Alastair interrupted, "just tell me you are not seriously injured."

"No, not seriously," she said. "I have a burn on my arm that will keep me from kneading bread or baking pies for a tenday, perhaps. So if you want a greenberry pie, you will have to wait till my arm heals."

She giggled at him then, and he felt an enormous tenderness.

"Would you bake me a pie some day, then?"

"Why, yes," she said. "I think you've deserved it, since you did not share in the feast we give our folk when a fire is safely out. I saved you some cold meats and some cakes, if you are hungry, though."

Alastair considered; he was desperately thirsty, but not at all hungry. "I don't think I could eat. But I could drink a whole rain-barrel of cold water!"

"That is because of your burns; but hot drinks are better for you just now than cold water," she said, and held a cup to his lips. It contained the same sharp-tasting herb tea she had brought round on the fire-lines. It relieved his thirst very well and he began to feel sleepy so soon after drinking it that he wondered if she had put some drug into it to make him sleep.

"You must rest," she said. "It took a long time to lift the burning tree off you. Luckily, you were only under one branch. It was the *leroni* who came at last and lifted it with their starstones, and they were desperate. At first we thought you were dead and Grandfather was upset because I would not stop crying so that they could bandage my own burns—" Suddenly she blushed and turned away. "But I must be tiring you with talk. You must sleep now," she said. "I will come back and bring your dinner later."

Thus admonished, Alastair drifted toward sleep

with a curious picture in his mind of the girl weeping—for *his* burns! He wondered if she had yet had time to inform her grandfather about the identity of his guest; did Lord Storn know that he was entertaining his oldest enemy under his roof—for Alastair was certain he was actually within the walls of Storn Heights. Well, he was helpless to do anything except trust to fire-truce, and with this thought he drifted off.

When he woke again—he did not think it was too much later—Lenisa had come back with a serving-woman carrying a tray. The woman helped hoist Alastair up in his bed, propped him against cushions and pillows, and Lenisa sat beside the bed and fed him spoonfuls of stew and pudding. When he had eaten several mouthfuls (he was surprised to discover how little he was able to swallow, for he had felt half starved), she tucked him carefully in. Then, over her shoulder he saw the lined face of Lord Storn.

"I owe you my gratitude, young Hammerfell, for the life of my grandniece," he said in a formal tone. "She is dearer to me than a dozen daughters, my only living descendant—" He paused, and his tone became more personal, "And believe me I am far from ungrateful. Though there have been many causes of controversy between us, possibly, now that you are my guest—though not by choice, we can speak about mending our differences."

He paused; and Alastair, who had spent much of his life in Thendara in formal training in protocol, recognized the pause as his cue to say something courteous.

"Believe me, I am grateful for your gracious hospitality, my lord; and I have always heard there is no quarrel so great it cannot be amended, even if it be between Gods rather than men. Since we are no more than men, it's certain that whatever lies between us can somehow be healed, given good will and good faith."

Lord Storn beamed with relief at Alastair's gracious little speech. He had changed from the rough working clothes he had worn on the fire-line; his hair was combed back from his brow, gray in color, but so smooth and gleaming over his high forehead that Alastair suspected it was a wig; he wore rings on his fingers and was clad in a rich gown of sky-blue brocade. He looked imposing, even regal.

"I will drink to that, then, Duke Hammerfell. Let me give you my solemn assurance, that if you seem willing to leave past grievances behind us, you have nothing to fear from me. Even though at your last encounter with my men you killed my nephew and threatened me with death . . ." Lord Storn's voice had begun to take on a dangerous edge.

Alastair raised his hand to stop him, anxious to protect his fragile safety.

"With respect, sir, I came on your lands for the first time this day. The man who so ungraciously threatened you and your policies was not I, but my younger brother—my twin. He was brought up by my father's old retainer, who was under the mistaken impression that my mother and I had perished in the fire that claimed Hammerfell, and that my brother Conn was the last survivor of Hammerfell blood. My younger brother is impetuous, and I fear he is deficient in noble behavior and good breeding. If he treated you without proper respect, I can only ask your pardon for him and attempt to make amends. I see no reason, sir, why this bitter and irrational feud should continue for another generation." Alastair sincerely hoped his little speech had appeased his ancient enemy.

Lord Storn smiled broadly.

"Indeed? Was it then your brother who raided my lands and killed my nephew? And he thought himself the rightful Duke of Hammerfell? Where is he now?"

"As far as I know, he is in Thendara, sir, with my mother, where I have lived these eighteen years since the burning of Hammerfell. We were reunited less than forty days ago. And I came north to look after the best interests of my people here on my ancestral lands."

"Alone?"

"Yes, alone, except—" abruptly he remembered. "My dog! I remember hearing her barking as I fell beneath the tree. I hope she was not hurt."

"The poor old thing would hardly let us touch you, even to treat your burns," said Lord Storn. "She is safe, yes; we would have taken her to my own kennel, but my granddaughter recognized her and brought her here."

"I saw her in the tavern, and we made friends, you remember," Lenisa said, smiling.

"My mother would never forgive me if anything happened to old Jewel," Alastair said.

Lord Storn went to the room door and opened it; Lenisa said "Dame Jarmilla, please bring in Lord Hammerfell's dog." She added to Alastair, "You see, she's in good hands—the hands of my own governess."

The swordswoman he had seen in the tavern came

in, holding Jewel's collar; but as Alastair struggled to sit up in bed, she broke from the woman's hands and leaped at him, swarming up on the bed and licking his face.

"There, leave off, there's a good girl," Alastair said, in considerably more pain from Jewel's display of affection. He pushed her head away, saying, "It's all right, old girl, no harm done. I'm really all right. Down, now." He looked up at Lord Storn. "I hope she didn't bite anyone in your household, sir."

Jewel sank down, lying near the head of the bed, her eyes fixed on Alastair's face, and did not budge.

"No, I don't think so," Lord Storn said, "though I think if Lenisa had not made friends with her, she might have attacked any who came near you; we had to bring her into the keep, she was barking enough to rouse the whole countryside. She won't eat anything, hasn't had a thing since you were injured."

"She wouldn't touch the food and beer served to all the firefighters in the hall when we came from the lines," Lenisa said. "Perhaps she was too worried about you to eat."

"No," Alastair said, "my mother and I trained her to take food from no hands but ours."

"I don't know if that's a good idea or not," said the swordswoman Jarmilla. "If you both died, the poor thing would starve herself to death."

"Well, she's never been out of my sight before," Alastair said. "And one doesn't exactly plan to get killed or hurt."

"No, I suppose not," Lord Storn said, "but there's an old saying, 'Nothing's sure but death, and next winter's snow'; we can't always stop to make arrangements for our descendants—or our dogs—before we get killed, especially these days."

"No, I suppose not," said Alastair, remembering quite abruptly that he was in the hands of the *same* Lord Storn who had burned his family home over his head before he was two years old, killing his father. Well, from what he had always heard, a guest was sacred in the mountains; but hadn't his older brother died within these walls? Could Storn's lack of care have had something to do with it? He couldn't remember, and in his present condition he could do nothing but trust Lord Storn—and Lenisa.

"I'd be grateful to you, *mestra*, if you'd give her something to eat in your kennels," he said, patting Jewel and saying to her emphatically, "It's all right, girl; go with her; *friend*," he repeated, taking Dame Jarmilla's hand and holding it under Jewel's muzzle, "You can go with her, girl, and eat your dinner, understand?"

Jewel looked at him as if she understood, and trotted along at Dame Jarmilla's side.

Lenisa smiled, "Then she is not like that Hammerfell hound of legend—trained to hunt down anyone of Storn blood?"

Alastair had never heard of such a hound and wondered if the tale were true. "By no means," he said, "though I dare say she'd protect me or my mother—or even, I suppose, my brother—to the death."

"I wouldn't think much of any dog that wouldn't," Lenisa said.

"Now, *chiya*," Lord Storn said. "No more idle chatter, there is something I must say to Hammerfell.

222

Young man, I'd like you to think seriously about the best interests of your tenants as well as mine."

"I'm always willing to listen," Alastair said courteously. There was something about Lord Storn which made him want to forget all the wrongs he had lived to avenge. It seemed somehow incongruous that he should be here to raise armies against this courageous old man; perhaps with diplomacy and understanding, war could be avoided. *Lenisa* was certainly not his enemy. He could at least listen without prejudice.

"This land here's played out, there's no living any more in farming," Lord Storn said. "I've been trying to help my tenants relocate, but they're stubborn as Zandru's devils; maybe together we can reeducate them. The new thing now is sheep—get the people out, put sheep in here. They must see it's better for everybody. There's no more money to be made in tenant farming. It's in your interest as well as mine. But think on it before you answer. We'll talk it over tomorrow." He stood up. "Hear the rain? Wish I could stay inside like you, snug in a warm bed with a friendly young hand to tuck me in, give me a nightcap of mulled wine. But I have to be off—ride the boundaries, make sure none of my good neighbors took advantage of the fire to move the marking-stones—oh, yes, it's been done, fire-truce or no—make sure the chemicals are stowed safe, the watchmen back in their places."

"I'll stay up and make you a nightcap of mulled wine when you're back, Grandsire," Lenisa offered.

"No, girl, go to bed and get your beauty sleep; you'll be needing it, now," he said, and kissed her roughly on the forehead. "Look after our guest, and

223

get to bed at a timely hour. Tomorrow, young Hammerfell, we'll talk, you and I. Sleep well."

And with a friendly nod to both of them, he walked out of the room.

15

Ardrin, Lord Storn, strode out of his castle, and for a moment hesitated; should he summon one of his paxmen to ride the boundaries with him? No, there was no reason for it; he had been surveying these boundaries every day of his life since his twelfth year, and he was reluctant to call any of his men out into the rainy night with him.

As yet the rain was soft, light; almost pleasantly cool after the heat and fatigue of the day. His clothing was thick and impervious to rain; he strode along checking each boundary stone almost automatically. He had a long-standing sense of unity with his lands; each acre was known for what it could produce, or what had been planted or done there in the past.

He thought with regret, *My grandsire grew apples in that field; now it is good for nothing but sheep. None of this land is useful for anything but sheep anymore. The wool industry grows daily in Thendara; farming*

*never made any of us rich, but sheepherding may indeed
do so.*

It was sad to turn away men who had been Storn
tenants for many years past, but he could not hold
them here to starve on dead lands; it was, after all,
necessary. They'd all prosper this way.

He would need a few fellows to be shepherds, but
he would be sure they were his own loyal men.

It's really for everyone's good, he reminded himself
comfortably. *We can't keep clinging to yesterday; and they
can find farmland in the lowlands or elsewhere, or work in
the cities. The manufacturers in the cities are crying out for
good workers, and can't get them. There'll be work for their
sons and their wives, too, as servants in city houses. Better
for everyone than clinging like hungry animals to worn-out
farms.*

He had not noticed that the rain was falling harder
and faster, and now he realized it was mixed thickly
with wet snow. He slipped and his feet went out
from under him; he managed to scramble up again,
but the snow was cold and heavy now and he tucked
his hands into the deep pockets of his cloak and
strode on, observing the fire damage and storing it
up in his mind.

He had walked a considerable way, and was beginning to wish that he had allowed Lenisa to prepare
him that hot supper before he went out; for the
sleet, still heavy, was penetrating even his thick cloak.

It seemed to him that he saw a light where, as the
old ballad had it, "Never a light should be." Unless,
perhaps, he thought with amusement, his dairy animals had taken to kindling lights in their pastures.
His first reaction was curiosity rather than alarm; he
went closer, wondering whether the fire in the pas-

ture might have flamed up again, only a spark perhaps but showing a long way at night.

The light wavered and he was no longer very sure he had seen it at all. A reflected glimmer of starlight off some random bit of metal; he remembered an episode in his youth when he had raised an alarm for seeing a light at night which had turned out to be a herdsman's belt buckle and pocketknife hung up on a fence, catching the moonlight.

Since that long-ago day he had always hesitated before coming to conclusions; and this wrestled in him with the ingrained custom of raising an alarm at once at any unexpected sign of fire or intruder, summoning help first and then investigating. Fire, night-runners or bandits, none of these were anything for a policy of *wait and see*.

Cautiously he turned his steps from the road in the direction of the light. He could see it again now, wavering faintly, and as he advanced, proud that his eyes were as keen as they had been a generation before, he resolved the flickers into reflections on glass.

But reflections of *what*, in the name of all Zandru's icy hells! In rain like this there was neither moonlight nor starlight. Only a few of his tenants were well enough off to have glass windows. He stepped cautiously up to the house and saw that, although the house appeared wholly deserted, a fire was burning somewhere within—in defiance of strict standing orders against any unattended hearths—and this was responsible for the fugitive light. He stepped up on the wooden porch, recoiling at the agonized creak of wood, and shoved his way inside. The warmth was comforting, but law was law and danger was danger;

he would cover the fire and save these people a fine and a lecture from the firewarden. His clothes were steaming as he approached the fireplace. Abruptly he recoiled, staring eyes wide with horror as his hands, stretched before him, encountered hanging, swaying forms.

Had they all hanged themselves? But why? He stepped back, bracing himself for what he feared to see by the firelight; then let out a gust of foolish relief. Empty coats and cloaks, hung from a high rafter to dry, no more.

He covered the fire with sand from a bucket near the hearth, wishing the farmer would come in so he could lecture him on covering fires at night when unattended. Where were they anyhow, to go out at night and leave an uncovered fire? Up to no good, he'd bet—well, perhaps he could tell them of his fright, which, shared, might even be amusing.

But after a short while, when no one returned, he went out again into the cold, to finish walking the boundaries. It was coming down harder now, a wet thick mixture of rain and snow, and it occurred to Lord Storn that it might be sensible to forget the whole thing and go back inside, spend the night by his tenants' fire, finish his checking of boundaries and damage in the morning. Why had he gotten it into his head that he could properly assess damage in a storm like this after dark? Had he been showing off, after all, for young Hammerfell? But no, the rain had been light and pleasant when he had started out, and he had felt the need of fresh, cool air and solitude.

The wind had an ominous moaning sound now which warned him with a lifetime's weather-knowledge to take shelter. Pride was one thing and lunacy was another.

He had better make for the nearest farm. There was a man named Geredd, a tenant of twenty or thirty years' standing, whose farm had actually been targeted for the new changes and the man given notice to quit; but he was still living there, as far as Lord Storn knew. He tramped on, stumbling at one point into a ditch and emerged covered with freezing mud. His boots were soaked because he had stepped into water over their tops and the mud had seeped down his shins to pool in his stockings. By the time he saw the lamp shining in Geredd's window, he thought no sight had ever been so welcome, and he halloed loudly to attract attraction before banging on the door.

A young man, with one eye covered with a black patch, wearing a ragged cap which gave him a fierce and wild aspect—Storn did not remember ever seeing him before—pushed the door open.

"What'll ye be wanting?" he asked suspiciously. "At a godforgotten hour like this when honest folk all be in bed?"

"My business is with Geredd," Storn said. "As I remember, this is his house; who are you, then?"

"Granfer," the man called sullenly, "somebody here be askin' for you."

Geredd, stooped and pudgy, and clad in wrinkled old homespun, came to the door. His face was apprehensive; but when he saw Storn the apprehension disappeared.

"My lord!" he cried out. "You lend me grace. Come in out of the cold."

In a very few minutes Storn was seated on a padded bench in the lee of the fireplace, his soaked outer garments and boots steaming in front of the hearth.

"I'm sorry I have no wine for you, sir; could you fancy a mug of hot cider, then?"

"With pleasure," said Lord Storn. He was startled by this kindness, after they had been warned to quit this farm by his factors; but he supposed clan loyalty went deep in these people; they were, after all, mostly his distant kin, and the habit of deference to the clan-leader and lord was very ancient. When the hot cider was brought, he sipped it gratefully.

"The young man who answered the door—the surly young fellow with one eye—your grandson?" he asked, remembering how the youngster had called "Gran'fer."

But Geredd answered, "My older daughter's step-son by her second marriage; no kin of mine, his father died four years ago. I give the lad houseroom because he's nowhere else to go; his father's people have all gone south to find work in Neskaya in the wool trade, but he says he's of no mind to be a landless or a rootless man, so he stays here—" He added anxiously, "He talks wild, but you know what young men are—all talk and no doing."

"I'd like to talk to some of these young malcontents; find out what's in their minds," Storn ventured, looking about the old, high raftered room, from which the sullen, ragged young man had vanished; but the old man Geredd sighed.

"He's always off and about wi' his friends; ye know, sir, how it is wi' the young folk, always thinking they can change the world. Now, sir, you mustn't think of trying to make it back tonight in this weather; you shall have my bed, and the wife and I shall sleep here before the fire. My younger daughter's here, too; they had notice to quit, but Bran—that's Mhari's husband, they have four little children under five, an' Mhari brought to bed with twins not a tenday ago, so I'm keepin' them all here—what else can I do?"

Storn tried to protest, but Geredd insisted. "No trouble at all, sir, none, we sleep here in the kitchen during the cold weather anyway; just now she's made up the bed with fresh sheets for you an' the best blankets," he told him, and led Lord Storn into the tiny bedroom. Almost all the space was taken up by an enormous bed covered with a featherbed and quilt, and a number of old and patched, but very clean pillows. Geredd's elderly wife came and helped Lord Storn out of his damp clothing, putting him into an also much-mended but clean nightshirt, patched and faded; his wig hung on the bedpost, and his garments, in various stages of drying, were strewn about the room. The old woman drew up the blankets about his shoulders, deferentially wished him a good night, and withdrew. Warm at last, no longer shivering, Storn settled down, hearing the sleet pounding the windows. Soon he slept; it had been a long day.

16

Markos's cottage was not large, but to Erminie it seemed cozy and homey, lighted dimly by torchlight. Outside, the night was starless and the sky thick with gray rainclouds, scudding along in their own mysterious light. Beyond the low stone wall she could see the ruined wall of Hammerfell, in what she supposed Alastair's city friends would have called romantic disrepair; Gavin had already used the phrase three times, somewhat to Markos's annoyance, and Floria had finally nudged him in the ribs and scowled him into contrite silence.

The cottage was weathertight, though not spacious, a low room reasonably furnished with a couple of narrow beds—on one of which Erminie now sat, her still-damp feet stretched to the fire.

Beyond this there was a small table with a couple of stout wooden chairs. Nothing more. Markos had laid out an old piece of embroidered linen on the table, and a couple of tarnished silver goblets; he brought the women food and wine. "I wish it were a proper Hall for you, lady," he apologized, but Erminie shook her head.

" 'Who gives of his best is the equal in courtesy of a king, though his best be but the half of a heap of straw,' " she quoted. "This is certainly better than any heap of straw."

Gavin was curled up on the rug at Erminie's feet, where the hearth-fire crackled, throwing out reassuring warmth. On the other side of the fire, on the second cot, Floria sat, a thick velvet robe over the thin white cloth of her Tower robe—which she had put on, like Erminie, because her riding clothes were soaked to the innermost undergarment. The half-grown puppy Copper was curled up in her lap. Conn sat on one of the wooden chairs, Markos hovered near the other, nervous and obviously still unsure that his cottage could adequately house the Duchess of Hammerfell. In the small space beyond the table and chairs, four or five men had crowded into the end of the room; half a dozen more had squashed themselves into the small inner room and were trying to crowd their heads through the door to be at least a small part of what was going on. These were, Erminie knew, the men who had ridden with Conn on his first foray and heard him acknowledged as rightful heir to Hammerfell. When Markos had called for their attention and introduced Erminie, they greeted her with a cheer that made the low rafters vibrate with the sound, and startled bats fluttered out from their lodging in the narrow space between the rafters and the thatch. Erminie had been warmed by this welcome, even though she knew perfectly

well it was not really for her. Even so, she was sure
Conn must have deserved it of them, and it spoke
well for her son if these people, twenty years without
a rightful lord, could even now be so loyal to the
family of Hammerfell.

*And in Thendara I never thought of them. I am ashamed.
Well, I must try and make it up to them. With King
Aidan's help* . . . She stopped there, drowsily wonder-
ing what after all these years she could, in fact, do.

Then, with a sigh, she remembered; Conn was not
their rightful duke either; that honor was reserved
for her older son, though Conn still bore his father's
sword. This welcome, really due to his brother, only
prolonged the people's belief that they should follow
him; and if it was personal loyalty to Conn, not loyalty to the house of Hammerfell, there could be
trouble ahead. Her heart ached for both her sons;
the one she had loved lifelong, and the one she had
suffered for loss of.

These heavy feelings were not suited to the moment; though, raising her eyes, she saw Conn's frown,
and wondered if he followed her thoughts and was
equally troubled. She raised her glass and said quietly, "A pleasure to see you again in your proper
place, my dear son. I drink to the day when your
father's house will be restored, and his Great Hall
rebuilt for you and your brother."

Copper, in Floria's lap, wagged her tail as if to
echo the sentiment. Erminie wondered where old
Jewel was now.

Conn lifted his glass, meeting his mother's eyes.
"All my life, Mother, since first I knew who I was,
and even when I thought you were dead, I have
dreamed of seeing you here; this night is joyous

indeed, for all the storm outside. May the Gods grant that it be only the first of many such occasions." He drank and set down the cup. "Too bad Alastair's not here to share it; it rightly belongs to him, but that day won't be long coming. Meanwhile—Markos, do you think we should send for Jerian's son—he's a fine hand to play the *rryl,* and the old man's four little daughters can give us a dance . . . Markos? Where's he off to now?" He looked round the room, searching for his foster-father.

"Don't trouble the fellow, my dear," Erminie said. "I need no entertainment; I am glad to be in my own country, and need nothing more. Though I am sorry to put poor old Markos to such trouble; his house is hardly big enough to hold so many. Floria and I have had five days of hard travel and want no finer entertainment than a good featherbed. If we want music, Gavin is here to sing to us," she added with a kindly smile at the young musician.

"But look, that man seems as if he wanted something with you—" she said uncertainly, seeing a tall burly man beckoning Conn from the shadowy far end of the room where she could just make out Markos as well.

Conn rose from his chair. "Let me just go and see what it is that he's wanting."

With his mug in his hand, he went off. Erminie followed him with her eyes, saw him approach the man, listen to him attentively for some moments, then spring backward spilling the contents of his cup. Then he scowled with an angry gesture, and after a moment he whirled, shouting.

"Men of Hammerfell!"

The cry at once drew all eyes to him; the men in

the room looked up in expectation, and the others crowded round the outside door shoved into the room, crushing against the fireplace and squashing into the very edges of the narrow beds where the women sat.

"They are on the march, those folk of Storn! Wouldn't you think they'd keep themselves within doors in this dreadful weather, but no such decency; Storn's bullies are out on the road in rain and snow, turning out old folk who've deserved better of him! Let's go and put a stop to it, lads!"

He turned toward the door and led the men, who swarmed after him, pulling on cloaks and shouting with enthusiasm. After a few minutes Markos came toward the women and said, "M'ladies, my lord sends his humble apologies, but he is needed; he begs you to go to bed and he will wait on you tomorrow."

"I heard him, Markos," said Erminie, and Markos' eyes glowed with pride.

"See how they follow him! They'd die for their young duke."

Erminie thought that Markos had assessed the situation very well, except that Conn was *not* their young duke . . . but this was not the time to bring up what this might be doing to Alastair's rights.

"Let's hope they will not be *required* to die for him, not yet anyhow," she said. The men had gone except for Markos, the old servant and Gavin, who had been crushed against the hearth and unable to move; he got up and would have followed, but Markos shook his head.

"No, m'lord; my master meant you to stay here and guard the women; think what would happen if the folk of Storn knew that the duchess was concealed here. At the very least they'd burn this place over our heads."

"As they did once before," Erminie said. She was not at all surprised that Conn had ridden off swiftly with the men he had known all his life, forgetting Gavin's existence; she, in fact, felt quite safe, and was grateful to the old man for saving Gavin's face.

The little room was very quiet after the men left, with only the crackle of the fire, and the heavy splashing of rain outside against the cobbles of the village street. Erminie finished her wine—it was not very good wine, but she was not much of a drinker and it did not matter to her—troubled about Conn riding in such weather, about the men following him blindly and thinking him their rightful leader.

"But of course he is," Floria said quietly, acknowledging her unspoken thoughts. "He has earned their loyalty and love and he will always have it, whatever Alastair may win in his own right."

Erminie recognized the wisdom in Floria's words, but she couldn't shed her worry.

"I love them both, too," Floria said, "and I am troubled for them both. Conn is even more troubled about Alastair than you are. Why do you think he rode off in such a hurry?" Erminie made no attempt to answer, so Floria answered her own question.

"Until all this with Alastair is settled, he does not want to be in the same room with me. He loves his brother and doesn't want to betray him."

At last it was in the open, and Erminie was glad; it seemed that she and Floria had been carefully walking around this topic almost since Conn had first come to Thendara. And since the night of the aborted handfasting, it had seemed to stand before every word she and Floria spoke to one another.

"Do *you* want to betray him?"

"No, of course not. I was brought up with him; I have always been fond of him. And so I was happy enough with the thought of him as my husband; I know he is fond of me and would be kind to me. But then Conn came to Thendara, and now everything has changed."

Erminie did not know what to say. As always, she who had been denied this kind of love and fulfillment, was tongue-tied and felt helpless before a young woman who took it for granted.

"I wish I could marry them both," Floria said, near to tears. "I cannot bear to hurt Alastair, yet without Conn, my life will be empty and meaningless."

Gavin said, with his crooked good-natured smile, "A hundred years ago in these mountains, I have heard, that would indeed have been possible."

Floria colored, and said, "Those were barbarian days; even here in the hills, such things are no longer allowed." Oh, how could she possibly choose between her old playmate, whom she had loved as a brother so long and well, and this his twin, who was so very like him—and so entirely unlike? It was not only that Conn shared the gift of *laran* and could enter into her heart in a way Alastair could never do—Floria knew it was more than that—she had never known passion, never known how to desire, until Conn swept so unexpectedly into her life and her heart. She was ashamed to admit it, but it seemed to her now that Conn was vivid and vital to her, Alastair only a dim and lesser reflection.

"In either event," she continued, trying for a lighter tone, "you will have me as a daughter—so does it matter to *you* which one of them I marry?"

"Only if you wish to be Duchess of Hammerfell," Erminie said softly.

And Floria replied slowly, putting it into words for the first time, "I'd rather have Conn than be Duchess of Hammerfell."

And now Conn had ridden out into the storm; she wished she could have ridden beside him, but it was expected of women that they should stay behind and wait for their men. . . . She wondered if the waiting and worrying weren't even more tiring than the doing itself.

She knew it would do no good for her to fret for Conn; it was his work to go where his people needed him. She smiled at Gavin and said, "Give us a song, my friend, before we seek our beds. We are certainly safe enough here, and I can see that the lady Erminie is weary." Conn, after all, had left his mother in her care; knowing him, she had no doubt that he thought it a post of honor.

The rain had stopped; the sky was clear with stars overhead, and it was bitterly cold. Conn rode with his men around him, knowing he was racing to prevent a wrong he hardly understood. King Aidan took it for granted that the lord of all these people had a right to determine their destiny.

Perhaps Lord Storn should not hold all this property, perhaps it was the system that was at fault; maybe all this land should be owned by the small-holders who farmed it; then they could decide how best to use it. But as long as this system was in fact the law of the land, who was he to keep the conscience of Lord Storn and say how he should deal with his own?

He had never questioned this before; he had always accepted that what Markos called *wrong* was actually wrong; now he was questioning everything. He did not know what was right, but he was beginning to feel more strongly that the land should be turned over to the farmers.

And he knew—and hardly knew *how* he knew, only that it must be through his mysterious bond with his brother's mind—that Alastair did not share his convictions, but took it for granted as something divinely ordained that he should have power over all these people who had been born his subjects. On this, he suspected, he and Alastair might never agree; but until this very night he had taken it for granted that he should submit to Alastair because of the foolish accident that Alastair had been born twenty minutes his elder.

In fact what difference did *that* make? If he was more fit to rule than Alastair. . . .

At this he shut off this line of thinking, quite honestly appalled by the treasonous twist his thoughts were taking. Since he had turned his eyes unlawfully on Alastair's promised wife, he was questioning everything—law, decency, the very foundations of the ordered universe he relied on.

He forced himself to think of nothing except the hoofbeats of their horses on the frozen stone of the roadway. A cry from Markos broke into his reverie.

"We're too late! See, they've burned them out—Storn's bullies. The place is afire."

"Steady on," Conn said, "some of them may still be

there. And if they've been turned out on a night like this, they'll need our help more than ever."

Even before he saw them, then, they could hear the sounds from the side of the road; soldiers in Storn's household livery, pushing and shoving a mixed group of men, women and children, half-dressed, a young woman in a nightrobe with two babies in her arms, other barefoot children clinging to the women; an old man striding up and down fuming and raging.

"I swear I deserved better o' my lord than this, after forty years!" An elderly woman with gray hair, obviously his wife, was trying to calm him.

"There, there, it'll all be settled when daylight comes an' you can talk—"

"But his lordship promised me—"

And Conn's eyes were drawn to another little man in a patched nightshirt, boots drawn on over bare feet, pounding his fists and yelling incoherently. Conn listened; one of the men was trying to get a coherent account of what had happened from the old man.

"They came while we were asleep an' turned us out in the rain an' fired the house. I told them—I *demanded* they stop and let it be, I told them—I ordered them to stop, told them who I was but they wouldn'a listen—"

The little old man's face was red as an apple; Conn wondered if he were about to have a stroke.

"And who are you, old grandfather?" one of Markos's men asked respectfully.

"Ardrin of Storn!" he shouted, red-faced.

One of Storn's soldiers failed to conceal a grin. "Oh, aye, an' I'm the Keeper o' the Arilinn Tower, but we have to dispense with protocol tonight; ye' can just call me 'yer grace.' "

"Damn it," the old man shouted. "I tell you I'm Ardrin, Lord Storn. I took shelter here—"

"Oh, shut yer flap, old man, you try my patience! D'ye think I wouldn't know me own lord?" the soldier demanded.

Conn watched the old man's face. It would otherwise never have occurred to Conn to believe what he said—but a telepath can tell when he hears the truth, and Conn was hearing it now. The old man really *was* Lord Storn—and what perfect irony, that Storn himself should be turned out in the rain by his own soldiers, and the very house where he sheltered burned over his head by his own orders. Conn did not blame the soldier at all—who would believe this ragged old man in a faded flannel nightshirt to be the most powerful man between here and Aldaran?

Conn went to him, bowed slightly, and said quietly, "Lord Storn, I see you finally feel the burden of your own proclamations!" He added to the soldier, "One old man's like another, without his fine clothes and wig."

The soldier looked closer. "Zandru's hells!" he swore. "Sir, I didn't know; I was only following your own orders—Geredd's family out—"

Storn snorted and seemed about to explode. *"My orders?"* he said tightly. "And did my orders say to put Geredd's family out in the middle of the night—in this storm?"

"Well," the soldier said uneasily, "I thought this might save us having to evict the rest of them this way. Make an example, like—"

"You thought?" Storn said. He looked pointedly at the shivering, crying children. "I must say that *this* gives me grave doubts about your ability to think."

Conn said, "Never mind that now. The important thing is to get these children to shelter." Storn seemed about to speak, but Conn turned his back and walked away, toward the woman with the swaddled children in her arms.

Lord Storn said roughly to the soldier, "Another time, listen when someone tells you something, man! Get back to barracks; you've caused enough trouble for one night."

The soldier opened his mouth to speak, looked at Lord Storn's angry face, and silently saluted, gave a sharp command to his men and they went away. Meanwhile Conn spoke to the woman.

"Twins," he said. "My own mother had just such an experience as this—and also by the courtesy of Lord Storn if I mistake it not—when my brother and I were not much more than a year old. Have you a place to go?"

She said shyly, "My sister married a man who works at the woolen mills in Neskaya; she an' her husband can take us in for a time at least."

"Good; then you shall go there. Markos—" he beckoned to the old man, "put this woman and the babies on my horse, and get one of your men—or two—to carry the smaller children. Take them to Hammerfell and give them shelter with one of our tenants; when it's daylight, get a farm cart and take them to Neskaya or wherever they wish; one of our men can drive them there and bring back the cart and donkey."

"But your horse, sir?"

"Never mind; do as I say, I'll make shift to get back somehow; I've got two good legs," Conn said, then asked the woman, "and when you get there?"

Marion Zimmer Bradley

"My husband's a sheep-shearer, sir; he's always in work, but we were turned out a few weeks ago with the babies coming—"

A rough-looking young man with sandy-red hair all awry in the wind, and dark eyes, came up beside the woman, and said to Conn, "I've always worked, all me life; but with four—no—six little mouths to feed, you can't tramp the roads. I kep' my house all my working days—and to be turned out—I never done nothin' to deserve it, sir, indeed I didn't. An' I'd stand up before the old lord himself and ask him what I done to deserve it."

Conn jerked his head sidewise and said, "There he stands. Ask him."

The young man scowled and lowered his eyes, but finally turned to Lord Storn and said, "Sir, why? What did we ever do to you that you'd have us put out by the roads this way? Twice now."

Storn stood very straight; Conn, watching, thought that he was trying hard to be dignified. It was hard indeed to be dignified by the road in a patched nightshirt that hardly covered his skinny old buttocks, though from somewhere he had found a horse blanket and was clutching it about his shoulders and shivering.

"Why, man—what's your name? Geredd didn't tell me, just that you were married to his older daughter."

The man touched his rough forelock.

"Ewen, m'lord."

"Well, Ewen, all that land's played out; no use for farming, an' it won't keep dairy animals; all it's good for is sheep. But sheep need space to run—acres an' acres. Why, you're a shearer, there'll be work in plenty for you, but we've got to get rid of all these

244

small-holdings and run the land together, can't you see? It's good sense—only a fool 'ud try to run thirty small farms on that played-out land up in the side hills. I'm truly sorry for all you people, but what can I do? If I starve because none of you can make a living, then none of us is any better off."

"But I'm not starving an' I've always paid my rents proper an' right up to the day," insisted Ewen. "I don't live by farming; why turn me out?"

Storn flushed red again and looked angry. "Yes, it may seem unfair to you. But my manager tells me I can't make any exceptions. If I let one small-holder stay, no matter how worthy—and no doubt you're one o' the worthy ones—then every one of them all will talk as if he had a special *right* to stay; and some of 'em have gotten so far behind I've had no rent for ten years, and some fifteen or twenty—before the big droughts began. I'm no tyrant—I've forgiven everybody here rent in at least one bad year. But enough's enough; there's got to be an end some-where. My lands are no good for farming and I won't keep farmers on them any more. No profit in it—and it does you folk no good if I go bankrupt."

Conn was struck by the inescapable logic and clar-ity of this. The Hammerfell estates were under the same crunch; would it really help if every small-holder were left alone to survive or go under on his own? Was Storn perhaps simply yielding to unpleas-ant necessity? He should talk at length with Alastair—and perhaps to Lord Storn himself. Storn, after all, had managed an estate in these hills for decades before he was born.

But there should be some way to allow for special cases, and if the land was no good for farming, and one man was holding all this land, should he not perhaps sit down with his estate manager and the tenants and decide fairly what was the best use of it, rather than one deciding for all, as Storn felt so ready to do?

Enough. He was *not,* in spite of having been trained for it, Duke of Hammerfell; he must consult with Alastair, and custom meant it must be for Alastair to decide. *Yes, even if he decides wrong,* said the voice which meant honor and law in his mind. Then the side of him which Markos had trained to tell himself: *I am responsible for all these men* reminded him that if Alastair cared nothing for them, he must still try to convince his brother to do what was right.

Storn was staring at him. The old man said truculently, "I suppose you are Hammerfell's brother, then; the other twin. Then you'll be the man who's been harrying my soldiers all summer and interfering with my orders."

Conn said, "Tonight, sir, we had no chance to interfere with your orders. Is it criminal to take a woman and six little children to shelter out of the rain?"

The old man had the grace to blush at that; but he continued, "Your men have been giving aid and comfort to anarchy—inciting my tenants to riot and rebel against me."

"No such thing," Conn said. "I have been in Thendara all this summer—nor have I ever incited anyone to rebellion or riot, in all my born days."

"And I suppose you didn't kill my nephew, either?" the old man demanded testily.

Conn was startled; in the heat of honest dispute he had all but forgotten the feud itself.

He said, "We did indeed kill *Dom* Rupert in the battle; but he was armed and attacking me and my men on grounds which had belonged for ages past to Hammerfell. I feel no guilt for that. I am not to blame for a feud which began before either you or I was born; I inherited this enmity—thanks to you it was my only inheritance, sir."

Storn scowled at him. He said, "There's truth to that, I suppose. Yet for years I thought the feud had been settled by the only settlement there usually is in such things—nobody left alive to carry it on."

"Well, that's not true," Conn said. "I'm here to say if you still want trouble, Lord Storn, my brother and I—" and then he stopped, remembering that Alastair was actually under Storn's roof.

In the abrupt silence, Storn remembered, too, and said quickly, "Have no fear for your brother; he's my guest, under fire-truce; he has saved the life of the only kin left living to me; my grandniece. He seems a reasonable person, and certainly I'd offer him no evil in return for that." After a moment more he said, musing, "Perhaps after all, young Hammerfell, this feud has gone on long enough—there are few enough of us left—"

"I'm asking no mercy from you," Conn said fiercely.

Storn's eyebrows met; he said, "No one will accuse you of cowardice, young man; yet there's enough trouble beyond our borders, perhaps we should not have enemies inside our very gates. The Aldarans and the Hasturs stand always ready to gobble up our domains while we quarrel—"

This made Conn think of King Aidan, whom he had so incomprehensibly come to love; yet Storn spoke of him as if he were the greater enemy of

247

them both. He said stiffly, "Mine is not the authority over Hammerfell these days, Lord Storn. It is not for me to say whether this enmity between our houses shall be honorably carried on, or honorably ended. Only the Duke of Hammerfell can answer to that, my lord. If you seek an end to this feud—"

"That remains to be seen," Storn interjected.

"If an end is to come," Conn amended, "it is for my brother to say, and not myself."

Storn scowled at him and then said, "It seems to me that you and your brother are like the man who didn't settle with his left hand what his right hand was doing, and tore himself into pieces trying to drive his team in two directions. I think you and your brother should settle between yourselves what it is you want; and then I will be ready to negotiate with you whether you want peace or war between us."

"I can hardly consult with my brother while you hold him in your castle, sir."

"I have said before this that he is my guest, not my prisoner; he is free to depart when he will, but I should be a sorry host if he left my roof before his burns were healed. If you wish to visit him and see for yourself that all is well, I pledge you that neither I, nor any man of Storn blood or allegiance shall offer either of you harm or insult . . . and you'll find my word as good as the word of a Hastur."

Storn was right; it was time to speak with Alastair. It went against the grain to trust a Storn; and yet it seemed to Conn that all of this could have ended long ago if anyone had been willing to trust anyone else. He had been impressed by the elderly Storn's openness and by his explanations of his actions; was he to trust his own feelings, or cling to an ancient enmity which had been set in motion before any of them was born and with which he had nothing to do?

"I will accept your safe-conduct," he said, "and I will go and speak with my brother."

Storn gestured to one of his men.

"Take young Hammerfell to Storn," he said, "and see that no harm comes to him, and that he may depart untouched when he will; my word of honor upon it."

Conn bowed to the old man; swung around looking for his horse, then remembered that he had directed Markos to take the young woman with the babies away. Well, he was young and strong, and the rain was beginning to abate. He strode away steadily toward Storn Heights, and not until he was out of sight did he even wonder where old Lord Storn would be housed this night.

17

Alastair and Lenisa found little to say after her grandfather left; perhaps because there was not much
which could be said while matters remained as they
were between them: Alastair pledged to another
woman, and Lenisa the grandniece of his oldest
enemy.

He wanted to tell her about Floria, but there was
really nothing he could say; it was a kind of arrogance to assume that she would have any interest in
his promised wife and an even worse arrogance to
assume that she would feel offended or resentful
because of this relationship.

The fact was that he wanted to tell her everything
about himself, but he had just been forcibly reminded
that she was a Storn, and not a woman to whom he
could in propriety express any personal interest, even
if he had not been pledged in marriage to another
woman. So they merely sat tongue-tied, looking at

one another sorrowfully. To break the painful silence, Lenisa finally reminded him that he had been admonished to rest because of his burns.

"I am not in pain now," Alastair said.

"I am very glad to hear it; but you are still in no condition to go out into the storm, or to ride on campaign," Lenisa reminded him. "I think you should sleep."

"But I am not even a little sleepy," Alastair said in a complaining tone.

"I am sorry for that, but still you know that you must rest; shall I go and ask Dame Jarmilla for a sleeping-draught for you?" she asked, as if she would be glad of something to do.

"No, no, don't put yourself to the trouble," said Alastair quickly, mostly not wanting her to leave him, for fear she might take this as an excuse to stay away.

All this time the old dog on the floor had remained motionless, only pricking up her ears now and again when Alastair spoke. Now she began to whine, prowling restlessly around the room. Lenisa looked at her curiously, and Alastair frowned, scolding her.

"Down, Jewel. Quiet, girl; behave yourself! Why, what's the matter with the creature? Jewel, lie down," he said sharply, but Jewel continued her restless pacing and whimpering.

"Does she need to go out? Shall I take her, or call Dame Jarmilla to walk her?" Lenisa asked, turning to the door. Jewel made a series of short rushes at the door, then stood there whining and imploring. As if in answer to the old dog's summons, Dame Jarmilla came in.

"Young mistress," she began, then broke off, "why, what ails your dog, sir?"

Jewel's whining became loud and insistent; Dame Jarmilla, trying to make herself heard over the sound, said, "There's a man outside who insists he is here to seek the Duke of Hammerfell—close relation to yourself, sir, judging by his face—"

"It must be my brother Conn," said Alastair, "That's what's wrong with the dog, of course; she knows Conn and was not expecting to see him here. Nor was I; I thought he was in Thendara." He hesitated. "May I beg you to receive him, *damisela?*"

"Bring him in," Lenisa said to Dame Jarmilla, who sniffed disapproval, but went, Jewel rushing after her. The dog returned in a moment, jumping and frisking around Conn, who came in, looking somewhat damp and bedraggled, for though the rain had abated briefly, it had not truly stopped, but instead turned to sleet. There were the beginnings of icicles in Conn's hair.

Lenisa looked at him with a childlike giggle. She said, "Surely this must be the first time in all the history of Storn Heights that we have under our roof not one but *two* Dukes of Hammerfell. Well, I suppose you can tell yourselves apart if no one else can. Which of you was it I met in the tavern in Lowerhammer, who cost me a bowl of porridge with honey?"

"It was I," said Alastair, a trifle annoyed that she should ask. "You might have known that from the dog."

"Really? But look how the poor girl is greeting your brother, as if delighted to greet her real master," said Lenisa, and at Alastair's scowl, added, "well, you cannot blame me for not making a distinction between you if your own dog, who knows you both much better than I do, does not."

This was so true that Alastair felt guilty for his own annoyance at it, and was also by reflex angry at Jewel for what seemed, and felt like, betrayal. He said sharply, "Down, Jewel; behave yourself."

"No need to be angry with the dog," said Conn roughly. "She's not done anything to be ashamed of. But of all the places I had expected to find you, brother, surely this is the last; snug under Storn's roof, while that same Storn's been out harrying our people out of their homes into the rain."

Alastair just scowled and said, "I thought you were in Thendara to care for our mother. Did you leave her alone and unprotected, then?"

"Our mother has many who wish to protect her," Conn said. "But she is here, safe, and Floria and Gavin are with her. When we realized you were hurt, and in Storn's hands, did you expect us all to remain in Thendara and do nothing?"

"Well, yes, I did," Alastair said. "After all, I am in no danger here; Lord Storn has been most courteous and hospitable."

"So I see," said Conn dryly, with a sidelong look at Lenisa. "Is his granddaughter included in his hospitality?"

Alastair scowled; Conn could read in his thoughts that he was more offended for Lenisa's sake than his own. Alastair said dryly that the question did not arise; that the *damisela* was his hostess and had tended his wounds kindly; that there had been no question of anything more.

"I know not how you deal with women in the mountains," Alastair said reprovingly, "but in Thendara, one would not speak so even about the daughter—or for that matter, the grandniece—of one's worst enemy."

"Yet I find you here alone with her at this godforgotten hour of the night; are you so badly wounded, then, brother, that you must be woman-watched all night?"

"In Thendara, one need not be at death's door to be trusted in the presence of a lady," Alastair said, and Conn could read the unspoken part of that: *This brother of mine will always be a country bumpkin, with no more knowledge of tact nor of gallantry than his own dog.*

Conn said, "All the same I must talk with you, brother; can we dispense then with the presence of the *damisela*?"

"I have nothing to say to you that couldn't be said in her presence, or in the presence of the Gods themselves, for all I have to say is simple truth," Alastair said. "Please don't go, Lenisa."

I don't want her out of my sight. Until this moment, Alastair had not clearly admitted that to himself; now he knew it. And Conn who heard his thoughts, said sharply, "And Floria, what of her? She is waiting for you at our mother's side, while you cannot even keep your straying fancy off Storn's own kin."

"You chide me for that?" Alastair said sharply, "when you cannot even keep *your* own eyes off my promised wife."

I thought Alastair had no laran; *how then does he read my thoughts? Is it as obvious as all that?* Conn demanded of himself with a sense of guilty dread.

Conn said gently, "Brother, I've no wish to quarrel

with you, above all, not here under this of all roofs. I have spoken with Lord Storn, and since you are here, I should imagine that you have, too. . . ."

Alastair's anger, far from being quieted by his tone, flamed instead.

So for all his talk of accepting me as duke and overlord, he feels that he will go behind my back and settle all this with Lord Storn without so much as consulting me; he feels that Hammerfell and the men of Hammerfell are all still under his orders!

So, Conn thought, *he feels that after twenty years spent in the city, far from Hammerfell, a fop and a good-for-nothing, he can walk in and settle this by diplomacy without reference to the long history which is between Hammerfell and Storn. What honor is there in that?* With all his heart he wished his brother could read his mind; instead it must all be laboriously put into words, and Conn knew he had small skill with words, while Alastair, skilled in city ways, knew exactly how to talk his way round the real issues.

And he's in love with this girl—Storn's grandniece. Does she know it? Does she have laran?

He said at last, slowly, "I suppose, Alastair, it's up to you to send out the word to raise what men are still pledged to fight for Hammerfell. After that, King Aidan—" he broke off short.

Lenisa said, interrupting him, "It must come to war, then? I had hoped, when you and my great-uncle talked together so reasonably, that some way could be found to bring an end to this long hostility—"

Alastair said, looking at Lenisa and avoiding Conn's eyes, "Is that what you want, *Domna* Lenisa, that we should make peace?"

Unexpectedly, Conn, who had been trying to remain reasonable, was so angry he could not contain his temper.

"This is why I feel the lady should leave us; there are many important things to talk about which cannot be settled by women," he rasped sharply.

Alastair said, "Your country upbringing shows discourtesy, my brother; in civilized parts of the world, women are expected to join with men in making important decisions which, after all, concern them just as much as their men. Would you seek to exclude our mother, who is a Tower worker, from any important decision like this? Or is it only that Lenisa is too young to share in making these decisions?"

"She is a *Storn,*" Conn responded angrily; and Lenisa leaned forward and said, "It is because of that that this decision concerns me. I represent half of this ancient feud; I inherited it as you did, I lost my father to it as did you—although, the Gods know, I hardly knew him—how can you say I am not concerned in it, that I should sit quietly on the sidelines and let others decide what's to be done?"

Conn began reasonably, *"Damisela,* I have no enmity toward you; only in name, quite literally, could anyone call you enemy. You have neither fought nor killed, you are this feud's victim, not one of its causes."

Lenisa said angrily, "You speak as if I were a child or feeble of mind; because I do not take up the sword and fight at my grandsire's side does not mean I know nothing of this ancient feud."

"Now I have made you angry, and I did not mean to," said Conn, "I was simply trying—"

"Trying to make me into a nothing, because only men have a right to speak out in such things," Lenisa raged. "At least your brother admits that I have a legitimate interest in what concerns my clan and my family! He believes that I am human and have a right to my own thoughts and to speak openly of what concerns me instead of whispering it to my husband for *him* to take my part!"

Conn said uncomfortably, trying to make a joke of it, "I did not know that you had taken up the vow of the Sisterhood of the Sword—"

"I haven't," Lenisa said, "but I feel I have a right to speak, for this feud concerns me as much as it does my grandfather; maybe more, since he is an old man and whatever may be decided will concern him only for a few more years at most; whereas I, and my children if I have any, must live with it for all our lives."

Conn said heavily, after a moment, "You are right. Forgive me, *Domna* Lenisa; do you feel, then, that my brother and I should deal with you instead of your grandfather?"

"I did not say that; you are making fun of me. I said only that it concerns me as much as it concerns my grandfather and therefore I am entitled to a voice in it."

"Well, go ahead and say what you've got on your mind, then," Conn said. "What do you feel about this feud? Do you want to carry it on for another hundred years because our ancestors hated and killed one another?"

Lenisa stared at the wall, and her jaws clenched as if she were trying not to cry. She said at last, "I would rather not think of Alastair as my enemy. Or you, either; I feel no enmity toward you, nor does my grandfather any longer; he spoke to your brother as a friend. What do *you* want, Hammerfell?"

Sentimental nonsense, Conn thought. *This is no more than a romantic girl's infatuation with a handsome man, when she has known too few of such.* Yet the straightforwardness with which she had spoken touched him; he admired her honesty.

Alastair reached out and took her hand, saying gently, "I would rather not be your foe, Lenisa. Maybe we can find a way to be friends." He raised his eyes suddenly to his brother's with a belligerent stare. "And now you may call me a traitor to Hammerfell, if you will—"

"No such thing," Conn said. "Maybe this old feud has served its purpose. One thing which Lord Storn said really touched me; he said that there were so many outside enemies that mountain folk should not quarrel among themselves. He said the Hasturs and Aldarans were pressing us from either side hoping to gobble up our kingdoms under their rule—and perhaps we should all unite against them. It would go hard with me to think of King Aidan as my enemy—"

"—and yet he has promised us help in regaining Hammerfell," Alastair said.

Lenisa rose and began to pace the room; Jewel prowled at her heels, her teeth bared, her toes clicking on the bare floor.

"Oh, he has, has he? And by what right does he offer that? What right has he to interfere in this matter?" she said, and it was perfectly obvious that she was so angry she could hardly speak. "I do not want to see all this land just another fief held under the Hasturs, who seem determined to spread their reign from Temora to the Wall Around the World."

"You do not know King Aidan," said Conn. "I do

THE HEIRS OF HAMMERFELL

not think he is personally ambitious; but he wants peace and order in the land. He hates these small wars and the bloodshed and the upheaval and turmoil which follow them. He would like to see this realm at peace."

"And when we are all subject to the reign of Hasturs," Lenisa said, "what will happen to such men as my grandsire?"

"The only way to know that," Alastair said, "would be to ask them both when they stand face to face."

"Perhaps that can be arranged. Indeed, if King Aidan comes hither it is sure to happen sooner or later," Conn said, "but we pledged ourselves to raise men here against Storn, so that the king could legitimately raise an army to put down rebellion from Aldaran." By revealing this much of King Aidan's plan he felt he was being disloyal.

"Why must we have Aidan's armies here, if we can settle this feud among ourselves and find strength in unity?" Alastair asked. "Surely even a threat from Aldaran concerns ourselves, and not any lowland lords, even the Hasturs."

Lenisa said, "Granted I do not understand all these things, but I have heard there was a treaty by which all this land is held under the Hasturs and we cannot make agreements among ourselves without their consent. When Geremy, the first of that name reigned in Asturias—"

"It seems, then, that the thing to do would be to try and bring Aidan here *without* his armies," Alastair interjected.

"And that's the question," Lenisa said. "How do we persuade Aidan to come here in peace?" She came and perched on the end of Alastair's bed.

"If the king's mind is set on making war in the mountains—"

"I don't think he *wants* to make war. My impression was that he thought it a distressing necessity which he feared he could find no way to avoid," Conn told her.

"Somehow or other, then, we must persuade Aidan to come here without his armies—" Alastair began, "but if we do that, he is likely to feel we are trying to lure him here unarmed for some traitorous purpose—"

"Rubbish," Lenisa interrupted. "Tell him he can bring all the bodyguards or honor guards he wants; but no armies to stir up trouble by riding all over the crops and being quartered upon poor folk in the village who have hardly enough to feed themselves, let alone to give to the army's quartermasters."

"Just a minute," Conn said, "I have spoken with King Aidan and I think he is well disposed toward us, or at least to our cause. But I have no power to bid the king to come or to stay. He has offered us armies, but I do not know if he ever had it in his mind to come here himself."

"Then somehow he must be persuaded to come," Lenisa said. "Is there anyone you know—your mother perhaps, who has spent all these years in Thendara— who has the ear of the king or perhaps some member of the royal family?"

Alastair said, "The king's cousin, Valentine Hastur, has been seeking for years to persuade my mother to marry him—but I would not wish to ask Mother to use her influence in *that* way. And I do not think she would do it if I asked."

"One of my closest friends is the queen's foster

son, the son of one of her favorite cousins," Alastair continued, "but he is in Thendara—"

"If you are speaking of Gavin," said Conn, "he insisted on coming with us, and he is in Markos's cottage at this moment, looking after Mother and Floria. Certainly he has the ear of the king, or at least of the queen—" Conn continued more sadly, "But the queen is in no condition to lend anyone aid. When we left Thendara she was terribly ill, and in grave danger for her life."

This unhappy news cast a pall over everyone, but through the momentary quiet in the bedchamber, a commotion could be heard in the hall, and a moment later Dame Jarmilla came in.

"Mistress, the lord gave orders you were to go to bed early; how many people are going to come here tonight and demand to see your guests?"

"I was expecting no one," said Lenisa, her pretty blue eyes wide and innocent, "but unless it is a band of armed mercenaries, let them come in, whoever they are."

Grumbling, Dame Jarmilla went to the door, and flung it open.

Gavin Delleray, soaked to the skin, his elaborately curled and dyed hair sagging and dripping onto his collar, came into the room.

"Alastair, my dear fellow! For no reason at all, the very strangest thing! I was sleeping in Markos's cottage, and I woke out of a sound sleep; I had been dreaming that I was in King Aidan's throne room and he demanded that I come at once—at *once*, mind you, in this rain and not even a decent umbrella to be had anywhere in the village—and see how you fared here." He looked apologetic, and bowed to Lenisa and Dame Jarmilla.

"On my honor, *mestra*, I mean no harm to anyone beneath this roof, or for that matter any other," he said. "I am a minstrel, not a soldier."

Oh, is that so? Conn thought, startled. *I wondered at the time why it was that Gavin insisted on coming with us; But I should have know that King Aidan would have wanted eyes and ears on this journey. Gavin himself did not understand what he was doing here; but I should have known. . . .*

Alastair and Lenisa had evidently come to the same conclusion. They were both talking at once, and Gavin held up a hand in entreaty.

"Please, I beg of you," he said, "let me at least dry myself a little by the fire before you enroll me in your intrigues."

Lenisa looked delighted.

"Some angel sent you to us," she said. "Or are you yourself an angel come in our need?"

Dame Jarmilla sniffed.

"The *cristoforos* say that angels may be found in strange places," she remarked. "But surely it is the only time in all of history that any God has had enough of a sense of humor to send an angelic messenger who dyes his hair purple."

Gavin stared. "Who, me? An angel? Lord of Light, you must indeed be hard up for messengers! What's this all about, then?"

Alastair sat up, reaching for a folded blanket across the foot of his bed, and flung it to his friend. He said, "My dear fellow, sit down by the fire and dry your clothes; and if the excellent Dame Jarmilla could be persuaded to bring a hot drink of some sort? If you take the lung fever, you'll be no good at all to any of us." Dame Jarmilla went to fetch the kettle hanging over the fire and busied herself with some kind of potion that steamed and smelled delicious.

"And when you get yourself dry," he began, "never in my life have I so much regretted that I have no *laran*; but perhaps it is enough to have a friend who has not only *laran* but the ear of the king. If you'll help us, Gavin, perhaps we can prevent war breaking out in these hills." He chuckled and added, "Maybe when it's over, you can make a ballad out of it."

18

They were awake very late, talking half the night about how Gavin should link with King Aidan and try to persuade him to come peacefully, with no more than his personal bodyguard and honor guard, for the purpose of burying the feud between Storn and Hammerfell which had raged for all these generations.

"But," Lenisa reminded them, "that may be the last thing the Hastur king wants; for if there is peace in the Hellers, he has small excuse to extend his kingdom into this part of the world."

"To that I can only say that you do not know King Aidan," Conn replied. "If you did, I think you would trust him as I do."

"It could be," said Lenisa, "but if Aidan is a mighty *laranzu*, able to read men's minds at a distance, perhaps he could make me wish to be his vassal even without my consent."

It was Alastair who answered that, for Conn had never thought of such a thing. He said, "I am not all that familiar with the mind of the king; but my own mother has been a *leronis* since I can remember, and if she were able to force obedience against a person's will, I would have been less of a rascal. She brought me up with the knowledge that the first law of *laran* is that it must never be used to force the mind or will; if Floria were here, she could quote for you the Monitor's Oath, which is the first obligation of any *leronis*—to 'enter no mind unconsenting, save to help or heal,' " he quoted.

"That is what I have heard during my schooling," said Lenisa, "but who knows what a Hastur—one of the sorcerer kings—might define as 'helping' or 'healing,' or as being for someone's own good."

Alastair looked at her, and to Conn it seemed that his brother's whole heart, such as it was, had poured itself into his eyes.

Shallow; he is a fool and shallow, if he would give up Floria for this one, Conn thought, *and an ancient feud with the honor of our ancestors at stake for the craven comforts of peace. War for a Hammerfell is an honorable endeavor; but what has this vaunted peace with Storn to offer us? We have yet to hear that Storn intends to return our lands, or rebuild our castle. Honor demands that we continue this ancient strife at least till we have avenged our father,* he thought. But though he had lived his life for the thought of revenge, he was confused, and Lenisa was looking at him almost as if she read his thoughts, with a sad look of skepticism.

He tried for a moment to see Lenisa through his brother's eyes, and she seemed little more than any of the simple country girls with whom he had played as a child, danced with at harvest and Midsummer festivals all during his childhood. Pretty, yes, he supposed she was pretty, with oval features, pink cheeks, shining fair hair looped into braids, wearing a simple tartan dress of blue and dark green.

In his mind he contrasted her with Floria; tall and elegant, with striking features, deep-set eyes, and soft speech. She was a trained *leronis*; a person could easily assume she would never brew a drink, or fetch mulled wine for a guest with her own hands . . . but this would certainly not be true, Floria had helped to housebreak and train the puppy Copper herself, and had not stinted the labor of her hands. Floria was no more a useless fine lady than Lenisa, and had her own component of skills to which she had been trained. But in addition, Floria was beautiful, noble and educated, a *leronis* in her own right, while Lenisa was only a pretty and unsophisticated country girl. Well, it would be easy to draw wrong conclusions about Floria; Lenisa, too, might have virtues which were not apparent, and if he knew her better he could value her at nearer to her true worth.

That night Conn slept on the floor of his brother's room; surely this was the first time, as Lenisa said—or was it the swordswoman Dame Jarmilla—that Storn had housed not one but two Hammerfells. He dreamed of King Aidan, and felt disloyal; he had displaced onto Gavin the task of making it clear to Aidan that the king's promised armies were not needed. But what, then, of the threat from Aldaran? And even so he wondered—was it only his country upbringing?—if indeed Alastair and Gavin were somehow in league against him. He didn't really trust these city people. And as he fell asleep, his awareness drifted through closed doors to where Lenisa slept, with Dame Jarmilla on a cot in the corridor, so that she could watch the door of Lenisa's room and make sure there was no unauthorized coming and going into Lenisa's chamber.

Alastair woke him early the next morning; snow was rattling softly against the window.

"You must take your horse, brother," he said, troubled. "She is in Storn's stables. Ride her back to Markos's cottage, for our mother should be kept advised of what we are planning. And I know not when it will be suitable or possible for me to leave here."

"And because of Lenisa, you don't want to leave," Conn said.

"You should be the last to reproach me for that," Alastair said, not without a flare of anger, "since it will leave Floria to fall into your arms—do you think I didn't know you were mad for her the first moment you saw her?"

"Can you blame me for that? And why should I not, since it's obvious that you don't love as you should."

"That's not fair,' said Alastair. "I do love her. I have known her since we were seven years old. Until I came here, I thought life could hold for me no happier destiny than to marry Floria—"

"Then why have you changed your mind? Do you now think it's better to marry this Storn girl—for political reasons?"

"One would almost think you did not want to bring this feud to an end," Alastair accused, now truly angry.

267

"I would have no objection to an *honorable* end to it," Conn said, "with the return of our lands and keep and assurances that no harm would come to our people. You may not care much about them; there is probably no reason that you should. Certainly you do not know them. But I have lived among them all my life and I feel honor bound to take care of them. Do you think you can do it just by marrying one of the Storn women?"

"*The* Storn woman," Alastair snapped, "She and Lord Storn are the only ones left of that kindred. With Storn dead and Lenisa married to a Hammerfell, the feud ends naturally, with no one left to carry it on."

"Are you planning to murder your host, then?" Conn snarled sarcastically. "I don't know what the custom is in the city, but here that sort of behavior is frowned upon."

"No, of course I don't—" Alastair shot back, as Gavin sat up in his bedroll by the hearth and groaned.

"What are you two fighting about now?" He raked his fingers through his hair, which was straying in all directions at once. "What time is it anyway? It's barely daylight out!"

"Conn is accusing me of a plot to murder Lord Storn," Alastair replied. "Pretty cheeky for my *little* brother."

"You certainly seem ready enough to forget your pledge to Floria," Conn pointed out, "so how can you expect me to understand the delicate shades of your definition of honor?"

But Alastair, rather than rise to the bait, sat thinking for a moment, and then said wonderingly, "The fact is that I am *not* pledged to Floria. I am sorry for

Queen Antonella's illness, but because of her sudden affliction, the handfasting did not actually take place—"

Conn said just as thoughtfully, "And of the guests there that night, how many knew to which of us Floria was to be pledged?"

Gavin looked amused, as if he knew something they did not. "And it's such a wonderfully traditional ending to a feud, for the two families to join together in marriage—I assume, Alastair, that you *do* wish to marry Lady Storn—the *damisela* Lenisa, that is?" Alastair nodded, and Gavin continued, "and if Conn wishes to marry Floria, I doubt if your mother will mind, since she will still have Floria as a daughter, so all you have to do is persuade Lord Edric . . ."

"And Floria," Conn interjected, "unless you think she's a bargaining counter to be traded about at her father's whim."

"Yes, of course," Gavin agreed. "You should both speak to Floria, but I am certain that she will agree to do her part in ending this dreadful feud. After all, if she married Alastair and the feud continued, she'd be losing her children to it. But will Storn give his consent?"

Alastair shrugged. "We shall simply have to ask him and find out," he said, as the door to the room was opened.

"Ask me what?" Lord Storn stood in the doorway. Although no one answered him out loud, he seemed to have heard the answer anyway.

Does he have laran? Conn wondered.

"Of course I do, boy," Storn replied. "The Storns have always had it. Don't the Hammerfells? He did not wait for either of them to answer. "So you want to marry my grandniece, do you" he said, turning to Alastair. "First, why don't you tell me about your promised wife, the one who's staying in the village with your mother."

"*Domna* Floria," Alastair said slowly. "Well, you see, sir, our families are friends, and I've known her since we were children, so when she was proposed to me as a bride, I thought myself lucky. She's a lovely girl. But then I met Lenisa, and—now I have fallen in love with her."

"Have you?" Lord Storn said consideringly. "That's all very well for the first few months, young man, but after that what keeps you together? I don't hold with all this nonsense about love and romance; never have, never will. A suitable marriage arranged by your parents has a much better chance of success; that way you don't have unrealistic expectations." He scowled. "Still, Lenisa has to marry—unless I'm prepared to let my blood die out altogether, which I am *not*. Aldaran of Scathfell wants her for his brother, but I'm not sure . . . I'll think about it, boy, I'll think about it."

He looked at Gavin, who was still sitting on the bedroll beside the fire. "I don't believe I've met you." Gavin rose hastily to his feet as Alastair performed the introductions. "So you're the Hastur king's cousin, are you?"

"Only by marriage, sir," Gavin said respectfully.

"And you're proposing to lure him up here to talk to us all?"

"If you agree, sir," Gavin said. "I wouldn't wish to bring King Aidan into any danger."

"Always danger here in the hills," Storn snorted. "If the feuds are quiet, and the bandits aren't raiding, it's the Aldarans, out to extend their territory. But I'll give you my word, your king is in no danger from me; I'll be happy to talk things over with him if he wishes." He scowled down at the bedroll. "Is this the best my household can provide for guests?" He stalked to the door and yelled. "Lenisa!" The echoes of his voice in the hall were followed by running footsteps as Lenisa came to answer him.

"Yes, Grandfather?"

He pointed an accusing finger at the bedroll. "Is that the best you can do for a guest? Have another chamber prepared for *Dom* Gavin, and one for Lady Hammerfell and her ward."

"Mother and Floria are coming here?" Conn gasped.

"With both of you under my roof why should they not be here as well?" Storn demanded. "Surely you don't think a peasant's hut the place to house your mother and your promised wife—or Alastair's promised wife—or *whoever's* promised wife she is! And I hardly think Hammerfell Castle is in any shape to house them. I have called them here myself."

Alastair glared Conn to silence. "Indeed, sir, we are most grateful for your hospitality."

Conn hoped that Lord Storn did not hear his mental addition. *Especially since it's due to you that we have need of it.*

If he did, however, he didn't show it. He merely said, "Since we appear to have a lot to discuss, we might as well do it in comfort. I've had quite enough of being out in the snow for the time being. Come, girl," he turned to Lenisa. "We'd best prepare to receive our guests."

"Is walking the boundaries *that* bad?" Alastair asked, and Conn realized that he knew nothing of the latest burning. When Lord Storn had left the room, he told his brother about it, thinking, *Perhaps it will be for the best for Alastair to marry Lenisa. At least she knows the customs of the Hellers, and can persuade him to follow them.*

"But do you really think our mother and Floria will be safe here?" Conn asked, as he finished his story.

"Don't worry about Floria," Alastair said unconcernedly. "She's not part of this feud."

"*Domna* Erminie should be safe enough," Gavin said, "King Aidan knows we're here, and would never stand for us to be harmed—I think we needn't worry."

That successfully silenced both twins; they knew no more powerful protector than the Hastur king.

Conn returned to the village at the ruined gates of Hammerfell and spent the morning exercising the horse that Alastair had ridden so long and hard. In the afternoon he escorted Ermine and Floria to Storn Heights. He was relieved to see that Erminie seemed at once to like Lenisa; it would have greatly complicated things if for some reason his mother had taken a dislike to her. He hardly dared to speak to or look at Floria; the idea that he might actually be free to marry her was almost more than he could take in. Indeed, the conference after dinner was a model of harmony. *Lenisa must have had a long talk with Lord Storn*, Conn thought with amusement. *He seems much more agreeable to her marrying Alastair than he did this morning.* And Floria had obviously noticed something, for she sat next to Conn at dinner and assumed a rather proprietary attitude toward him. Conn was not surprised to find that he liked it, although he

wondered if he had Gavin to thank for her obvious
change in attitude. What had Gavin told her about
this morning's discussion?

This question, at least, was quickly answered. When
they sat down in the solar with their mulled wine, it
was Floria who opened the conversation in a direct
and frank manner. "I understand, Alastair, that you
do not wish to marry me."

Alastair gulped and looked uneasy. *Even in Thendara,
they cannot teach a graceful and courteous way to jilt your
betrothed,* Conn thought with some amusement, *for all
their elegant lowland etiquette.*

"I have and always will have the greatest respect
for you, dear cousin—" Alastair began, "but—"

"It's all right, Alastair," Floria said gently. "I'm
willing to release you from the betrothal, which, after all, was never made formal. I simply wanted to
have it made plain to everyone that this is what we
both want."

"Both?" Alastair said lightly. "Am I to have you
for a sister, then?" Everyone looked at Conn.

"Yes," Conn said buoyantly, "if the lady wishes it,
nothing would make me happier."

Floria put out her hand and took his, smiling
brilliantly. "Nothing would make me happier, either."

"And I suppose that now you expect me to consent to my grandniece becoming Duchess of Hammerfell," Storn growled, obviously having a bit of trouble
articulating the words.

"I would certainly prefer to marry her with your
consent, sir," Alastair said politely.

"And without it? Are you saying you'll marry her
whether I give it or not? Is that what you're saying?"

273

Storn turned to glare at Erminie. "A fine son you've raised, my lady! What do you think of all this?"

Erminie looked briefly at her hands, clasped in her lap, then lifted her head and looked Storn in the eye. "My lord," she said sweetly, "it seems to me that this feud has gone on for too many generations, and all those who began it are dead. I've lost my childhood playmate and my husband both to it, and for many years, I believed I had lost one of my young sons as well. You've lost all of your kin save Lenisa. Haven't there been enough deaths—both your people and mine? Whatever the original offenses may have been, surely by now we've shed enough blood between us to wash clean all the Hundred Kingdoms! If my son wishes to marry your grandniece, I rejoice at the chance to bury this old feud forever, I swear Lenisa will be as a daughter to me, and I give them my blessing. I implore you to do the same, my lord."

"And my alternative, I suppose," Storn said with the appearance of bitterness—but his eyes twinkled, "is to be the ogre of the piece; to refuse and let you go and raise up a rabble against me, and then the Hastur king will come with *his* army, and there will be burning and destruction all over both our lands— and then when I die you'll take the girl anyway, assuming you both survive the fighting."

"Put like that, sir," Gavin said quietly, "it doesn't sound like much of an alternative. But must you put it that way? Can't you think of it as a chance to be the hero who brings an end to all this fighting?"

Lord Storn scowled. "That doesn't sound like much of an alternative either. My own father'd be turning over in his grave. Well, he didn't live his life for my good pleasure, I see no reason I should live my life for his. I don't approve of love matches, myself; but here you are, lady, to speak for your son, and I have to give my great-niece to somebody, I suppose. Very well, girl," he addressed Lenisa, "if you want to marry him, then I won't be the one to stand in your way. Better to make Storn and Hammerfell one kingdom than lose both to Aldaran. You do want to?" he glared at her with his fierce eyes. "You're not just going along with this because you think it's romantic, or some such rubbish? Well, marry him, then, if it suits you."

"Oh, thank you, Grandfather," she cried, hugging him.

Alastair rose and extended his hand. "Thank you, sir." He swallowed hard. "I can't tell you how grateful I am. May we name our first son after you?" Alastair blushed furiously but stood firm.

"Ardrin of Hammerfell? My great-grandfather would be doing handsprings in his grave, but—well, yes, if you like." Storn tried not to look pleased. He took Alastair's hand briefly. "But mind that you always treat her well, young man; even when this first infatuation wears off, always remember that she is your wife—and, the Gods willing, mother of your children."

"I promise you that, my lord—Great-uncle," Alastair said fervently. It was obvious that Alastair didn't believe he would ever feel differently about Lenisa, and Erminie was looking indignant, but at least the fact that he'd said it seemed to make Lord Storn feel a bit better about the whole business.

"Well, that's settled," he said. "I suppose you'd better send word to that king of yours about it. You can tell him I offer him hospitality—but I've only got room for thirty or so of his guards in the barracks and I can't ask my people to accept strange lowlanders quartered on them, with all else they've got to bear these days; mind you tell him that, young man," he admonished Gavin.

Gavin nodded, settled deeper in his chair and closed his eyes.

"Doesn't he need his matrix?" Lord Storn muttered.

"Not to talk to the Hastur-lord," Erminie whispered softly.

Alastair found himself wondering about the unknown *laran* of the Hasturs. But everyone else took it for granted; they all sat in silence for several minutes, waiting for Gavin to open his eyes. After about ten minutes he did and reached for his wine glass. Floria shoved the plate of biscuits toward him, and he took one and ate it before speaking.

"He'll be here within a tenday," Gavin reported. "Queen Antonella is doing much better than expected, so he feels he can leave her. And since he canceled all his engagements to sit with her while she was ill, nobody expects him to be anyplace else. So he'll slip quietly out of the city with twenty of his guards—no need to strain your hospitality, Lord Storn—and come straight here."

"Very well," Storn said. "Lenisa, you'll see all made ready for His Grace's visit."

"I'll help, if you permit," Floria said, looking shyly at Lenisa with a tentative smile.

Lenisa hesitated for a moment, then returned the smile. "That would be very kind of you," she said. "I do not know what a Hastur king may expect in the way of protocol—sister."

Floria knew the girl was torn between shyness and a fear that the Thendara *laranzu* might despise her as an awkward country girl.

"Oh, you need not worry about that, my dear," she said, giving Lenisa a spontaneous hug. "King Aidan is the kindest of men; within half an hour you will be thinking of him as your favorite uncle, as if you'd known him all your life. Won't she, Gavin?"

19

Conn found himself feeling strangely uneasy about the end of the feud and King Aidan's coming visit. Maybe he had a suspicious nature, but it all seemed too easy to him, too good to be true. Being told he could marry Floria was like a beautiful dream but one he kept expecting to wake from. Riding through the hills a few days later, checking to see how his—no, Alastair's—tenants were doing, it struck him that everything that had happened since he left for Thendara seemed like a dream—something he couldn't quite believe in.

He confided his anxieties to Gavin, and Gavin laughed. "I know what you mean," he said. "If this were a ballad, there would have to be another complication, preferably with a great battle, to make a satisfying ending."

"Well, I certainly don't want that," Conn said. "By the way, how goes it with King Aidan and his Queen?"

Gavin, who had been checking in with the king each night, replied, "The lady is safe in Renata's hands, and while her recovery may be slow—and it's hardly likely she will ever be her old self—it's unlikely she will be gravely incapacitated either. As for the king, he crossed the Kadarin late yesterday and should be reaching the foothills this evening."

"You must be a powerful *laranzu*," Conn said, "to reach him that far away."

"Not really," Gavin said. "I actually have very little *laran*; it's mostly the power of the king that holds the link. It seems that *you* are the truly powerful *laranzu*; in fact, you could probably survey the condition of the lands and tenants from here," he gestured around the solar, where they were sitting, "and save yourself many hours out on horseback in bad weather."

"I like riding," Conn said calmly, "and as for bad weather, you haven't seen any of it yet." But he thought about what Gavin had said. "You really think I could see much from here?"

Gavin shrugged. "Try it," he said.

Conn took out his starstone and focused on it, lying back against the pillows. Suddenly he seemed to have risen and crossed to the windows, but when he looked back, he saw himself still sitting in the chair. He took another step forward and floated through the window and down to the ground. He was starting to walk down the road from the castle when he remembered some old stories he had heard, about *leroni* who flew on the mountain winds, using large gliders. He didn't have a glider with him, but then, he seemed free of his body at the moment, so perhaps . . .

Apparently simply thinking about it was enough; he found himself floating over the trees. Should he go to Hammerfell? No, he'd ridden all over those lands yesterday and the day before—and he had always wondered what lay on the far side of Storn's borders.

Several minutes of drifting brought him to a point over a large stone keep. *Scathfell*, he thought, remembering Storn's comments about Aldaran. On the wings of thought he moved over fields and hedges, crowded with flocks of woolly sheep. Near the main part of the keep many men were gathered. *It's not harvest festival nor a hiring fair*, he thought, *can it possibly be time for a roundup, a sheep shearing?* But as, impalpably, he moved closer, he noted that none of them bore shearing scissors and that most of them were armed with swords and pikes. Half a dozen men in what looked like Aldaran livery, with the blazoning of the Aldaran emblem, the double-headed eagle, were mustering the men into squads that looked alarmingly like an army. . . .

But why was Scathfell raising his men like this? There was no conflict in the hills, except his own family's private feud, and Aldaran had never interfered in that. But raising them he certainly was, to judge by the look of it. Conn could not at the moment imagine why.

I had better go back, and perhaps send someone out with a glider, if only to gather more information about what is happening in these hills. He was beginning to understand that there was more to ruling Hammerfell than administering the tenants or even making decisions between farms and sheep.

Maybe I should have a long talk with Lord Storn and

find out more about the business of a great estate like this one. Although of course this is really more Alastair's business than mine; Mother expects me to return with her—and Floria—to take my place there in the Tower for training. But am I to be a laranzu *for the rest of my days?* he wondered. It did not seem like the kind of work he would be satisfied to do forever; and yet he knew in his heart that if he remained here, he could only dilute Alastair's authority with the men who had come to think of Conn as their young duke. But it did not seem right for him to desert his people, or to stand peacefully by while Alastair adopted Storn's policy of turning men off the lands to seek work in Thendara or elsewhere, in favor of the endless sheep.

He had been trained to be responsible for these people! Did Alastair have the *least* concept of what it meant to be Duke of Hammerfell? For that matter, did his mother even know anything about it? She had married into the line when she was a young girl. He could not blame her; but the fact was that she probably knew almost nothing whatever about it. For a short time Conn drifted, caught up in his personal dilemma; but Scathfell was mustering, and he must somehow act—he must get back to Storn Heights and Gavin.

Thinking about Gavin, Conn found himself suddenly back in his body in the solar. His friend swiftly gauged Conn's mood and said, "What's wrong?"

"I don't know for sure that anything's really *wrong*," Conn answered, "but I don't understand what's going on. . . ." He described what he had seen at Aldaran.

Gavin looked grave and said, "The lady Erminie must hear of this."

Conn didn't know what Erminie could do about it,

but Gavin seemed so sure that he did not protest. Erminie came into the room at Conn's summons, took her own starstone, and went to see for herself. When she opened her eyes again they held a look of fear. "But this is terrible! Scathfell is arming, and marching against King Aidan's people. He has at least three hundred men."

"Against Aidan! But he has only an honor guard," Gavin said. "Perhaps twenty men at best."

"He will think we lured him into these hills without knowing," Conn said swiftly. "Someone should ride at once to warn him—"

"But no one could reach him in time," Erminie said despairingly, "unless . . ."

"Well, I could *try*," Gavin said without much hope, "but it is hard enough when it is night and all is quiet—"

"Three hundred men," Conn said in dismay. "King Aidan could not face so many with only his honor guard even if we armed the bears and rabbits."

He was restating an old proverb; but to his surprise Erminie smiled.

"We can do that," she said.

20

For a moment both young men stared at Erminie as if she had taken leave of her senses.

Then Gavin said, "You're joking, of course?" But he did not sound sure.

Erminie said, "I never joke about such things. Were you joking when you told me Aidan has only an honor guard with him?"

She sounded positively hopeful; for the first time, Conn realized the vast implications of *laran* power. He could feel, as within himself, his mother's unwillingness to use all she knew; and with the knowledge came a kind of sympathy for her. Suddenly he knew the difference it could make, *would* make, not so much in the battle (which he did not yet understand), but in the way people would forever after regard his mother or anyone else who called upon such powerful forces.

Although she had worked for many years as a

leronis in the tower in Thendara, there she was one of a group, and people took little more notice of her *laran* gifts than of her skill at needlework. In Thendara, she was Erminie first, and a *leronis* second. Here in the mountains, where *leroni* were scarce, doing something this dramatic would make her visibly different, forever alienated from those who would be her neighbors. She would never be allowed to forget it.

She looked up at Conn. "You must help me," she said, "all of you must. This is going to be complicated, and we have so few of us with any *laran:* me, the two of you, Floria, Lord Storn . . . Conn, do you know of anyone else on these estates who has *laran?*"

Conn shook his head, while Gavin protested, "But, lady, I have so little *laran*—I never had any training —I'm not good for much of anything!"

"What little you have, we need," Erminie said grimly. "But for the moment, you can run errands. Find Storn, Floria, Lenisa, and that swordswoman governess of hers, and bring them here—quickly, please."

Gavin ran from the room, and she turned to Conn. "We need Markos, and you're closest to him. *Call* him."

Conn started to rise from his chair, but she gestured him back impatiently. "No, we haven't time for you to ride out and find him. Concentrate on him— call him like that! *Think* at him, make him feel that something is terribly wrong and we need him here at once. If he starts calling up the men on his way over, so much the better; we'll need them all."

Conn concentrated, furrowing his brow with the effort. *Markos, come to me; I need you.*

He was quite surprised when Markos appeared,

and more so when his stepfather clearly thought nothing of it, taking it for granted. Gavin came back, with Lenisa and Dame Jarmilla; Alastair with them.

"Alastair! I'm glad to see you up and about," Conn said.

Dame Jarmilla said crossly, "He shouldn't be, you know; he's still as weak as a kitten."

Erminie explained quickly what she meant to do; to transform any wild animals she could find into the semblance of an army. "There would not be a proverb about it if no one had ever done it," she said.

"It is not a *laran* I've ever heard of," Gavin said.

"It was better known in the old days than now," Erminie said. "Shapechanging has given rise to many legends; but I have never done it; there were those in my family who, they say, could transform themselves at will into wolf, hawk—I know not what. It is dangerous for humans to do this; if they keep that form too long, they can take on the characteristics of the beast-kind. A part of it is simple illusion, of course; they will not be as human as they look. They will be able to carry no weapons but those nature has given them. And in the case of a rabbit, that is not very much. Still, they can be useful to us nonetheless."

"I don't know anything about it," Conn said, "but we will be grateful for anything you can do to help us; one blood feud at a time is enough. How will you get them?"

"I can call them to me," Erminie said. "So could you, I think; do you want to try?"

But Conn was too far out of his depth to try anything of the sort. And gratefully left that duty in the hands of a more experienced *leronis*.

"Bring them to me now and I will do what I

must," Erminie said, and Storn seemed to understand. He picked up his starstone, and a little later when Conn looked out the window, he saw that the clearing around the building was rapidly filling with the wild animals of the woods.

There were rabbits and rabbit-horns, hedgehogs and squirrels, and there were two or three small animals that even the woods-bred Conn did not recognize. But there were also bears.

Erminie studied them all, thoughtfully. After a time she got up and went out, moving among the animals. "When I change them, it will not give us the army we need except in illusion," she said, when they came out to join her. "The rabbits will still *be* rabbits, and will run away rather than fight if they are threatened."

That, Conn imagined, made sense. But what of the *bears?* He and Floria were still closely in rapport; and she said quietly, "I hope the appearance of a vast army will stop those of Scathfell without need for confrontation, I do not relish the task of controlling a bear in human form!"

Conn didn't either. "Not in any form!" he said; but by that time Erminie had approached the nearest of the animals. She threw a little water on it and said in a low voice, "Leave the form you wear and put on the form of a man."

As Conn watched, the animal, groaning in protest, stretched out, and a small man stood there; clad in brown and gray, he was bucktoothed and—as Erminie had said—he was essentially still a rabbit; but in form, at least, he *looked* like a man. Now Conn knew what she had really meant when she promised to arm the bears and rabbits against Scathfell.

When Erminie had finished her work, it seemed that an army stood before them—but, he understood, it was still an army of wild things. Alastair understood this, too, and said, "They cannot really fight for me, even in human form—"

"We hope they will not need to fight," Erminie said. "But I can give you a bodyguard who *will* defend you to the death." And so saying, she called Jewel to her; the old dog came, and as she had done in Thendara, looked long in her face; then, as she had done with the other animals, threw a little water in her face, saying; "Quit that form you wear, and take the form your soul seeks."

"Why," exclaimed Dame Jarmilla, "It's a woman!"

Erminie said, "Yes, but she is like you—a warrior." She said to Alastair, "She will fight for you as long as life is in her body; it is in her nature to defend you."

Alastair looked at the red-haired woman who stood where the dog had been. She was roughly clad in leather and wore a sword at her waist.

"*This* is the—this is *Jewel?*"

"This is the form Jewel has taken to guard you," his mother answered. "This is the true shape of her soul, or at least this is akin to how she thinks of herself." And Alastair remembered that Jewel had guarded him since he could remember. In fact the old dog was one of his earliest memories.

"But if she is not to fight—"

"I did not say *she* would not fight," replied Erminie. "It is her nature to defend you—I said we hope it will not be necessary for the other creatures to fight; they will *look* like an army, and that is probably all we really need, but they could never really defend us."

Jewel crouched at Alastair's feet; he expected at

any moment that she would begin licking his hands, and wondered how he would respond if she did; she was still a dog, but she did not *look* like a dog; she looked like a woman warrior. Only her eyes were the same: wide, and brown, and devoted.

21

Alastair waited in the bushes for sight of Scathfell's army. His own force—the pitifully few real men and the "army" his mother had raised by giving the bears and rabbits human form, waited with him; so many that if Scathfell—or his military advisors—caught sight of them he would turn and run—or so Alastair hoped.

But if Scathfell—with the use of his *laran*—could tell what had been done, what then? Alastair could not hope to win any kind of military victory with such an army; they could only run away. An army composed mostly of rabbits would, he thought with dry humor, be very good at running.

Jewel slept at his feet; with nothing to do but wait, she had curled up on the ground and fallen asleep. This, more than anything else, reminded him that whatever form she might wear, she was still essentially his old dog.

And this made him wonder a little; his mother had

said Jewel would defend him. How could this strangest of warriors defend him better than a good dog
could? Though he loved her, Alastair would be the
first to admit that as a human she didn't look like
much.

Before he left Thendara, his mother had spoken
of changing Jewel's form, but said at that time she
could protect him better as a dog.

But now Erminie felt he could be better protected
by Jewel in human form—what was she expecting?

He did not have much time to ruminate. Before
long he heard a distant rumbling; he had never
heard such a sound before, but he needed no one to
tell him what it was. The sound was quite unmistakable—Scathfell's army on the march. Alastair could
also hear the far-off military sound of trumpets and
drums. Aidan had nothing like that, only his honor
guard—alone and without anything to protect them,
as Gavin said. The unfairness of it made Alastair's
blood boil.

At his feet, Jewel stirred and stretched. Alastair
said tightly, "I guess it's time, old girl," and she made
a little sound of excitement; neither a growl nor a
whine, but something of each. Alastair felt partly
excited and partly afraid; *his first battle. Would he be
killed? Would he panic? Would he come through it and see
Lenisa again?* He half envied Conn, who at least had
some experience with such things.

Then an arrow came screaming toward him; and
instead of thinking about his first battle he was in the
thick of it.

Erminie had told him what they were going to do;
it was an old trick in the mountains. Beyond the
thicket where he was hidden he heard the few other

men—and the great many bears, rabbits and hedge-hogs in human form—crashing about in the under-brush, making a great deal of noise and sounding as if a large army lay concealed there. The only un-questionably human sound—and the one which made the rest sound human, as opposed, Alastair reflected, to the noises of the wild animals they really were—was the ululation of the drone-pipe played by old Markos, reverberating in the distance as if there were many more of them. Alastair had never real-ized how hard it was to tell one war pipe from a dozen when the sound came at you through the hills and underbrush.

Through the trees he heard Scathfell give the or-der to withdraw. Aldaran, or whoever was command-ing his forces, had not been expecting to face half a dozen regiments, and judging by the sound, that was what lay in wait for him under cover of the bushes. Alastair had heard of this sort of thing before—there was an old story of how eleven men and a piper had driven off a couple of regiments—but it had never been attempted on this scale. He knew Scathfell's army could see a great body of men milling just behind the cover of trees. Sooner or later, Scathfell would begin to wonder why they did not close, but before he had a chance the few men they had among them, a scant half-dozen and a few women, let fly a hail of arrows and crossbow bolts from cover. They seemed like far more than they were; and taking Scathfell by surprise could do no harm; by taking the offensive they might succeed in driving them off before Scathfell and his armies fully knew what they were about.

Alastair looked around him. Jewel crouched at his

feet, but it was only fair that Conn, who was known by the few loyal men, should be in command of them—they should have the "young duke" they had fought with before to rally them. Gavin, Alastair knew, was riding to intercept King Aidan's party and make sure that he did not blunder unaware into the battle.

And I am left to command the bears and rabbits. Alastair reflected with some bitterness; whatever came of this, he would get no glory from his first battle. A commander skulking in the bushes, in charge of a horde of transformed animals, wasn't terribly heroic. And the worst of it was that there was nothing he could do about it; anything that he *might* do, except for crashing about and making noise in the bushes, would reveal the trick to Scathfell, and whatever came of that would not be good.

So Alastair chivied his forces, such as they were, through the bushes, helped by Jewel. Obviously enough of her dog's nature remained for her to enjoy chasing rabbits, whatever form they were in, although she never allowed the chase to take her far from Alastair.

The situation, though precarious, was stable for the moment.

And then their luck changed.

It was, as everyone told Alastair later, no more than unavoidable chance that Jewel chased one of the rabbits onto the path in front of one of Scathfell's men. The man promptly set on it, running through with his sword what he thought was a soldier; and when it died, it turned back to its natural form. The man's cries of, "Sorcery! It's a trick!" alerted his fellows, and before Alastair could call for help, a good number of them charged into the bushes, all set to slaughter a bunch of rabbits.

The rabbits, naturally, panicked and ran all over the place. The hedgehogs and squirrels also turned tail, but the bears were another matter entirely. It seemed to Alastair no time at all before the soldiers started running into bears in their quest for rabbits. And while both rabbits and bears appeared to be unarmed humans, that was only their semblance. Rabbits were still timid and defenseless, but the bears were quite the opposite. Running into a bear, even in human form, was a terrifying and potentially deadly experience. The bears still had claws and were not happy about being bothered. Numerous soldiers died, mauled by the claws and teeth of enraged bears, and their dying screams told the others that this thicket wasn't the easy fight it had appeared to be.

Scathfell's men drew back to join the main body of their army, which, Alastair noted, was somewhat smaller by now. *Good,* he thought grimly, *Conn and the men must have done some damage in the confusion. I only hope that Gavin managed to reach King Aidan in time.* Then Scathfell's bowmen started shooting at random into the thicket in which Alastair and his "men" were concealed. But this tactic had some unexpected results. The rabbits who were struck usually died, but the bears were far tougher. Not only did they stay on their feet, they tended to charge into the road and maul a few more soldiers before they fell. Yet Scathfell must have decided that this was still his best chance; the arrows continued to fly.

Alastair was sorely tempted to take refuge behind the nearest large rock and wait for it all to be over, but he sternly reminded himself that he was Duke of

Hammerfell, and the Duke of Hammerfell did not hide behind a rock during battle. After all, hadn't he fought for Hammerfell hundreds of times? Even if they had only been pretend battles in his nursery, he knew that a duke must set a heroic example to his men. Despite his fear, he continued to move his troops around, trying to make enough noise so that Scathfell would believe his arrows were having little effect.

Then suddenly an arrow flew toward Alastair from the direction of the road, and before he knew what was happening, Jewel threw herself in its path. Had she still been in dog form, the arrow would have passed over her head and hit Alastair, but in her present form, it hit her squarely in the throat.

Alastair threw his arms around the stricken Jewel, kneeling, sobbing, cradling the body of the old dog who had taken the arrow meant for him. He no longer cared about the sorcery by which this had happened; he knew only that for him the most personal casualty in this battle had been the dog who had fought more fiercely in his defense than any warrior, and had died for him. Jewel's slayer was standing over him, stunned; in an instant Alastair had his sword out and even before he knew what he was doing, the man lay dead.

Then Gavin was with him, reaching to take the dead dog's body from where it lay.

"Don't," he said urgently, "I'll carry her myself." In his heart he knew this was just the kind of death his gallant dog would have wished for.

Cradling Jewel's body in his arms, Alastair could not help but wonder if Erminie had known—if Jewel herself had not known.

22

There was not much to the battle after that; a few minutes later Scathfell's forces asked for a parley. Alastair got hold of himself again, dusted off his clothes and strode into the clearing, with a flag of parley, concentrating on looking as impressive as he could. After a time a tall, burly mountain man, with hair like flame and the double-eagle crest of Aldaran emblazoned on his tunic, came to him and said harshly, "I am Colin Aldaran of Scathfell; you, I believe, are Hammerfell."

"Yes, but probably not the one you were expecting." Alastair said sharply, and Aldaran smirked.

"Save me the tale for when we are seated around a fire somewhere," he said roughly. "I have heard just enough to be sure I would not understand. For now I want to know why you have joined against me with the lowland men and the Hastur king."

Alastair thought about that for a moment. "If you

295

will tell me why you and your men were marching in full strength against King Aidan and his honor guard, who had come into these hills as a private person to settle an old feud between Hammerfell and Storn—"

"A likely story," Scathfell snarled derisively, "do you truly expect me to believe that? Even here in the mountains we know that the Hastur-lords want to rule us all."

Alastair fell silent, feeling confused. *Did* King Aidan really want to rule in the Hellers? It had seemed to Alastair that the king had quite enough to keep him busy in the lowlands, and just wanted to see unnecessary bloodshed ended.

Colin of Scathfell looked at Conn, who had come up to join them, and said, "Both alive? I had heard that the twins of Hammerfell were killed many years ago. Now I know this will be a long story—I am eager to hear it sometime."

"You *shall* hear it, and as a ballad," said Gavin, who joined them. He looked sadly at the body of the old dog which Alastair had laid at the edge of the clearing. "And she will be a character in it—the dog who fought as a woman warrior to defend her master. But I think Aidan should join this parley, and Storn as well." He gestured to the two men who were approaching them, accompanied by Erminie, Floria, Lenisa, and Dame Jarmilla, "Then will all the parties to this feud be with us."

Colin of Scathfell smiled. "That is inaccurate; I have no feud with anyone in these hills. Or elsewhere, as far as I know; though my cousin to the south seems to be trying to make one with me. But now tell me why you armed every bear and rabbit in these woods against me. And I will consider peace with you."

"Gladly," said Alastair. "I have no quarrel with Aldaran—at least none that is known to me. One blood feud at a time is enough! We armed to aid King Aidan, who is here with a scant two dozen of his bodyguard, to arbitrate between myself and Lord Storn. He has no quarrel with *you*—although who is to say what he may say when he finds you have raised an army against *him* when he came here all but unarmed. And that I, too, would like to know."

"So we come to that again,' said Colin of Scathfell with some exasperation. "I marched out against the Hastur kings who are eager to bring Aldaran under their rule."

King Aidan entered the clearing with his honor guard of ten men, a few pipers, and Valentine Hastur. Colin glared.

"If we go over all the causes which lie between Hastur and Aldaran, we shall be here till tomorrow sunset and accomplish nothing. I came here," King Aidan said, "to settle the feud between Storn and Hammerfell—and for no other reason."

"How was I to know that?" demanded Scathfell.

"Be that as it may," Aidan said, "and probably will—I am *only* here to settle for all time this feud between Storn and Hammerfell; it has gone on for generations too long, and few of either family remain—no one alive knows the rights and wrongs of it, nor can it matter now. Tell me, Storn, will you lay your hand in friendship within that of the Lord of Hammerfell and pledge to keep the peace in these hills?"

"I will," said Storn solemnly. "And more than this;

I will give him the hand of my great-niece Lenisa, which will join our lands as one and settle it for a few generations more."

"I will gladly marry her," said Alastair formally, "if she will have me."

"Oh, I think she'll have you," said Storn dryly. "I've listened to the sentimental rubbish she talks about you to her governess when you are not there to hear. She'll have you—won't you, girl? "

Lenisa said, "If you call me *girl* in that tone, and give me away to settle some old feud, I will take up the blade and live and die unwed, as a Sister of the Sword! Will you have me, Dame Jarmilla?"

Dame Jarmilla laughed and said, "What would you do if I said yes, you silly girl? I tell you, you had better marry Hammerfell and raise up a half-dozen daughters; then let *them* take the sword if they will."

"Well," Lenisa said, "I suppose, in that case, if it will really settle this feud—"

"You suppose you can force yourself to it," said Alastair. "And I have already said that I will marry you if you are willing. So that is settled."

"And while we are speaking of marriages," Valentine Hastur said, "now that the heirs of Hammerfell are reinstated at last, which of you must I ask for the hand of your mother?"

"Neither," Erminie said firmly, "No one can say I am not of age; my hand is my own to bestow."

"Then you will marry me, Erminie?"

"I am most likely too old to give you children—"

"Do you think I care about that?" he said fiercely, and enfolded the blushing woman in his arms. Edric stared angrily at her and said, "You know perfectly well I was only awaiting the end of the battle to ask you myself—"

"Oh, Edric," she said, "you know I love you like a sister; if my son is to marry your daughter, will we not be close enough kin?"

"I suppose so," he said grimly. "And so it seems that everything is settled—"

"One thing is *not* settled," said Conn, speaking up for the first time, "this clearing out of men because it is more profitable to raise sheep—this sending of my men out to die away from their farms must cease."

Alastair said, "I remind you, brother that they are not *your* men."

"Then," said Conn, facing his brother squarely, "I plead with you for them—or I will fight you for them. I was brought up with these men and I owe them my own loyalty—"

"I cannot promise to do what you wish," said Alastair. "It is clear that these hills are no place for farming. And if you were thinking with your mind and not with foolish sentiment you would know it. It will not do for us all to starve, and if you challenge me, I will be forced to remind you—you are a land-less man, brother."

"No! It will not be so!" Aidan interrupted, "Recently I came into the overlordship of a property on the border to the south, where the weather is more clement and the farmland still good. I bestow it upon you, Conn, if you will be my true man."

"I will," said Conn gratefully, "and any man who is forced from Hammerfell—or from Storn—may come there and have lands to farm if he will. And if *you* will—" he turned to Floria. "As a landless man I had nothing to offer; now I have, thanks to King Aidan. Will you come and share it with me?"

Floria smiled brilliantly at him. "Yes," she replied. "I will."

"And so all this ends as a proper ballad should," Gavin said, "with the making of many marriages. But *I* get to make the ballad of it!"

"By all means, dear boy," Aidan said, beaming. "You had better put your mind to making that ballad."

Gavin grinned.

"I've already started it," he said.

And everyone in the hills has heard the ballad of the twin Dukes of Hammerfell, and of the old dog who died to save her master in the last battle—but like all true ballads, it has changed a good deal between that day and this.